C000102625

IMMORTAL GAMES

THE IMOGEN GRAY SERIES BOOK 2

LAURETTA HIGNETT

CHAPTER 1

I could hear the screams from down the block.

Unholy shrieking, gutwrenching, tortured screams, and terrified, frantic shouting. Whatever was in Terry and Sandy Becker's house, it was making a hellish racket, that's for sure. It sounded like the audio reel from *Night of the Living Dead* was being blasted down the street.

Father Benson called me ten minutes ago, begging me to come. I didn't want to. I'd tried so many times to wiggle out of helping him with his Evil Spirit Exorcism and Pest Removal side-gig business, but I was worried he'd get hurt if he took on too much.

And there was a *lot* to take on. Since the Dip had widened over Emerald Valley, we'd seen all manner of beasts accidently falling through the portal to wreak havoc on this little town.

Benson felt vindicated. He set up his side-gig years ago, because his parishioners had often reported strange noises and odd occurrences. Galvanized by memories of his predecessor – the vicious, sanctimonious witch-hunter Father Sampson – Benson decided he needed to investigate the hauntings, banish any stray ghosts, and exorcize rogue demons.

Most of them turned out to be confused racoons. Not anymore, though. Now that the Dip had widened and the flow of energy reversed, it was accidentally sucking in mythical creatures and cryptids that weren't paying attention to where they were going in their own dimensions. Consequently, Father Benson had a lot of callouts for his business.

So far, I'd managed to bag them all and explain patiently to him that they were normal, average animals. However, it was getting harder and harder to explain away the unnatural phenomena.

I wasn't even sure I had to anymore. I had been vaguely worried that Benson would have a heart attack and die if I told him the truth. But not only did he seem to take everything in his stride, he always seemed quite disappointed when I inevitably explained the otherworldly beast we'd been called out to catch was actually just an unusually big lizard or a very, very loud toad.

Last week, I had to catch a cu sith – a beautiful green fae dog – who bounded happily around Susan Keene's back yard trying to avoid me, like it was a game. He dropped slurries of drool that instantly bloomed into huge bushes of perfect Irish Littlebell roses.

I caught the big dopey thing eventually. I led him to the town square and cable-tossed him straight back through the portal. I scurried back to Susan Keene's house, trying to come up with a story to explain the roses and the vivid greenness of the cu sith. When I got there, Father Benson was teaching Susan how to deadhead the roses before the spring.

Nevertheless, I was worried about him. He was very old and decrepit. I didn't want him to die of shock. Despite being annoying, he made me laugh.

I didn't think I could get him to stop the fight anyway. He was quite dedicated to fighting the Forces of Darkness and wouldn't be talked into having a rest. He called me to help him often, though, and because I was trying to get to know the townsfolk so I could find my father, I always answered.

Walking up the sidewalk towards the little townhouse, I spotted Benson sitting outside on the porch, mopping his brow.

I gave him a wave. "What've you got for me today, Father?"

His hand trembled as he put his handkerchief away. I couldn't tell if it was excitement or fear that made his hands shake. "It's not a swarm of murder hornets this time, Imogen-me-good-lass. This is Terry and Sandy Becker's house," he said, pausing as an anguished shout shook the windowpanes. "Terry called me a couple of hours ago, says he's got a vengeful ghost stalking him. I show up, and the man's being chased around his house by a long-haired hippy woman in a white dress and long nails that would look fabulous if there was a bit of polish on them, y'know, but they're black as night and look like claws. She's in there trying to claw his heart out," he said, jerking his thumb behind him.

He gave a big sigh, sounding disappointed. "It's not a ghost; we got a *human* problem, a hospital escapee, or something like that. I called the police station, but Gary says he's out investigating something important, and if Terry Becker can't handle a crazy little girl by himself, then he wasn't much of a man to start with."

"Hmmm." I didn't know Gary, but I already hated him. And judging by Terry's screams of terror, I didn't think there was a *just* a crazy little girl in there.

I cocked my head. A baby's cry floated to my ears, sounding like a distant echo. "Is Sandy Becker at home?"

"Nooo, she'd be at work. She's a hairdresser at Curl Up And Dye, the salon down on Main Street."

"Do they have a baby?"

"They got a little 'un, a boy, he's at the daycare."

I sniffed the air. The faint smell of frangipani hung in the air; underneath that, the heavy, sickening odor of decaying flesh. It *could* be an air freshener covering up the smell of a dead racoon under the house, but I was never that lucky.

I leaned sideways, peeking through the front window of Terry and Sandy Becker's house. The living room was a mess; a cereal bowl lay upturned on the carpet, the TV was smashed on the floor, a game console's control cords tangled up and wrapped into a ball. Claw marks ripped through the wallpaper. A little blood-splatter, too, trailing into the kitchen. The only spot in the living room that hadn't been completely wrecked was in the corner. There, I could see a kid's play area – a little desk with nicely-organized craft supplies, a cute toddler stool and some toys neatly stacked onto shelves.

I mentally ticked off all the evidence, grimacing. Pale woman, long black hair and fingernails, trying to kill the man inside. Faint baby cry, smell of frangipani. I was pretty sure I knew what it was.

"Father," I said to Benson. "I might need your help with this one after all. Have a seat for a minute, while I go check it out."

He sat back down in a huff. "I'm not calling Gary again. That man's an ass."

I tried the front door; it was unlocked. I tiptoed into the living room, picking my feet over the scattered debris, and moved slowly towards the kitchen, where sounds of fighting had escalated. I stuck my head around the corner, taking in the scene.

Terry Becker was on the kitchen table - crying in terror,

pinned down, spreadeagled, and writhing underneath the most terrifying woman I'd ever seen.

Just as I thought. A pontianak.

Long, black hair covered her face completely, obscuring any other features. Her white gown was loose and billowy, flowing over her thin chest and her unnaturally bulging belly, the pale white gown contrasting the black of her hair and claws. She had Terry pinned with one hand, his t-shirt pushed up around his neck, and she was using the claws on the other hand to delicately mark out the shape of his liver on his pale, trembling belly. Tiny gashes slid open when she struck his skin with her claws. Her body trembled with anticipation, ready to plunge her hand in and rip out his liver.

He spotted me in the doorway behind the monster, his eyes wide with terror. "Help. Me." His shaking voice was barely a whisper.

The pontianak pulled back her hand, ready to plunge it into his flesh.

"Nope," I said firmly. I stepped forward and grabbed her by her hair. "No, that's not polite." I yanked her back.

She gave a howl of rage and fell off the table. "You can't go around feasting on the flesh of men," I told her sternly. "Nuh-uh."

Immediately whirling around, she swiped her long claws through the air, hissing at me. The long black hair swished back and forth as she whipped at me, cutting at my head, then my torso. I caught a glimpse of her eyes through the curtain of hair, glowing red. She was fast; I kept my eyes on her flashing claws as they whipped this way and that, trying to cut me so she could feast on my internal organs. Behind her, Terry clambered off the table and huddled into a ball near the refrigerator, sobbing.

This bitch was *so* fast; the bulge in her belly didn't slow her down at all. She came at me in an intense, furious rage. She nicked me on the shoulder with her black claws; it burned where they struck me.

I stepped back and glared at her. She moved, arms outstretched lightly in front of her, hissing like a snake, ready to strike. Her hair-covered face snapped in the direction of Terry, crying on the floor.

"You want to eat him, huh?" Her head whipped back between me and Terry, her bloodthirsty instincts warring between going for him, and defending herself from me. "You'll have to go through me first." I squared up and pulled out my knife.

Wailing like a banshee, she whirled her claws around and came at me again. I blocked her strikes with my knife; the claws flashed with sparks where they hit the metal. I pushed her back, testing her strength, but she rallied and lashed out again. She was light but strong, and filled with such an indescribable, overwhelming rage, it gave her a power that could very well be inexhaustible.

While I fended off her razor-sharp claws, I tried to decide what the hell I was going to do with her. She wasn't a cryptid or a mythical beast; she was a spirit creature. I didn't even know if I could do any damage to her. As it was, my knife-strikes were missing her by millimeters, and she was easily dodging my kicks. I needed to regroup; to think for a moment. She could fight, she could kill, she could eat, but I doubted she was thinking very clearly. I just had to trap her for a few moments, so I could figure out a plan.

Terry sobbed next to the refrigerator. Glancing over, I spotted a child safety lock on the refrigerator door.

Regrouping, my knife flashing, I started an advance, slashing and thrusting, driving her into the corner. Terry wailed again, and scrabbled into the wall as I backed the creature towards him. His terrified flailing distracted her for a moment, drawing her attention.

As soon as her head was facing away from me, I whipped open the fridge, grabbed a hank of her long black hair and shoved it inside the fridge. I slapped the door shut and flicked on the child-proof lock.

The pontianak thrust forward towards Terry, and gave a strangled yell as she stopped short, trapped. She yanked again, then turned, and scrabbled with the refrigerator door, trying to get her hair loose.

Benson was right; her long nails would probably look pretty with a slap of polish on them, but they were no good for delicate picky jobs like flicking open a child-safe lock. Her nails made the *clack clickety clack* noise as she struggled to get herself free.

Terry wailed in the corner, trapped.

Whoops. I probably should have gotten him out first. The pontianak slashed at him with her claws, missing by miles, in between trying to get herself free. As she struggled, her snow-white dress billowed out around her, stained with little spots of Terry's blood, and an embroidered logo on the left-hand side of her chest.

Wait. *What?*

Pontianaks didn't have embroidered logos on their death-shrouds. They were astral spirits; bloodthirsty, carnivorous, vengeful ghosts appearing in the form of a pregnant woman who will never give birth. They sometimes manifested as beautiful women to lure their prey, and then turned into terrifying creatures with black hair and red eyes, and used their razor-sharp claws to feast on the internal organs of your typical fuckboys.

This spirit was a classic pontianak, and they didn't come with any sort of company logo.

I frowned, looking at her closer. Edging forward, I

watched carefully as she alternated between slashing at a crying, moaning Terry, and trying to get her hair free.

I peered at her dress. The logo was a pair of little scissors. The words below it: Curl Up And Dye.

Aha. This was interesting.

I put my finger on my chin, and turned to the pontianak. "Wait here. I'll be back in a flash." Leaving the sobbing Terry on the floor with the trapped spirit slashing at him with her claws, I stepped out of the kitchen and went back outside.

Benson sat out on the porch, fingering his rosary. I plonked myself down next to him. "Is Sandy Becker pregnant?"

"Why, yes she is. Only a few weeks, she tells me. She's confessed she was feeling a wee bit overwhelmed with it all."

I'd never been pregnant before, or had kids. I couldn't imagine how hard it would be to stand on my feet all day cutting hair, while growing a tiny human inside me for two-hundred and eighty days, getting heavier and more uncomfortable as the days went by, with another tiny human waiting for me to serve it when I got home. It would be like being a slave, an incubator and a hairdresser all in one. "Tell me more."

Benson frowned. "I would never break the sacred seal of the confessional, lass."

"I understand."

"But yes," he went on cheerfully, "Sandy's been having a terrible time. Almost twelve weeks pregnant and sick as a dog, you know? Morning sickness has her puking up every ten minutes. It's taking her twice as long to get through her haircuts in the salon, has to keep running to the bog."

"Poor woman. And she has another kid?"

Benson's face crumbled up. "A hellraiser, but a sweet boy. She loves him dearly."

"What about her husband?"

He frowned. "Marriage is on the fritz, that's what she's been in the confessional for. She's working full time, pregnant, looking after the toddler when he needs her at the night-time too, because Terry's a forklift driver and needs to sleep properly or else he might cause an accident."

"Does he?" I frowned, thinking for a moment. "Come on, Father. I'm going to need your help."

"Is it a ghost?" Benson's face lit up like a beacon. I'd never seen much of his eyes underneath his mass of wrinkles in his scrunched-up face, but they were now bright blue and shining with delight. "An actual, real-life ghost?"

"Sort of. You'll see. I know how to get rid of it, but I'll need your help." I led him back into the kitchen, watching him carefully in case he had a heart attack.

I didn't need to worry. Benson's mouth dropped open when he saw what was in there.

His big gummy grin was an odd reaction to the sight of the horrifying, vengeful spirit trying to slash her other-worldly black claws through one of his local parishioners. Luckily, the pontianak hadn't managed to get herself free; her long, stringy black hair was still stuck in the refrigerator. Terry had his face pressed into the wall, covering his head with his hands.

While Benson was gaping, I casually rummaged around the kitchen, finding a big salt shaker in the pantry and a fruit bowl on the counter. I plucked out a banana and an apple. I took a leisurely bite out of the apple and marked out a circle of salt around the pontianak, keeping well clear of her slashing claws.

Just in time, too. She'd worked out how to use her goth nails to click open the child-safe lock on the refrigerator. She lunged at Terry, but the salt circle brought her up short.

I grabbed Terry by the back of his shirt and dragged him

out of the corner. He curled himself up into a ball on the floor.

The pontianak seethed, pacing around the small salt circle, her movements jerky. She hissed at us. The sound cut through the air with an eerie preternatural timbre.

"Benson," I said. "Have you got your exorcism stuff with you?"

"Sure do," he rummaged in his pockets. "Bell, rosary, book, holy water. I'm ready to go."

"Go ahead, do your thing."

He flicked open the pages of his book and began to chant, periodically splattering the pontianak with holy water. His voice grew in volume and confidence. The pontianak screeched and writhed in the circle. Finally, with a teeth-rattling shriek, a real, warm human body fell out of the pontianak, fainting to the floor.

I caught her just in time. She was small and curvy, with pink streaks in her short blonde hair.

Benson's eyes boggled. "Sandy?"

Her eyelids flickered and popped open. "What–" She swallowed. "What happened? Who are you? What's going on?"

Trapped in the salt circle, the pontianak let out a guttural snarl. Sandy blinked, and focused over my shoulder at it. Her mouth dropped open. "What... is... *that?*"

"Oh," I said, still holding her. "That's a pontianak. She was in *you*. Or, more accurately, you were in her." I pulled her up into a sitting position. "Now, I think we all need to have a chat."

Terry sat up and backed away until his head hit the kitchen wall behind him. "What the hell! What the *hell* is that?" He looked at me. "Who are you?" He shook his head, bewildered. "Sandy, what's going on?"

I waved. "I'm Imogen. I work with Father Benson here to

get rid of evil spirits, and mostly trapped racoons. That there," I pointed at the evil spirit, jerkily darting and hissing in the circle. "Is a pontianak. It's a ghost, of sorts. It got here, to our town, by accident, but I don't think it randomly chose your house. Or your wife."

"What's it got to do with Sandy? Sandy, doll, why aren't you at work?"

I sat her up, handling her gently. "I don't know," she whispered. "I dropped off Dexter at daycare, and I was headed to work... I think I had to puke again, so I ducked home..."

"Oh, I don't think it was *her* who summoned the pontianak, Terry," I said. "Tell me, what were you doing today?" I asked him cheerfully. "What's your schedule?"

"I don't work today," Terry shook his head confused. "I was sleeping in. I do four days at the distribution center."

"Why is Dexter at daycare, then?"

He looked at me blankly. "What?"

I repeated myself patiently. "Why is Dexter at daycare?"

His eyes blinked slowly. "Dexter is at daycare when Sandy is at work."

"Why?"

"Because..." he looked at me with an *isn't it obvious?* expression. "Sandy's at work."

"Why don't you look after him?"

"Hey," he said, obviously offended. "I babysit him some days. When I work, I do long hours, at least nine hours a day. It's a tough job, real physical. I need the downtime."

"Nine hours, huh? That's rough," I said sarcastically. "How many days does Sandy work?"

His face turned cautiously blank. "Six. Her mom watches Dex when she works on the Saturday."

"What do you do on Saturdays?"

"I've got my fishing club. Hey," His eyes narrowed at me.

"What's with the questions? What's this got to do with that... that *thing* in the corner?"

"So you never look after your own kid?"

He glared at me. "Hey, I'm a *good* dad. We all hang out on Sundays, we do family stuff together, I play with him in the evenings, when Sandy's getting dinner ready. I'm a *great* dad," he repeated defensively.

"She cooks *every night?*"

Terry didn't reply. I made a show of looking into the living room, where the gaming console and tv were smashed to pieces, and the cereal bowl on the floor.

"And now she's pregnant?" I paced back and forth across the kitchen floor, eerily aware that I was matching the pontianak's back-and-forth behind me. "She's pretty sick, yeah? Have you been getting up in the night and looking after Dexter when he needs someone?"

"He never wants me; he only wants her. Besides," he added sullenly. "She's always awake, she's up puking in the toilet anyway. There's no point in me getting up too. There's no point in *both* of us being tired."

Benson knelt down, his knees creaking, and patted Sandy's arm. I looked down at Terry hard, for a full minute. He sat on the floor, his expression sulky.

Finally, he shifted uncomfortably. "Okay, it sounds bad when I put it like that, but I'm with my kid a lot, you know. I'm a *good* dad. I help around the house a lot, I fold my own laundry, I take the garbage out and mow the lawn."

"Once a week," Sandy mumbled. A pale blush appeared under her pallor.

"What was that, my child?" Benson patted her cheek.

"Once a week," I said loudly. "Terry does one fifteen-minute job, once a week."

"I can't cook," he said sulkily. "She knows it. I'm no good

at doing the cleaning. She's good at it, so she does it. Besides, I never do it the way she wants."

Her voice was feeble beside me. "He won't learn."

Ugh. I could never get my head around mortal relationships. Men and women were ridiculous, what they did to each other, and what they put up with.

It wasn't that long ago that society had drawn strict lines between what a man would do and what a woman would do domestically. The man would have a job, a simple nine-to-five, and the woman would keep house and make babies.

Those lines had shifted and blurred. At first glance, you'd think it was because of the women's suffrage movement, but that wasn't it. This society was moving into late-stage capitalism. In the past, one man's wage would feed and clothe an entire family of six, and buy a house, with money left over for holidays and trips to the movies once and a while.

As the cost of living went skyrocketing, and wages limped lethargically behind it, men weren't bringing home enough money for the family to survive anymore. So, the wives went out to work as well. But the reorganization of domestic labor didn't go with it.

Women were told that they could have it all - a career, a family, a fulfilling life. It just meant they were *doing* it all, while a lot of men were reveling in their weaponized incompetence, just like Terry, here.

I looked down at him in disgust. He thought he was a good dad. The bar was on the floor.

"That's it." I straightened up and moved over to the salt circle. "I'm letting the pontianak out." I put my toe in the circle, as if I was going to scrape out the side of the salt. "I think you deserve to have Sandy eat your internal organs."

"No!" He screamed, scrabbling to his feet. "Don't do it!"

"It came here for a reason, Terry, and that reason is not just vengeance. It's justice. I can't believe you can look me in the eye and tell me you think you do enough around here?" I knelt down and grabbed him by the chin. "She's growing another human inside herself. She's a literal *goddess*, and you can't be bothered to get up to take your toddler to the toilet at nighttime? You're a worthless sack of shit," I spat out. "Sandy's wrecking her back at work almost every single day, and you think you do a hard job because you sit on your ass and drive a *forklift?*"

Terry's eyes wildly swung between the pontianak, and me. "I have to lift boxes, sometimes! It's hard, physical labor!"

"So is being a hairdresser." This asshole just wasn't getting it. "Let's try something," I said. "Hold your arms up like this." I brought my hands up and out, to around chin height. Terry looked at me sullenly, but copied me once I raised my eyebrow and made a reaching gesture towards the salt circle. "Good man. Hold it there. Now, let's do some math." I squatted down and brought up the calculator on my phone. "You're at work four days a week, nine hours a day. I'll make it ten, just to give you some leeway. That's forty hours a week. Sandy, how many hours a day do you work?"

"The salon is open from nine-to-five and nine-to-one on Saturdays. I open three days a week."

"Okay, you need another half hour to open..." I tapped on my phone. Terry's arms were falling. I smacked the floor and he jumped. "Arms up. Okay... so that's forty-five point five hours. So she's already doing far more hours than you."

"My job is much more physical..."

"Arms *up*," I snapped at him. He lifted them back up to chin level. "Now, let's do domestic labor hours."

Terry looked at me sullenly. "That's not fair. Mowing the lawn takes ages. I fix little things that get broken around here, too."

I made a show of looking at the broken lamp on the counter. "How long has that been sitting there?"

"Three weeks," Sandy whispered.

I tapped at my calculator. "I'm going to give you half an hour for the lawn, another hour a week to fix stuff around the house. What else do you do?"

"I fold my own laundry and put it away."

"I stopped doing it for him," Sandy's voice was getting louder.

I ignored her. "Who does the laundry, though? Who does Dexter's laundry?"

He didn't answer. I tapped on my phone. "I'm going to go with six loads a week, just to be conservative. Washing, hanging out to dry, bringing it in, ironing, it all takes about half an hour to an hour, more if you have to hang it out to dry. Now, the cooking."

"I take care of it on a Friday."

Sandy sat upright. "He picks up a pizza."

I glared at him.

"Okay!" He slammed his arms down on the floor. "I get it. I could probably do a bit more around the house."

"Arms *up*," I snapped.

"I can't! My arms are tired."

"Now you know how Sandy feels every single day. She holds her arms like that for at least half an hour at a time, probably over eight times a day. Am I right, Sandy?" She nodded. "If you can't do it for ten minutes, then her job is far more physical than yours."

"It's *her* fault," Terry whined. "She never liked how I cooked, or how I did the laundry."

"Oh, I can imagine," I said. "I bet you never checked all the pockets before you washed anything, so the whole load was covered with tissue paper. You would have been washing pants with your jocks still stuck inside them, or with socks still rolled into balls. I bet you even hung clothes out without giving them a shake first."

"I asked *so* many times," Sandy muttered. "He never did it properly."

"Yeah. Now you know. It was on *purpose.*"

Terry shook his head frantically. "It wasn't!"

"Yes, it *was.* You deliberately do things badly, so you won't have to do it again. You're a sack of shit, Terry," I said, getting to my feet. "I'm letting the pontianak out."

"No!" Terry screamed and scrambled up to his feet. "I'll do better, I promise! Sandy... Sandy, stop her!"

"No, please," Sandy grabbed my arm. "Don't do it."

I glared down at her. "You want to be married to that sack of shit for your whole life?"

She cocked her head. "Oh, no, it's not that," she said. "I've thought about divorcing him *so* many times. I was always just too busy to follow through with it, and my faith has always told me I should try and stick it out. No, I just don't want to be blamed for murdering him if that thing possesses me again."

I paused. "Ah. Righto. You don't have to worry; I can help cover it up. I know at least eighty ways of disposing of a body. No one will ever find him."

Benson chuckled. "Well, I'm not sure if I can idly stand by and watch a murder." He patted Sandy on the cheek. "But, my child, I think Jesus himself would give you a high-five if you left Terry in the gutter."

"Sandy..." Terry crawled forward and took her hands. "No. Don't do this. I'll cook every night. I'll... I'll... take lessons, or something, I'll follow recipes."

I put my hands on my hips. "And if you screw it up, you'll start again from scratch, and keep going until you do it right."

He swallowed, and nodded. "I will. And I'll do all the laundry. I'll do it right, I promise. I'll even separate the colors."

There was a moment of silence, as Sandy thought about it. Finally, she pursed her lips. "Okay. This is your last chance, though, Terry," she said. "The only thing holding me back from taking Dex and going to live with Mom was my marriage vows."

Terry's eyes flashed; a calculating look came over them before it disappeared abruptly, replaced by pleading, puppy-dog eyes. "You can't break your vows, baby. You know you can't. It's you and me, forever."

Benson kicked him in the ribs. "You've some thick bollocks, Terry. You've broken your vows every single day since you wed. You promised to honor her, and you've proved yourself a dishonorable fecker, you have. You broke your vows, so she's released from hers."

Sandy gazed up to him with round eyes. "Is that how it works, Father?"

"If I say it does, it does."

"Well," she said. "I'll give it one more chance. One more chance," she glared at Terry. "You hear me?"

I flipped the banana in my hand. "If that's your final decision... And it's a stupid decision, mind you," I added, pointing the banana at him. "If you hang on a minute, Sandy, I'll give you an insurance policy." I stood up. "Do you have any Tupperware containers?

Sandy automatically started to open her mouth, but she stopped herself. She looked at Terry and raised an eyebrow.

He went red, and mouthed like a goldfish. "I... I don't know," he said finally.

"Learn," I snapped. I turned to Sandy.

"Third drawer down."

I opened the drawer and rummaged around a neat assortment of Tupperware containers. She even had the matching lids attached to each one. I pulled out a small, rectangular container, and dumped the remaining salt inside it.

I turned, and faced the pontianak. It was still pacing in the circle, hissing. I aimed and tossed the banana at her. It hit her in the chest. Instantly, she disappeared in a blinding white flash.

The banana thumped to the floor.

I grinned. That was good. I was sincerely hoping that would work, otherwise I had no idea how I was going to get rid of her. According to legend, pontianaks usually slept in banana trees during the day. It was daytime now, so I hoped she'd be nice and cozy there.

I placed the salt-filled Tupperware container inside the circle, gently lifted the banana and nestled it inside the salt, making sure it was covered completely. That should keep her trapped, and hopefully asleep. I clipped the lid closed, and lifted it into my hands.

"I'm going to keep a hold of her," I said, cradling the container to my chest. "I'm going to keep an eye on *you*, Terry. Sandy might have given you another chance, but I haven't. If I find out that you're not pulling your weight in this relationship, I'm going to let her out, you hear me? And I'll help Sandy get rid of your body."

Sandy stood up and pulled me into a hug. It was awkward and uncomfortable, but I bore it with good grace.

"Thank you," she whispered, her voice trembling. "I was at the end of my rope." She let me go, and turned to Benson. "Thank you too, Father. You really are the best exorcist of your time."

Benson glowed with happiness. "That's not all I'm good for, my child! I'm going to stick around and give you two some marriage counseling. It is sorely needed. Terry, pop a Band-Aid on those scratches and make some coffee. This is going to take a while."

I chuckled. Terry looked miserable. "This is where I say my goodbyes," I said. "Sandy, keep me posted."

"I will." She smiled at me warmly.

I turned and walked out of the kitchen, and out of Terry and Sandy Becker's house, cradling the Tupperware container to my chest.

If only all my problems could be solved by murderous, vengeful ghosts.

CHAPTER 2

The bell of Marigold's shop door jangled merrily as I slammed it open. "I've got a live one here!" I shouted, sweeping in and plopping the Tupperware container down on top of a display stand basket filled with dried roses.

A low, rumbling growl answered me. I looked up.

Marigold stood at her apothecary shelves, elbow-deep in amber bottles, restocking her flashy beauty products. Behind her, at the counter, Backman loomed, her muscled arms crossed over her chest, glaring at me.

"Oh, hello Barbara," I cooed at her. "I didn't see you there."

"Don't call me Barbara," she growled back. "You call me Backman. Or *sir*," she added menacingly.

I laughed. "Or Winnie? Or Yogi? Or Paddington? Or-"

"Shush, you two." Marigold pushed her round gold-framed glasses back up her nose. "What have you got there, Imogen?" She tiptoed over to me excitedly.

Backman bristled. "Mar, don't touch it."

Backman had been a little more than overprotective of her wife since she had offered herself up as a sacrifice to get rid of the Bloodlord. Against my better judgment, I'd managed to take Marigold's place, but Backman had glued herself to her wife ever since, hovering around like a menacing bodyguard, snarling at anyone who even dared come close. Since Marigold didn't mind, it was kinda sweet. And it was fun for me to provoke her.

Marigold stopped three feet away from the Tupperware container and peered at it. "I'm not going to touch it," she said patiently to Backman. "What's in there?"

"It's a pontianak. I pulled it out of Sandy Becker. It was trying to eat Terry Becker."

Marigold looked confused.

"It's also known as a kuntilanak," I explained. "Depending on where you're from."

"Oh, a kuntilanak." She peered at the container. "I know what they are. It was possessing Sandy?"

I nodded. "Honestly, I should have probably left it in her."

"I wouldn't blame you. Her husband is one of those 'fun guys' who are absolutely useless. I was at her salon a few months back and he called her in a tizz. He'd taken Dexter for a walk to the playground but forgot the diaper bag, and hadn't thought to pack some water bottles and the snacks. He fully expected her to run home, grab the bag, pack some snacks and bring them over." She shook her head. "If a Kunti-lanak came through the portal and was attracted to anyone, it would be him."

"He's a kunti-la-whack."

That's why I preferred to call it a pontianak. It was hard to not make stupid jokes if we kept calling it a kuntilanak. I might be a few hundred thousand years old, but I was still horribly immature. It also rankled that I was too dumb to come up with anything better than kunti-la-whack. There were so many opportunities there, I was sure, but I just couldn't think of them.

"Do you want me to put it back through the portal?" Marigold asked.

"You're not going near that thing," Backman growled.

"It's fine. I don't want to send it back, anyway. I'm going to hang onto it, as insurance. I told Terry I'd be keeping an eye on him."

"Oh, wow," Marigold said. "If only all our problems could be fixed by murderous vengeful ghosts, huh?"

I grinned at her. "*Exactly.*"

"This is a problem, though," Marigold said, frowning. "We've had far too many things come through the portal lately. It's beginning to get too much attention. The normies are going to start noticing. It might cause a panic."

I shrugged. "So far, so good. Benson helped me get the pontianak out of Sandy. He seemed to take it all in his stride."

"That man is as crazy as a cut snake, Imogen. He's been seeing ghosts for years. No," she said. "I'm not worried about Terry or Sandy either. I think we can handle a couple of ghost sightings and a handful of demonic possessions. It's just the otherworldly creatures that are going to be a problem. There's too many coming through. No one here would bat an eyelid at a ghoul moaning in your attic, but if the locals see a griffin marching down main street, there's going to be a panic."

Backman stirred, uncrossing her huge arms. "Mar and I spent the morning rounding up a clan of pukwudgies at the OE Center," she said crossly. "I've been pulling little poison arrows out of my hide ever since."

"Hmmmm. I don't think it's anything to worry about. So far, it's just been cryptids and local astral spirits," I said. "The things that are closest to our dimension. They would find it the easiest to come through. You're not going to get to fight a griffin, Backman, sorry to disappoint you. There's probably nothing to worry about."

Cryptids - like Bigfoot, and the pukwudgies - were in a dimension so closely aligned with ours that it practically overlapped. It wasn't very difficult for them to appear without the portal, if they wanted to, usually only briefly. That's why they were spotted so often on Earth.

It was harder for the astral spirits like the pontianak and the wendigo, as the earth's telluric field kept them more firmly out. They could fall through the portal, though, if they blundered through it, or if they were attracted by something they wanted. Hunger and greed, in the wendigo's case. Fuck-boys, for the pontianak.

I frowned, remembering the cu sith. They were dogs from a fae realm, and that was a lot further away from our dimension. You needed specific ingredients and special talents to create a world key to be able to go between worlds. Only the most talented fae could do it, and they couldn't bring more than themselves through the portal to our dimension. Even *then*, they couldn't come here without an invitation from someone in our world.

To make things more complicated, there were a lot of different types of fae, in many different worlds. Generally, the closer they were to our realm, the more human-like they were. The further away the fae realm, the wilder and stranger they were, and the more likely they were to make trouble if they managed to make their way here.

I bit my lip, thinking. The fae were tricky. They were more powerful than humans, magically speaking, and very culturally different to us. The few times I'd had to deal with the fae had been... interesting, to say the least. They had convoluted manners, they took offense very easily, and they had the most bizarre sense of humor.

My humor tended towards fart jokes and gentle teasing. A fae practical joke could involve a frozen corpse, a pack of wild dogs, or an afternoon of ethnic cleansing.

23

If it were easy for a fae to come to Earth, it could be extraordinarily dangerous. And that dumb, slobbering cu sith pooch had just fallen through the portal. I wasn't sure if the invitation rule extended to fae dogs or not.

I tapped my chin, thinking. "Maybe we do need to do something. The little beasts are fine; they're kind of fun. It's the big scary ones that might cause a panic." I turned to Marigold. "Is there anything we can do, in the magical sense?"

Before she could respond, the bell on her door jangled, and Leroy walked in.

"Hi, guys. Hi, Imogen. I thought you might be here."

I frowned. "Why aren't you in school, buddy?"

He raked his hands through his shoulder-length hair, tousling it in an artful manner. The kid had just turned thirteen, and I was starting to worry about him. Worry about him *more*, I mean, because not only had I rescued him from a life of horrific child abuse, plunging him straight into another dangerous existence where he had to help avert the apocalypse with his natural-born magical talents, but now, to make things worse, he was starting to show signs that he was going to be a ridiculously good-looking kid.

In my experience, there was nothing worse than a powerful, handsome, emotionally damaged man. It was a recipe for disaster.

The gorgeous boy in question slumped on the counter. "I got kicked out."

"Kicked out of school? Why?"

"I might have gotten into a fight."

I narrowed my eyes. "You *might* have? Leroy, seriously? What happened?"

"We had an assignment in art class. We had to infuse a piece of art with as much emotion as possible, however we could. The subject was our moms. We had to draw our mothers."

Ah.

Leroy's mom was a junkie who often sold him to various scumbags, like pedophile businessmen or hungry vamps. It culminated with her selling him to a Blood Witch who planned on torturing him to death. That's where I found him.

I had intended on leaving him there. I tried to, but he was determined to stay with me.

I often have nightmares that I succeeded.

"Aw, kid." I rubbed him awkwardly on the head. "That's rough. Did you refuse to draw her? Or did you draw her, and someone teased you?"

"Not... exactly."

"What do you mean?"

He frowned and swung his bag off his shoulder. "You're going to hate this." He pulled out a folder, opened it, and turned it around to show me.

The top piece was a drawing of me.

He'd got my physical features perfectly. Very long, very thick black hair, big, almost-black eyes, with tiny flecks of white that looked like stars in the sky. Pointed chin, full lips, shining brown skin. He'd made me look much more beautiful than I actually was. There was no hint of my creeping insanity, no indications of my social bluntness or my non-existent emotional intelligence.

He'd made me look like a goddess. Somehow, he had also infused the picture with a lioness fierceness that I was sure I didn't have.

I pursed my lips. "It's disgusting."

He chuckled darkly. "I knew you'd say that."

"You got my nose wrong. And I look like I need blotting

paper for my oily skin." I looked up, catching his eye. "So, what happened? Why did you get into a fight?"

He shrugged. "I didn't expect all the jokes, that's all. I should have drawn my actual mom, as an evil monster, or something, and I would have gotten a bunch of sympathy. Instead, I drew you, and I got a bunch of kids hollering about how much they want to bang my mom."

I suppressed a grin. "Okay, that's gross."

"One kid was being so disgusting about it, I couldn't help myself. I smacked him in the mouth and split his lip. I'm excluded for the rest of the week," he said. "Mr Somers said he had no choice, but he'd call you, and arrange homework so I can keep up."

"Yeah, well, he owes me," I muttered. I thought Sam Somers would disappear once I rescued his dog and gave it back to him, but he was obviously the responsible type who wouldn't abandon his kids in the middle of the school year. "He better take you back and think harder about the kind of assignments he sets in future."

"He didn't know about the art assignment, to be fair. Mrs Calloway set that assignment, she doesn't know about me."

I nodded, still a little restless. I'll have to drop into the school and have a chat with Mrs Calloway. Make sure that Leroy wasn't triggered at all. "You can hang out with me, or with Marigold here. Help her with the shop."

She smiled at him widely. "That would be great. You can help us with our portal problem."

"What problem?" Leroy looked far too interested.

"Settle down there, Mr Fisticuffs. Magical theory only. No practical, okay?"

"Okay," he said sulkily.

Marigold walked over to her bookshelf, reached up on her tiptoes and tickled the bottom of a thick book on the highest shelf, trying to wiggle it off. Backman stepped behind her automatically and lifted her as if she weighed nothing. Marigold plucked the book out without dropping it on her head. "We're looking for a way of filtering the portal. We can't close it, of course, because that would mess up the flow of the telluric field and put our whole world in danger."

"What else can we do?" Leroy asked. "A magical net, to keep things out? I think I saw a spell—"

"I don't know if a net is a good idea," I cut him off. "Things get stuck in nets."

Marigold flicked through the pages of the huge, dusty book. "I was thinking of a version of a *don't-look-here* spell. Something that will broadcast from our reality, out through the portal, that says: *Go Away! Don't come near here, you'll have a bad time!*" She shrugged. "Or something like that."

"You'd just have to modify a *don't look here*," Leroy said, trying to read the book from upside down. "That would be easy."

"It's more complicated than you think, Leroy. Setting the intention is easy, but you have to think about how those intentions are received once they go through the portal. Sometimes, what you put out isn't what is taken in."

"Okay," Leroy nodded, spinning the book around to face him so he could read it properly. "Where would you anchor the spell, anyway? The portal is twenty feet in the air..."

I tuned out. It wasn't really my problem. I mean, there was a *slight* chance an army of Dark Elves would march through the portal and wage war on the earth, but I just added that thought to my lingering background anxiety. Other than that, I didn't mind all the mythical creatures stumbling through the portal. It gave me a chance to check out the locals.

Somewhere, living here in Emerald Valley, was the reincarnation of my father. I was desperate to find him. He was the only person who would know how to cure my immortality – my curse – and I needed to find out how to do it.

I knew that he knew how, because he'd done it himself. He hadn't always been human, but he died a human.

I barely remembered my childhood, because it was thousands and thousands of years ago. Little memories remain, though; how beautiful my mother was, her big eyes and glowing dark skin. I remember how fascinated my father was with every single aspect of our new human society. I remember how he used to be able to move huge rocks when I was a little girl, but when I got older, he could only roll small boulders before getting tired. I remember how his eyes glowed, and how different he looked from the rest of us, even though eventually he had the same dark hair and brown eyes and bronze skin. He became more and more human with every day that went by, and then finally, he died, just like a normal human.

I never died. I just got hurt and grew my body parts back.

My mother had never reincarnated, choosing instead to merge with the great Oneness when she died. I still missed her.

My father, instead, chose to come back to experience life, over and over again, as different people. I've caught up with him only a handful of times, always as an older man – father-figure type – because I don't think I'd recognize him any other way. Every time I found him, he was stubbornly human. Each time, he died before I could get him to a good witch, someone who could help him access his higher-self knowledge, so he could tell me exactly what I needed to know.

It was heartbreaking and soul crushing, and the worst thing about my existence. Far worse than growing back severed limbs or stuffing my intestines back into my gut. I got to experience losing my father over and over again, every few thousand years or so.

I wasn't going to lose him again.

A few weeks back, I blackmailed a Blood Witch to find him, and found out his reincarnated soul was living here in Emerald Valley. Or, more specifically, he *had* been here, and he was going to be here again soon. I was looking for someone who hadn't been in Emerald Valley when I arrived; someone who had maybe gone away, and either moved back, or would move back soon.

The list of suspects was surprisingly long, and, considering I didn't know what form his soul had taken, I didn't have much to work with. He could be a local rich kid sent to boarding school in Switzerland who would come back for spring break. He could be a local shopkeeper on his honeymoon. He could even be one of the billionaires that flew in and out of the country club.

I had no idea. All I could do was talk to as many locals as I could and try to find someone who felt like my dad.

It was hard, since I have the emotional capacity of a cucumber. I don't have gut feelings; I don't have any instincts. I can't sense magic, not even like Normies do – raised hair on the nape of the neck, tingling sensations, that sort of thing. Nothing.

Nothing... until I access my deeper powers. Within me, I had the strength to move mountains, to run as fast as the morning light falls on a town when the sun rises. I can instantly read the emotions of everyone in my line of sight. I kept it buried deep down, because every time I'm in a pickle and I'm forced to access my deeper powers, a terrifying, jealous god breaks out of the Dip, chases me, catches me, and tears me to shreds.

I mean that literally. He pulls me apart like a bitter punter would rip up a betting slip after his horse falls at the last fence. I always spend the next few years in horrendous pain, regenerating from one of those tiny bits.

I don't know who he is, and why he hates me so much. I don't know why he hunts me whenever I use my full powers.

All I know is that I'm *done*. I can't keep going like this anymore. Done. Finito. Can't take another bit of pain.

Things are slightly better these days, I had to admit. I lost the lower half of my body only a few weeks ago, and my friends got the local vet – a lovely man named Jamieson – to put me in an induced coma so I wouldn't feel anything. I regrew everything in record time; three weeks, instead of the usual years and years.

It was nice having people to take care of me. I glanced around the shop, looking at Marigold and Backman and Leroy. Well, I guess the first one was a friend, Backman kinda hated me for putting Marigold in danger. Leroy appeared to like me, which was nice.

They were bickering about the spell. "Okay, I've had enough," I said. "I'm going home."

Backman crossed her arms, a funny smirk on her sergeant-major face. "Getting ready for your date?"

I grimaced. "It's not a date. It's an exchange of information."

"It's a date. You're having dinner."

"To exchange information." Rafael Stefano Di Stasio had finally agreed to fill me in on some vampire politics I was curious about, provided I told him exactly what I was doing in Emerald Valley. "And for him, it's breakfast," I added. "Dinner for me, so we're not even on the same page."

Leroy popped open a can of soda and laughed. "It's a date, Imogen," he said, taking a gulp of soda. "The king has been asking you out for weeks now."

"Harassing me, more like. He's only after a little entertainment. I'm a novelty, and he's bored."

I felt weird when I thought about Rafael Stefano Di Stasio, so I tried not to think about him often. He was the Northern Vampire King, one of only four vampire monarchs in the world. A billionaire with thousands of companies, millions of employees, and his own private army. He was also weirdly obsessed with me, which made me very nervous.

"He likes you." Marigold grinned. "A lot."

"Yeah, well, if I've learnt anything in my lifetime, it's this: When it comes to powerful men, there's a fine line between liking someone, and locking them in an underground dungeon until rats nibble their feet off because you won't give them a B.J."

Leroy spat out his soda.

"He wouldn't do that, would he?" Marigold rubbed her chin thoughtfully.

"It's been done before, believe me," I said. It was the reason I only dated human men. If I couldn't knock him unconscious easily, I didn't want to date him. "He's a vampire," I added. "They're all batshit crazy. Look at Sonja; she keeps a jerry can of gas in her Maserati just in case Rafael gives her the go-ahead to set me on fire."

"Oooh," Leroy made little kissy-faces at me. "Rafael, huh. Rafael, your *boy*friend."

"Eat a dick, Leroy."

"Don't talk to me like that, *mom*."

"Ugh. Let's just go home."

* * *

IT WAS past lunchtime when we stepped out on the street. I'd left my van at Terry and Sandy Becker's house and walked to Marigolds, holding the pontianak-banana carefully in my hands, so Leroy and I walked back down Main Street towards the lake to go pick it up.

31

I had just stepped off the sidewalk to cross the street, when a police cruiser stopped suddenly in front of us, hitting the siren as it screeched to a halt. Leroy flinched at the loud noise, and moved back onto the sidewalk, his fists clenched at his side.

That made me angry. I stayed on the road and glared at the cruiser.

After a long moment, the door opened, and a cop got out: A big white guy with a ruddy face and thinning hair. He was tall, and carried a lot of weight, but not enough that would slow him down. He moved with a slow, deliberate swagger that made my blood boil.

I knew there were only two cops in Emerald Valley. I hadn't met either of them yet; I didn't really want to. I'd heard of them, though. They were both men. One was younger, mid-twenties, a pleasant man who was more interested in hanging out in the forest testing his survivalist skills than catching litterbugs. He mainly stuck to policing the roads coming in and out of Emerald Valley and stayed away from the town.

This was obviously the other one – Gary, the asshole cop who wasn't interested in helping Father Benson with his 'crazy little girl' problem earlier. Anyone who would refuse to help Benson was already an asshole in my books. Even *I* couldn't turn him down.

He swung his body around the cruiser and fronted up to me.

"Step back on the sidewalk. Now," he snapped, jabbing a finger behind me.

I crossed my arms. "Why?"

He glared at me with beady eyes. "Because I said so, that's why."

"I was about to cross the road."

"Well, that's jaywalking, for starters." He pulled his shoulders back. "I could charge you."

"You can't. The law was changed, it's only a secondary offense now. You can't stop me for jaywalking." I knew the law. I broke it often enough; it was good to know it.

His piggy little eyes narrowed further. "I stopped you for something else. You're a suspicious person, I have to ask you some questions."

"Imogen…" Leroy's voice trembled behind me.

None of Leroy's experiences with cops were ever good ones, and he was still just a kid. I turned away from the cop, stepped back up on the sidewalk, and patted his shoulder. "It's okay, buddy."

The cop followed me, pulling out his notebook. "Name?" He pointed at Leroy.

"You don't have to answer him, Leroy."

"He does. It's school hours; he should be in school, so if you're responsible for him, you could face criminal charges. Name," he snapped again.

"Leroy Mahoney." His voice wobbled.

I shushed him, but the cop snapped again, talking over me. "Why aren't you in school, Leroy?"

"I got excluded today."

"Why." The cop didn't look at him, and didn't phrase it as a question; he scribbled in his notebook, frowning.

"I got in trouble in school for fighting."

"Did you?' The cop glanced over at me and gave me a disgusted look. "And you're responsible for this boy?"

Damn it. Legally, of course, I wasn't. Leroy would still be registered in the foster care system back in California.

A real tingle of fear shot through me.

I lifted my chin anyway. "Yes, I am. I'm looking after him."

"Is that right?" He snorted. "Name?"

"Imogen Gray."

"You got a license, Imogen Gray?" He said my name in a

stupid baby voice. I clenched my fists. I'd never wanted to punch someone in the face more than I did right now. "Some ID?"

"I do, but I don't have to show you," I said stubbornly.

He gave a laugh and scribbled in his notebook. "Yes, you do."

"You have no cause to stop us, and no reason to ask us any questions. We've broken no laws," I lied furiously.

"I don't need a reason to stop you," the cop chuckled humorlessly. "And I *do* got a reason to ask you questions. Like I said, you're a suspicious person."

Leroy had started to pant, the beginnings of a panic attack. I was beginning to feel some things myself; my chest felt like it was going to explode. I was *so* furious.

It wasn't the first time I'd been stopped by the cops. I was a young woman who appeared to be mixed-race, and for some racist cops, that was enough to stop me. The difference was, every time I'd been stopped before, I was alone. I had nothing to lose. It was so easy for me to break my cuffs, flip the police cruiser and run away. Easy, and fun.

This time, I had something to lose. It was a horrible feeling.

The cop glared at me. "ID," he snapped.

My mind whirled. Leroy had already given his name, which screwed everything up. It was hard for me to concentrate on what I should do. If this cop had Leroy's full name and enough motivation, he could look him up.

His mother had formal custody of Leroy, and she sold him to the Blood Witch. He'd escaped with me, but his social workers would be doing follow-up visitations with his mother. She would have reported Leroy as a runaway, to cover her own ass. There would be an alert out on him.

Last time he was seen in California, we were running

away from two dead bodies in an alleyway. If there were cameras… Facial recognition… Holy shit, we were *screwed*.

I folded my arms over my chest, hoping to bluff it out. "I'm not giving you my ID. Tell me, what do you suspect me of doing?"

"Oh, there's a lot of crime happening around here right now, Imogen Gray." The cop did the stupid baby voice again. "It just so happens that I'm investigating what happened to the statue in the town square. The one of Sir Humphrey, the founder of this town," he said, watching my face carefully for my reaction. "As you know, it got destroyed. It was smashed up by a sledgehammer or something, left in pieces on the ground." He squinted at me. "You know something about that?"

I raised my eyebrows. "What is that supposed to mean?"

"What do you think it means?" He looked right in my eye and smiled smugly. "We had a beautiful statue of this town's great founder in our town square, and it got smashed to pieces. We've got CCTV footage. It's fuzzy, but we've got someone working on getting it cleaned up. What do you think that footage is going to show?"

I knew what it would show. I was there. I didn't *personally* destroy the statue, but I'd been right beside it when the weight of dark knowledge from the Tashk crushed it, then broke it to pieces.

I stayed silent.

The cop waited a full minute. His smug smile vanished. "Right. Where were you that night?"

"What night are you talking about?"

"You know what night I'm talking about."

"No, I don't." Behind me, I could hear Leroy slump to the ground, and put his head in his hands. I worried about him so much that I couldn't think straight.

"August fifth. Where were you?" His voice sharpened.

35

"I don't know. I don't have my diary on me."

"You know what, I'm losing my patience with you." He put his hand on his belt. The holster was unclipped; my eyes involuntarily hovered on his SIG Sauer, just like he intended. "Give me your license, right *now*."

"No."

"No? I don't think you know who you're talking to, here, girl." He shifted his weight, looming over me. "I can make your life hell, you know that? This is a small town, and you think you can come in here and bust up our statues and parade around the main street like you're something?" He spat on the pavement, right in front of me. "Give me your ID, or I'll arrest you right now."

"On what charge, officer?" The familiar, slightly accented voice came from behind me. I gritted my teeth.

The cop squinted behind me. "Who are you?"

Sonja stepped up beside me, moving with her cold preternatural grace. "I am merely a curious citizen of this town, officer..." She stepped forward, pretending to peer at his badge. She would have been able to read it from a mile away. "Harmann. Officer Harmann."

"Oh yeah?" He ran his eyes over her. Sonja was beautiful in the same way that a robot sex doll was beautiful. Interest warred with suspicion in Harmann's eyes. "You don't sound like a citizen."

"I am originally from Berlin, officer, but I assure you I am now a citizen of this great country. I am very interested in the legal processes here, I must admit. I am... *attracted* to the idea of law enforcement. On what charge are you arresting this woman?" Sonja jerked her head towards me.

Harmann tore his eyes away from Sonja and stared at me. I did my best to keep my face as blank as possible. I could almost see his brain ticking over.

There was no charge he could arrest me for, not yet

anyway. He had no evidence that I'd done anything. If someone had reported me as a suspicious person, he would have told me already. He could still arrest me, but it could lead to problems later if he actually had something to arrest me for.

After a long moment, he tucked his notepad back into his pocket. "Nothing, for now. Once that CCTV footage gets cleaned up, I'm coming to look for you, Imogen Gray," he mocked. "Nothing goes on in this town without me knowing about it."

He backed away, maintaining eye contact with me, while he opened the cruiser door. "I'm watching you, you hear me? You and your bully kid," he added, nodding his head towards Leroy. He got in, slammed the door, and hit the siren. He chuckled when Leroy jumped in fright at the loud noise. The cruiser drove away with a skid of wheels.

Asshole. I crouched down next to Leroy. "Are you okay, buddy?"

His face was pale, his eyes pinched closed. "Yeah," he said in a little voice. "That guy was disgusting."

"Yeah, he was. Typical power-trip asshole."

"He felt horrible. Almost like Tony Dangillo, the commando guy. He loved having power over other people too, like it was his life's mission to have everyone squirm underneath him. But he's dumb, y'know."

Sonja sniffed. "It is a terrible combination, to be power-hungry, and to be so stupid." She looked down at me. "You are welcome, by the way."

I gritted my teeth. "I don't need your help, Sonja. I could have knocked him into next week, and you know it. No one would ever find him."

She didn't smile. "You should have done it already. You have made a costly mistake. Now your name is in his database. You are known to him, and so is your ward."

It didn't matter to me. I'd gone by many names over the years, usually a variation of Im, which is what I was called when I was born. At the time, it meant 'star', which were the most beautiful and mysterious things in the prehistoric world.

"It's not my real name, anyway," I shrugged carelessly. I patted Leroy's shoulder. "Why did you give him your real name though, buddy? I thought you were smarter than that."

Leroy looked up at me sharply. The pale, worried look on his face disappeared. It was replaced by a slightly pissed expression. "First of all, Imogen," he said. "I panicked. I don't have the best experiences with cops, as you know."

"Yeah." I bit my lip. "Sorry."

"Second of all, Mahoney is not my last name."

I squinted at him. "What?"

"I panicked, and my real first name came out," he said, eyeing me suspiciously. "But I caught myself, and gave him my made-up last name. It's the name I use for school, anyway, so he'd be able to crosscheck my story and it wouldn't get flagged as suspicious."

"Oh."

"Do you…" He squinted back at me. "Do you actually not know what my real last name is?"

I shrugged. "I guess I never asked."

"Did you not even think about what name I used on my enrollment forms at school?"

I chuckled awkwardly. I'd let him sort that out; application forms were boring, and I hated them. I put Leroy in touch with my forger on the dark web, and he ordered what documents he needed to get himself enrolled in school.

The kid was smart. Far smarter than me; it was embarrassing. My stubbornly average brain was a sore spot for me; it was wildly unfair that I would be so old, with so much experience, but still forget stupid little things. "Okay, I get it."

I threw up my hands. "I should probably keep tabs on stuff like that."

He grinned, his color returning to normal. "Don't sweat it. I can't expect you to remember everything. You've got a lot on your plate."

"Yeah," I frowned. "I don't really need this cop on my back, either."

"He cannot harm you." Sonja sounded disgusted. "He is a worm beneath our feet."

I sighed. "I wish that were true, but he's obviously obsessed with the statue of Sir Humphrey being destroyed. He's going to want to pin that on someone." I bit my lip and looked up the street in the direction the police cruiser had disappeared. "Maybe I should just kill him."

"Imogen. *Imogen.*" Leroy waited until I was looking him in the eye. "No. You can't murder the local law enforcement officer because he's asking awkward questions."

"Spoilsport," I muttered. I wouldn't have even thought twice if Leroy hadn't been around. "Well, I can't leave Emerald Valley right now; my dad is here somewhere, and I have to find him."

"You cannot leave Emerald Valley at all," Sonja declared.

I glanced at her, puzzled. "What?"

"My King would forbid it. For reasons that only he is privy to, he desires your company, so you are not permitted to leave Emerald Valley."

"Oh, honey, I don't give a *damn* what your king wants," I told her. "In fact, that makes me want to pack up the van and take off right now."

She curled her lip, her version of a smirk. "You will not. You have other commitments, you said so yourself."

I huffed out an exasperated breath. "Sonja, why are you even here?"

She held out a large shopping bag. The paper was suspiciously thick and glossy, and the embossed logo on it was familiar. Gucci.

"My King directed me to bring you a dress to wear this evening at dinner. I do not understand why, but you will be dining on the patio at the country club. There will be other guests around. I suppose my Lord does not want you to embarrass yourself in front of the other members."

"Did he?" I took the bag off her and peered inside.

The box inside was gift wrapped. I roughly wiggled the ribbon off so I could see the color of the silk inside. Bright, emerald green. "Well, that's not creepy or controlling *at all*."

Sonja smiled, flashing her teeth at me. Her prominent canines glinted in the sunshine for a second, then she slammed her mouth shut again. Vampires were allergic to sunlight; the younger ones couldn't tolerate the daylight at all. It got easier as they grew older and their skin hardened. Sonja herself was covered head-to-toe in shiny polyester-blend workout gear, with a cap and aviator sunglasses, and her skin glistened with SPF, so I assumed that she was only a few hundred years old. "I do not understand why your feelings matter at all, but I know that he will be pleased that you like it."

I wrinkled my nose. "Thanks, bestie. That's sweet."

"I'll send the car for you at seven." She turned to go.

"I'll drive my van up whenever the hell I feel like it," I sang back.

Sonja turned back and glared at me. I raised an eyebrow. Just as I thought she was going to say something, and we could get into a nice little sparring session right here on Main Street, she let out a breath and turned away again.

Darn. I cracked my knuckles. "I was hoping she'd make a move. I need the release."

"Imogen," Leroy whined. "You can't. Not now, anyway. Harmann might be watching."

"Hmmm." I glared up the street. "I need to think about what to do with him."

"You can't kill him, Imogen."

"I can, actually. It would be *stupidly* easy."

"Yeah," Leroy furrowed his brow. "That's not what I mean. It would be... wrong. Yeah, he's an asshole. He's dumb, and he's on a power trip. But he's not, like, evil."

"Evil is a spectrum, kid. He's on that spectrum."

"Then so are you!"

"I never said I wasn't."

"He doesn't deserve to die."

"None of us deserve it. Some of us aren't that lucky," I shot back.

Leroy shut his mouth and glared at me.

I didn't like him being mad. I threw up my hands. "Okay, fine. I won't kill him. It would create more problems than it would solve, anyway. He'll be putting us in his database as we speak. I need to stay here in the Valley and find my dad."

Leroy was silent for a minute, watching me carefully. I knew what he was thinking. He knew why I wanted to find my dad. I hadn't even had to explain it to him. He was smart, he figured it out.

He knew that if I managed to find my father, I'd find a cure for my immortality. Then, I'd die.

That's what I wanted.

I *used* to want it immediately; as soon as humanly possible, so to speak. But with Leroy right in front of me, I was happy to put it off.

I just wanted to know that there was an end. That's all I wanted. An ending. And I had a pretty good reason.

If you were to ask someone what their worst nightmare was, they'd tell you a variety of things. Dying alone, losing a kid, not finding true love, having a snake come up the toilet and bite you on the vagina... There were lots of 'worst nightmares.'

I'd done them all. I'd experienced every single worst nightmare that anyone could come up with. Anything you could think of... it had happened to me.

That wasn't the worst part. The worst part was this: For me, it would only get worse.

If I didn't find a cure for my immortality, then eventually, I'd live to see the end of the world. I'd be crawling in the dust, mourning everyone I ever loved, choking as the oxygen disappeared from the world, screaming as the scorching rays of the sun blazed through my skin once the atmosphere disappeared. And I'd float through the scattered remains of the earth, weightless, tortured for all eternity.

I swallowed heavily and shoved the Gucci bag at Leroy. "Here, kid. Put this on eBay, would you? Start the bidding at three grand."

He took the bag. "Why are you going to dinner, if you don't like him? Why don't you just say no?"

I *could* have said no. I'd said no before, when he'd asked me, and he hadn't been sulky or vindictive about it. That's if you don't count Sonja and Brick showing up to kidnap me for daring to decline his invitation. Both vampires insisted that Rafael didn't ask them to do it, and they were punished for taking the initiative.

Rafael was more the type to take no for an answer, for now. He would be quietly confident in the fact that he always got what he wanted. He would sit back and wait for whatever he wanted to fall in his lap.

I wasn't going to fall in his lap. No way.

I should have said no to going to dinner this evening. I don't know why I didn't. Rafael made me nervous in a way that I hadn't experienced in centuries, and I couldn't quite figure it out. Powerful men had always made me nervous, so maybe the feeling I got from being around him was just that – just nerves, a slight concern that he was going to go psycho on me at some point. But I didn't think so.

I knew Rafael enjoyed me as a novelty; a puzzle to be worked out. I was new, a shiny toy, something to break up the dull monotony of existence.

I could have said that he was the same to me. He was someone new to torture.

"You gotta keep your enemies close, buddy," I told Leroy, leading him back to the car. "Besides, I'm not passing up a free meal."

CHAPTER 3

The enormous wrought-iron gates of the country club were closed when I arrived for dinner. I stuck my head out the van window and glared at the cameras on top of the pillars. After a second, the gates cracked, and I drove in.

My battered van was not going to fit in well at a million-dollar-a-year-membership country club. Sonja was going to be furious. She tried to pick me up, like she told me she would. I waited at home until I spotted her Maserati driving up to my cabin, then, I deliberately got in my van and drove past her car as she was coming in, giving Brick, Sonja's mate, a cheerful wave as I drove by.

The road into the country club was paved in glittering white marble granite, of all things. I wondered what my tires were doing to it, and how often they'd have to replace it.

A grand palace stood before me; marble columns, turrets, the beautiful, classic structures of pre-Christian Rome. It had been Rafael's heyday, so the architecture made sense. I had noticed that about people in general – they tend to stick to what was fashionable in the time they came of age. It was lucky that Rafael wasn't born in the seventies, or else we'd be dealing with some ugly postmodern brutalism.

I chuckled to myself. No wonder I was comfortable in my rustic wood cabin.

I turned into the wide driveway around an enormous fountain, wondering where to park.

A valet appeared out of nowhere and approached my van. "Good evening, ma'am," he said, opening the door for me and standing back respectfully. "Mr Di Stasio is expecting you."

I didn't unbuckle my belt. "Where do you park the visitors' cars?'

The valet looked at me warily. "We have an underground car park beyond the squash court, just over there," he said, pointing. "Your vehicle will be quite safe, I promise."

Underground. I didn't like that very much. If you had to run, it was far harder to ram your car out of an underground car park than it was to bash your way out of a street-level park, or even a multi-story carpark.

The valet waited patiently. "Listen, Gerald," I said, reading his name off the little tag on his chest. "Is there anywhere else I could park? I might have to make a quick getaway."

"I can have your ride back to you within thirty seconds of you requesting it, ma'am," he said with a reassuring smile. "We've timed it."

"Yes, but thirty seconds can count for a lot when you're in a hurry. You know that, don't you, Gerald?"

He nodded. "I do, ma'am. I will put it at the front entrance of the car park, if that pleases you. So there will be no delays in getting your vehicle out."

"Do you *have* to put my van in the carpark? Is it a rule?'

His genial grin slid slightly. "It's the procedure, ma'am. They're well looked after, I swear."

I tapped the steering wheel, frowning. "I don't want to get you in trouble, Gerald," I said. "I'll tell you what. I'll just wait another few seconds, then the person that I *do* want to get in trouble will be here…"

Right on cue, Sonja's Maserati raced up the marble road and screeched to a halt next to me. She got out, moving like a smooth, efficient robot. "What are you doing here in that monstrosity? I was supposed to pick you up."

I grinned at her. "I told you I would be driving."

She glared back. Instructions contrary to her master's orders did not compute. "Get out," she jerked her head.

Brick appeared behind her. He ran his eyes over my van, his eyebrows furrowed. He did not know what to do either.

"Just a sec." I pulled a steering wheel lock from under my seat and snapped it on, firmly locking it in place, and tucking the key into my bra.

"What are you doing?" Sonja's pale face was turning purple.

"Locking my van, of course, silly." I held her gaze calmly, while my hands found my gear lock and snapped it on my transmission with very practiced movements.

"You can't leave your van here!"

I smiled. I noticed Gerald had vanished. Smart man. "Of *course* I can." I opened the door and got out, beeping the lock behind me.

Her eyes bugged. "You're not wearing the dress!"

"It was too cold. I'm warm-blooded, unlike you." I tutted. "You didn't do your research properly." Instead of the beautiful Gucci dress, I was wearing black cargo pants, a long-sleeved black crop top, a short black jacket, and my Doc Marten boots. I had thought about adding a beanie, but I was having a good hair day, so I'd left it loose.

She ran her eyes over me in disgust. "The country club is heated to perfection, and that dress cost ten thousand dollars. I'll have to find you something in my quarters."

I looked her up and down and stuck my nose in the air.

"I'm not wearing Lululemon to dinner, Sonja. That would be inappropriate."

Brick cleared his throat behind her, and murmured in Sonja's ear. "I can tear off the gear lock and steering wheel brace easily. I can also probably carry the van into the car park, but it might damage the van, and the locks would be useless. Do you think our Master would–"

"Oh, he would punish you," I said cheerfully. "I'd be wildly unhappy if my ride got damaged. For reasons that I don't understand, your boss is trying to suck up to me at the moment. If he punished you for kidnapping me, what do you think he'd do if you wrecked something I love?"

The vampires stared at me; Sonja white with fury, Brick vaguely confused.

Finally, Sonja stirred. "Leave it," she spat through clenched teeth. "Come. I'll take you to our quarters to change."

I followed her as she led me through the vast, shining white marble corridors. We walked past serene courtyards, over a pure green lawn in the middle of an enormous atrium, and through a lush greenhouse where I spotted some delicate orchids and a species of carnivorous lily, both of which I hadn't seen in thousands of years. I thought they'd gone extinct.

Finally, we reached the end of a long corridor. Sonja placed her thumb on a keypad near an almost-invisible door.

I glanced down at it. Questa lock, activated by a drop of blood. The security system here was insanely expensive and almost impenetrable. If the blood signature was wrong in any way, if the blood was too old or cold, or if the thumbpad was tampered with in any way, the door would bolt shut, and could only be opened again by a keymaster.

The keypad beeped, and the door swung open.

Sonja and Brick's quarters were huge, and very odd. I'd expected minimalism, hard lines and neutral tones.

"Wow," I said, moving into the room and poking around, ignoring Sonja's irritated huff behind me. "This isn't what I expected, Sonja. I thought you'd be more minimalist. This is *max*imalist."

An enormous circular bed lay in the corner, its cover a big swirl of gold and red. The wardrobes on one side of the room were paneled in dark oak and gilt-edged, one of them open, spilling gaudy silk scarves out of a top drawer. The walls were striped red and white, and decorated with framed posters of PT Barnum's first circus; the Bearded Lady in one, the Dog-Faced Boy in another.

I stopped near the poster by the bed. It had the Strongman, a ridiculously over-muscled freak, holding a beautiful blonde woman over his head.

I frowned, and looked closer. The Strongman had a thick black mustache, but if I stuck my finger over it and refocused...

I turned, and stared at Sonja. "Is that... Brick?"

She glared at me.

"Come on, Sonja," I cajoled. "Tell me. I won't hold it against you. In fact, I might be nicer to you if you tell me a little about yourself and Brick. Is that him?"

She huffed out a breath. "Yes."

"He was the Strongman in PT Barnum's circus? Wow," I said, staring back at the poster. "I never got to see it." I'd been in China for a good part of the nineteenth century, searching for a cure for my immortality. "I heard of it, though," I said. "PT Barnum was a bit of a scam artist, wasn't he?"

"He was a lot more than that," Sonja replied, her voice tinged with darkness. "He owned all his oddities; they were his slaves. Even Brick, who could have smashed him into the ground even as a human, was owned. Brick's mother was a

Bearded Lady, one of many. He was born and grew up in the circus. They were his family, and he loved them, but he was not permitted to leave. He became the Strongman to try and break his way out using his strength, but Barnum kept his mother and refused to release her. She died before Brick could see her freed." Sonja's face hardened. "Barnum sold tickets to her autopsy."

"Oh." I peered at the picture again, and pointed to the beautiful blonde doing a back-bend on top of Brick's outstretched hand. "Is that you up there?"

She nodded. "I was in America on business for the General and had thought it appropriate to sample some of the New World's frivolous entertainment. I met Brick." She clamped her mouth shut.

I stared at her, waiting for her to go on. "So, what happened?"

"The General recalled me."

I waited patiently. Sonja met my eyes stonily. I sighed. "Why do I have to drag this out of you?"

She took a deep, unnecessary breath. "The General recalled me... And I did not come."

My eyes widened. "Oh. Oh, *wow*."

"Yes."

General Lucius Claudius Agrippa was the Vampire King before Rafael, and he'd ruled over his territory with an iron fist. No one dared go up against him. If any vampire within his territory set even a toe out of line, not only would Lucius kill said vampire, but he'd also kill the rest of that vampire's nest, as well as their human companions, their workers, their postman, their hairdresser, and basically anyone the vampire had ever spoken to. He'd been cold, methodical, secretive, brutal and uncompromising.

"You mean to tell me you deliberately disobeyed orders from your king, for *love?* Ew, Sonja," I teased her.

She threw a wad of gold silk at me. "Put this on."

I let the dress hit my chest and fall to the floor. "No. Tell me more. What happened?"

She sighed heavily. "I hid in the circus with Brick for a few years, then I turned him. We went on the run together. We hid in other kingdoms for a long time, staying out of sight, watching desperately as General Lucius expanded his territory, sinking his hooks deep into other kingdoms as he did so. We debated what to do, over and over again. We could not hide for long in other kingdoms, we knew that. We were traitors, and not worth enough for another ruler to keep, knowing we'd defied our king. Finally, in an act of madness," she said, shaking her head. "I managed to get a message to the General's son, begging him for help. I'd served him before I met Brick, briefly, so he knew of me. I told him the truth, and begged to be allowed to come home."

The ghost of a smile appeared on her lips. "My Master concocted an elaborate lie to explain away my hundred-year absence and the sudden appearance of Brick, and we were able to return. My Master didn't have to help us, you understand." Sonja stared at me hard. "He had no reason to. I had defied his father. But he helped us. He brought us home and granted us permission to mate."

"So that's why you're obsessed with Di Stasio," I breathed out. "He took away everything that you ever feared and gave you everything you could ever want." Lucky for some. "Nice. Did you ever wonder why he did it?"

Sonja shook her head. "I would never question him. It is not my place to ponder why my Master does as he does. I do know, however, that he has knowledge far beyond anything that the General ever had. He has wisdom that exceeds the ancients," she said, her eyes gleaming. "Whatever purpose he had in granting us our wish, it is guided by his pure divinity."

I rolled my eyes. "Give it a rest. He's not a deity."

"No. He is better, because he is *real*." She looked at me in disgust. "It is not for me to question why he does anything. I usually do not even consider it, although I do not understand why he bothers with you."

"It's my sense of humor," I told her. "You should try it."

She stared at me with her psychopath eyes. "Put on the dress."

"No."

She clawed her hands. "I will strip you naked and sew you into it."

"You can try," I said, skipping backwards a step so I'd have room to move.

Her hands came back down. "You said you would be nicer to me if I shared information with you."

"I said that I *might* be nicer to you. *Might*."

"Put it on," she growled.

"I'll tell you what, Sonja. We already know that your judgment is horribly impaired, and when left to your own devices, you make terrible decisions. So, tell me. Did Rafael tell you to make me wear this dress?"

She glowered at me.

"Did he?" I put my hands on my hips.

"No," she ground out the words bitterly.

"Then I'm not wearing it."

"You're dining on the patio. You must wear a dress." She lifted her chin. "Those are club rules."

"Do you mean to tell me that I'm going to be dining with a handful of billionaires who will be sitting around wearing silk Gucci dresses?"

She nearly rolled her eyes. "No, you moron. The men must wear jackets and ties."

"Well, I'm already wearing a jacket..." I backed up until I was near the wardrobe, and snagged one of the scarves that was hanging out of the drawer. I quickly flipped it around my neck in a practiced motion. "I'm assuming a cravat will be okay?"

Sonja bared her teeth at me. "You have three seconds to put down my scarf and put on the gold dress. If you do not, I will strip you naked and wrestle you into it myself. One…"

I held eye contact, my fingers tying the scarf in a knot, tucking the ends underneath my shirt.

"Two…"

I pulled at the silk at my throat to create the perfect cravat puff.

Sonja opened her mouth. "Th–"

I bolted. One moment I was standing still, the next, I was through the door before Sonja even saw me move. I whipped the door closed behind me and mashed my fist down on the thumbpad, smashing it two inches into the marble stone. The door made an ominous *clunk* noise as the bolts within the doorframe slid through the reinforced steel frame.

A fraction of a second later, I was rewarded with a satisfying *thunk* as Sonja hit the door, attempting to smash through it.

I chuckled, turned around, and skipped away, idly wondering where the dining room was.

CHAPTER 4

The security at the country club caught up with me in seconds. Luckily, they were a lot more amenable than Sonja was. I was escorted to the dining room by an army of helpful employees.

The patio was set on the east wing of the country club. Elevated high above the sprawling golf course, it provided an excellent view of the rest of the valley, and the pretty little town below. The height gave the patio a heady atmosphere, as if we were all gods in Olympus, gazing down at our subjects.

Despite being entirely in the open air, the patio was perfectly heated. There was no indication of a breeze, or even a waft of smoke from one of the braziers that burned in the corner.

Twenty or so other members and their guests milled around, talking in groups at the bar before being escorted to their tables. The men were, predictably, in stiff dinner jackets and bowties. I grinned happily when I spotted a few cravats instead of ties.

The women were extraordinary; supermodel-beautiful, in

figure-hugging gowns that flowed effortlessly down their gorgeous bodies. They must be guests, of course; not members. Even the world's highest-paid supermodel couldn't afford the million-dollar-a-year membership fees.

I glanced around, and spotted two sharp-eyed older women, both in structured designer dresses. The sight made me feel oddly reassured. In a lot of the exclusive clubs around the world, women were not admitted as members.

A staff member appeared at my elbow. "Madam," he said quietly. "Mr Di Stasio is waiting for you at his table. Would you permit me to escort you?"

I nodded, and followed him outside, ignoring the outraged muttering of the other members and guests as they watched me walk past, still in my cargo pants and cropped jacket, with the stupid makeshift cravat at my throat.

As we weaved our way through the tables towards the eastern end of the patio, the grumbling quickly subsided. One by one, the guests realized where I was headed, and who I was with, and obviously felt it safer to keep their mouths shut.

The waiter led me to what I would call the feng shui power zone in the east corner. We would be separate from the other diners, and elevated on a slight platform. From here, I would have an excellent view of all the people on the patio, as well as the restaurant entrance.

I'd spotted Rafael the moment I'd walked into the restaurant, although I'd done a stellar job in pretending that I didn't see him. The Vampire King was easily the most impressive thing in the room – vibrating with astonishing handsomeness, radiating wealth and privilege. Everyone else on the patio held themselves carefully around him, as if we were all planets and moons, and he was our sun.

He might as well have a choir of angels standing behind him, singing odes to his magnificence. The dinner jacket he wore clung to him perfectly, highlighting his impressive height and muscular body, and his crisp white shirt offset his tanned skin, complimenting it perfectly.

It was the tan that gave me goosebumps. Vampires don't tan unless they are really, really old. The only way a vampire gets to be really, really old is to be extraordinarily powerful.

A human would look at Rafael and think: *Wow. Gorgeous, powerful, rich.*

Someone who knew better would look at him and think: *Old. Powerful. Run.*

I swallowed roughly. I forgot about it until I laid eyes on him. No, I forgot until I actually thought hard about it. He was dangerous, and that was something that you didn't see when you first laid eyes on him.

At first, he blinded you with his magnificence. The danger was there, nonetheless, and even though I couldn't feel it instinctively, I knew for a fact that if I irritated him enough, he could make my life a never-ending torture. I kept forgetting that. I should behave myself.

It wasn't just me that was in danger. Leroy, too. Rafael knew all about Leroy already, and Marigold. He'd been completely aware of the shifter school on the other side of the valley, and he knew exactly who Backman was. They posed absolutely no threat to him at all, so he ignored them.

And there was Benson. He didn't count though. Rafael seemed to genuinely like him, which was odd in and of itself. Benson was not a particularly likable person. I liked him because he was crazy, and it made me feel relatively stable when I was standing next to him.

I have all these friends now. How the hell did that happen? It had been centuries since I'd let anyone get close to me. It always ended in pain, every single time. I learnt my lesson for hundreds of years, but here I was again, with something to lose.

What would happen if any of us offended Rafael in some way? His father, the General Lucius, had once burned London to the ground to get rid of a couple of vampires who insulted his wife. I had no idea what his son was capable of. Rafael was the only surviving child of Lucius, so I assumed he'd be every inch the iron-fisted dictator that his dad was.

I'd known a lot of power-hungry maniacs in my lifetime. I'd been one myself, on a few different occasions, when the madness got too much, and I couldn't control myself. I knew what we were capable of. What kind of monster was Rafael Stefano Di Stasio?

Standing beside Rafael, almost dulled into invisibility by his insignificance, Brick stood upright, holding out a screen so Rafael could see it. Both watched the screen carefully. Brick's face was mildly alarmed. Rafael's expression was smooth and cool, as usual, although I thought I could detect a hint of a twinkle in his eye. Whatever he was watching amused him, but he wasn't going to show it.

I clomped up to the table in my Doc Martens. Rafael glanced up and watched me approach. The twinkle in his eye grew, but he still didn't smile.

Brick's mouth fell open as his king rose and held his arms out.

"Miss Gray," Rafael murmured. His voice felt like tequila kisses under a stormy sky. I shook my head to get the image out, to try and focus. What the hell was wrong with me? "Thank you for joining me," he added, tilting his head back, regarding me carefully.

"Eye eye, your Fangliness," I said, saluting him.

I could have kicked myself. So much for not provoking him. I wasn't even sure why I was being such a dork; it wasn't even my style.

His gaze swept down my body. "You look... dazzling, this evening. I particularly like your tie." The side of his mouth twitched, but he quickly smoothed out the beautiful lines of his lips, and settled into his usual smolder. "You did not like the dress I gave you?"

I shook my head. "I'm sure it was nice, but I'm more comfortable in my own clothes."

"Understandable. I merely sought to alleviate any discomfort you might have in dining here without an appropriate dress. I did not mean to insult you."

"Oh, there's no offense taken." My bank account would get a boost once Leroy sold the dress. "Sonja is a little miffed, though."

Brick's fists clenched; he made an odd grunt. Rafael's lip twitched again, but he controlled it. "Yes, she is. We are currently watching her on the security cameras. She is attempting to punch her way through a solid marble wall."

I peered over at the screen. Sonja's fists were a blur, whirling back and forward on the marble near the door, breaking off little chunks at a time. She looked like her head was going to explode. "Why don't you get the keymaster to open the door?"

Rafael glanced up at me when I said the word keymaster. Yes, that's right, Your Fangliness, I know everything there is to know about your security systems.

Brick cleared his throat. "She dented the steel bolts in the frame. We can't open it."

I chuckled. She wouldn't have known that I'd punched out the keypad, triggering the bolts, so she thought she could bash the door down. "She was going to strip me naked and sew me into the dress, you know."

Rafael's eyes flared. He composed himself quickly. "Is that right? I apologize. Sonja can be a little…"

"Insane?"

"I was going to say… proactive. She has, as you might say, a lot of initiative. It works well in most aspects of my business." He hitched his shoulders languidly in an elegant shrug. The lines of his crisp white shirt shifted, highlighting his powerful shoulders.

"How does that normally work out for you in your love life, though?" I asked sweetly. "How many of your dates begin with the girl in a sack, slung over Sonja's back, and dumped at your feet?"

His eyes twinkled. He pressed his lips together. "None."

"Do you mean to tell me that she doesn't always kidnap your dates when they refuse to dine with you?"

"So far, no one else has refused."

"Well, what happens if one of your girlfriends won't let you pick her up in your ride?"

"That has not happened, so I cannot say."

I frowned. "So… what do you do when Sonja makes one of your dates wear something that they don't want to wear?"

"It is not often I give a dress to my dining partner, Imogen," he said, one eyebrow lifting slightly. "Usually, I do not need to, as my dates tend to always have appropriate dining attire. I've seen your wardrobe, you know," he said, the hint of a smirk playing on his lips. He'd had the roof of my cabin fixed, of course he'd have someone snoop around and report back. "I knew you did not have a cocktail dress to wear. I merely sought to remove that problem. That green dress was bespoke. I gave the atelier your measurements. You might have liked it if you had tried it on."

He had a gown specially made for me, just for our date this evening. I frowned. Controlling, or thoughtful and generous? Possibly both. Oh well, it was still going on eBay.

Rafael waved a hand at the table. "Please, sit."

A waiter appeared at my side and held out the chair for me. "Oh, thank you," I said. I pulled the chair back further, swung it around, and nestled it on the other side of the table, next to Rafael. I was halfway to putting my butt in the chair when I froze, realizing how it must look.

Rafael shifted away slightly, and sat down next to me, holding my gaze. "I see you cannot have your back to the room either."

I shook my head. "I'll never be able to relax."

"You are a warrior."

"A worrier, more like."

"That's what I said."

"Ha. No, I meant like, I'm a worrier. You're a warrior."

He nodded patiently. "Yes."

"I mean worrier, not warrior. Oh, geeze." I smacked my head. The two men at the table next to us were signing contracts; I leaned over, my arm outstretched. "Can I borrow this?" I plucked the pen out of his hand and flipped my napkin. It wasn't paper, but it would do. "See, warrior. And…" I scribbled the word into the napkin. "Worrier. As in, I worry a lot." I pitched the pen back to the man next to me. "There you go. Thanks."

Rafael clenched his teeth; the muscle on his jaw pulsed, squaring out his jawline. "Senator Broad and Mr Xi are signing a peace treaty."

"That's nice. Good for them." I smiled.

"It means the end of a civil war that's been raging for decades. You just took the pen out of their hand."

"I gave it back." I shrugged.

Rafael pressed his lips together again. "You could have just said, worrier, as in, I worry a lot."

"But I didn't, okay? I felt the need to make myself understood, for some insane reason."

Rafael looked away. It took me a while to understand the expression. I still wasn't *completely* sure, but it looked like he was trying very hard not to laugh.

I coughed to cover up my awkwardness. "To answer your

question, yes, I am a warrior too, I suppose. A fighty one, I mean. I can't sit with my back to the room."

He waved his hand, gesturing at the table. The waiters quickly descended and moved the plates and cutlery around, so that I would be sitting next to Rafael, not opposite him. "Unfortunately, I cannot sit with my back to the room either, so you will have to sit next to me."

"What could you possibly be scared of, Your Majesty? This is your domain, and your people, with your friends."

"This is my domain, yes, and my servants are all mine. But none of these people are my friends, Imogen. I keep them close so I may understand them."

I gazed at him frankly. "Why did you invite me here today?"

"I thought we would share information," he said, holding out his hands in an expansive gesture. I made the mistake of looking at them.

Big hands. A little calloused in a couple of telltale spots; he worked a dagger as well as a sword. Thickened skin on his knuckles told me he punched hard things, often. He was a warrior. I had no idea what his fighting skills were like. I knew his father trained every day. Stories of him regularly killing his sparring partners had reached my ears on a few different occasions. I thought his son might be a pampered pen-pusher, but it looked to me like he knew his way around a blade.

Also: Big hands.

"What kind of information?" I asked warily.

"How about this; you ask me a question, and I'll ask you a question?"

"Okay."

"I'll go first. I know you are immortal. I know you are slightly faster than a vampire, and possibly match an average vampire for strength. Do you have any other abilities?"

Argh. He just wanted to assess me as a threat. "Unless you can count being a terrible driver as an ability, then no, I don't. I'm strong and fast, and I can grow back anything you dare to chop off."

He furrowed his brow. "Have I said something to offend you?"

I shook my head. "Nothing that I shouldn't have expected." I straightened up. "My turn. What happened to your dad?"

Rafael answered automatically. "He has abdicated the throne."

"Bullshit."

He cocked an eyebrow. "Can you tell I am lying?"

"Ha. No, I just don't believe you."

He frowned for a second; my eyes flared. Again, I'd forgotten to not piss him off. "Sorry," I said quickly. "Honestly, I don't think anyone who knows the General would ever believe that he stepped down voluntarily. It's not his style."

Rafael shifted in his chair, turning to face me fully, his dark eyes somber. "You speak of my father so casually. Did you know him?"

"Oh, no way. No *way*. No offense, but I know who to avoid, if you get what I'm saying." I picked up my salad fork and started fiddling with it, avoiding his intense stare. "I don't like to attract too much attention, if I can help it. Powerful men tend to fixate on me, then try and destroy me when they can't use me. It's not fun." *Please don't be like that.* I cleared my throat, hoping that I hadn't said the silent part out loud. I had not. Good. "To answer your question, no, I don't know your father. I keep up to date with the supe gossip, so I know who to avoid." I frowned. "Honestly, I would have avoided you too, but you blocked the road with your cavalcade and refused to move even when I honked my horn at you."

He pressed his lips together and looked away again. When he turned back, his eyes were shining. "You did *not* do a good job in avoiding my attention, Imogen. Sonja and Brick are both elite security operatives, and you stripped them naked and sent them home covered in mud."

"I couldn't see any other option. I could have killed them, I suppose." I shrugged. "I thought about it. It would have made everything worse, though. I knew that sending them home buck-naked might get your attention, but I was hoping there was a chance that they'd be too embarrassed to tell you what happened. Instead, you showed up yourself, and forced them to apologize." I smirked. "You're like an angry dad whose kid stole something from the store."

Rafael looked down at his plate. Miraculously, there was food on it. I'm sure it hadn't been there before.

I peered down at my own plate. On it sat a delicate shimmering scallop and a sliver of cucumber, nestled on a saffron-yellow cream.

Where did that come from? I hadn't even seen the waiters move. Nobody asked me what I wanted to eat, although I didn't expect anyone to. Fine dining, I'd noticed, had come full circle. In the old days, the host brought out everything they'd cooked, and if you liked it, you ate it. When restaurants became a thing, you were always asked what you wanted to eat, and if you had any dietary needs. Now, you go to a nice restaurant, and they bring out heavenly food and call you a stupid pig if you don't eat it.

I forked up the scallop and shoved it in my mouth. *Delicious.*

I looked up again, Rafael was staring right at me. His plate was untouched. I nodded towards it. "Are you going to eat that? No?" Leaning over, I speared the scallop and popped it in my mouth.

Rafael let out a sigh. "You are absolutely bizarre."

"Sorry, I just assumed that you weren't going to eat it. Because you're a vampire, y'know? I didn't want it to go to waste."

"No, I mean I still cannot figure you out. When I came to see you for the first time – after you sent Brick and Sonja home naked – I wasn't trying to intimidate you. I was worried. I was concerned that I might have a goddess on my hands."

"A goddess?"

"You're not a vampire or a shifter. They didn't know what you were, and they were alarmed. You were stronger and faster, you knew that they would burn in sunlight, and you played with them like they were your toys. My father often spoke of a goddess who manifested during a battle between the Romans and the Gauls, around 4BC, and you reminded me of her." His eyes roamed around my face for a moment, assessing me carefully. "According to my father, this goddess could foresee the outcome of every battle. She was a terrifying creature; blazing black eyes and huge nose. She often took the form of a crow."

I squinted. "Are you talking about Cathubodua?"

Rafael put a hand over his face, covering his eyes. "Of course you know her. Why wouldn't you know a goddess?"

I chuckled awkwardly. Gods and goddesses very occasionally manifested on Earth, when the portal was near and the planets aligned properly. They're not very powerful while they are here, but they are unpredictable, which makes them dangerous. There's nothing like the intense stimulation of a world war to get a goddess all riled up for manifestation. "I mean..." I said to Rafael, shrugging. "I don't *know* know her. I heard about it. That's all." I pressed my lips together and looked away.

I'd been in Belgium at the time. I heard about the manifestation of Cathubodua, so I ran in to see if this goddess could put an end to my immortality. I figured I'd take the chance.

Unfortunately, death was her talent, so she knew immediately that I couldn't be killed. She was a good sport, though, so she decided to try to kill me the best way she knew how – she took me to the nearest alehouse and tried to drown me in beer. Cathy, like all war goddesses, was fond of a drink. When she dematerialized two weeks later, the only thing I was in danger of was alcohol poisoning and strep throat from kissing too many Gaulish soldiers.

Rafael didn't need to know any of that, though. I cleared my throat. "So, the great Vampire King, Rafael Stefano Di Stasio was scared that a crazy goddess had come to screw up his kingdom. Instead, you got me, a two-hundred-thousand year old immortal woman barely clinging on to her sanity."

He shrugged languidly. "Not so different from the goddess."

"A goddess has magic. I have none."

"I don't know if I agree with you there."

I furrowed my brow. He didn't elaborate.

"You know," I said idly, swirling my wine in my glass. "I *was* worshiped as a goddess for a couple of hundred years. In Germany, around 40,000BC, somewhere around then, anyway. I'd just regenerated from being crushed by a landslide, so my mental state wasn't that great. I had a big fuck-it attitude going on back then."

Rafael's eyes sparkled. "Tell me."

"There's not much to tell. It's not a good story. I sat in a big palace, and people brought me things. They carved statues of me. If I was unhappy, I'd rip out some spinal columns. I lived like that for two centuries, being worshiped as a goddess." I looked into my wine glass, lifted it, and drained it. "Eventually, someone got pissed enough with me to cut my throat while I was sleeping. They threw my body into a lava pit. It wasn't a good time, Rafael. I wasn't a good person." I shrugged. "I'm not a good person."

Rafael was silent. He watched my face carefully.

Why the hell did I tell him that story? I hadn't mentioned it to anyone in a long, long time. His face showed no emotion while I told it. He didn't seem disgusted with me.

"No goddess has ever been blessed enough to be humbled like you have," Rafael murmured softly. He was silent for a moment, then he shook his head. "It is hard for me to comprehend how it is possible that someone like you has been walking the earth for so long, and I have not heard of you before."

"I try to keep on the down-low," I muttered. "Lucky for me, soon enough, everyone that I know dies and is forgotten. Even Cathy, the goddess. She was the biggest thing to happen in thousands and thousands of years, but now no one has heard of her, except for maybe the oldest creatures in existence, like you. All I have to do is wait it out, and I'll be forgotten again. I keep to myself as much as possible. As soon as I stick my head above the parapet, it gets shot. Unlike a normal person, I don't die. It's a curse."

His deep brown eyes bored into mine. "I have spent several evenings reevaluating my opinion of immortality since I met you," he murmured, his voice low, like the rumble of distant thunder. "Immortality has always been the Holy Grail for creatures such as I. Powerful mortal men, too, would do anything for the chance to live forever."

"Careful what you wish for," I muttered. I took a deep pull of my wine, which had been mysteriously refilled.

A tingle shot through me. I'd definitely drained my glass before, but now it was full.

Was I actually here? Was I imagining everything?

I looked down at my body. My legs were still there. My entrails were inside my belly, where they belonged. Two arms, check, check.

Quickly, I ran through my routine - I tapped the table, sniffed my wine, and focused on the sound of the two men talking at the table next to us, just for a second. I surreptitiously picked up my phone and pushed the camera app. Rafael appeared on the screen.

Okay, we were good. I was actually here, dining with the Vampire King. The waiters must be invisible, then.

I glanced around quickly, and saw a waiter shimmy around another table and refill their water glasses as quickly and gracefully as a hummingbird sipping nectar from the flowers. The two men, deep in discussion, didn't notice him. The waiters weren't invisible; they were just very good at their jobs.

I sighed in relief, and turned back to Rafael.

He had cocked his head and was looking at me oddly with a deep frown on his face. "Are you okay? Is there something wrong?"

"Oh no, no. I'm all good."

"You looked like you were worried about something."

I shook my head. "I'm fine. Reality is normal. I'm sorry," I said, and waved my hand. "Please, continue with what you were saying. Something about how people stupidly think immortality is the best thing since 'skip intro?'"

He hid a smirk. "My father, in particular, desired immortality above all else. He spent thousands of years searching for ways to make himself immortal. He chased sorcerers, dug up tombs, had witches brew spells, all for the chance to live forever. And here you are, in all your glory, fallen into my lap and revealing it to be the empty curse that it is."

I patted my cheeks to see if they felt as hot as they seemed. "Yup, it's a curse all right." I fumbled with my fork, and looked down. The hummingbird waiters had visited us again; my plate had been refilled: A sliver of blood-red beef with the skinniest piece of asparagus arranged artfully around it.

Mindlessly, I speared it up and shoved it in my mouth. It was so delicious that I didn't even think about it – I leaned over and forked up Rafael's piece. The beef was on the way to my mouth, when suddenly, his hand was around my arm, freezing me in place.

The shock was electric. His hand was firm, but gentle, stopping me easily. There was an intense strength in his hand, like an immovable iron cuff had suddenly manifested around my arm. I glanced up, and got caught in his intense gaze. I was locked in place.

For a second, I wondered if I was in trouble. Then, the hint of a smile played around his lips.

I scowled. "You're not going to eat it!"

"On the contrary, I still enjoy human food."

"You do not!"

"I do."

"Liar."

His arm flexed, and I tensed, testing his strength. With an unfathomable amount of force, he slowly brought my hand to his lips, and put the fork in his mouth. I watched, mesmerized, as his tongue swirled the delicate meat off the silverware.

I felt a hot flush in my cheeks. He chewed with relish, holding my stare the whole time.

I broke eye contact first, and cleared my throat awkwardly. "Most vampires I've ever known are disgusted by human food. They're all about the blood, they talk about it like they're sommeliers at Balthazar." I picked up my wine glass and swirled the contents. "Oh, this one is a fine 1967 Latvian vintage, well-aged, top notes of cinnamon and CrossFit workouts with undercurrents of dark chocolate and a hint of high cholesterol."

Rafael put his hand over his face. "Stop," he mumbled.

I frowned. "Stop what?"

The hand disappeared. He exhaled heavily. "One of the reasons Sonja is so unsettled–"

"Do you mean psychopathically unstable?"

"–Is because she is worried. Vampires are measured by their consistency. Especially old vampires, as you know. We are monitored carefully for signs of change. When a vampire changes, trouble is sure to follow."

"I know. Old vampires eventually go mad, and have to be put down before they kill too many people and attract too much attention from the Normies. What's your point?"

He glared at me. "You seem to have an uncanny ability to amuse me."

"You make it sound like I'm pulling teeth."

"Vampires are not known for their sense of humor, Imogen. We do not smile easily, and we laugh even less."

"Bullshit. Vampires laugh all the time. Granted, it's not really like, *I'm watching an old episode of Seinfeld and having a good chuckle kind of laugh.* It's more like, *I'm cutting off the head of my enemy with a spoon and laughing maniacally while I do it* kind of laughing."

Rafael leaned towards me. "You must understand. My kingdom has been a little... unsettled, with my father abdicating the throne." All the mirth had disappeared from his face. "I am being watched very carefully. As you know, my father ruled the North with a firm hand."

"That's an understatement. A firm hand, filled with nuclear weapons, maybe."

He lifted his chin. "I am not my father. My enemies know this, but they do not know what kind of ruler I will be. They are watching me, waiting to see where my weaknesses lie."

I looked him over. If you put a gun to my head, I couldn't tell you where any of his weaknesses were. He projected an insane amount of strength.

I could see what he was trying to tell me, though. I was amusing, like a jester, the Fool in a royal court. He couldn't be seen to smile at me, because that would be perceived as either weakness, which would endanger his new kingdom, or indicate madness, which would put his life at risk.

"I got it," I said shortly. "I'll try to be more like Sonja. A mysterious sex robot." I took a sip of my wine, and smoldered at him.

He leaned away from me, and exhaled. "*Dios mio*, don't do that, either." He shifted in his seat. "You will be the death of me, Imogen."

"Well, then. Lucky for you," I said shortly. I felt weirdly irritated. "Tell me, Rafael. Why did you really invite me to dinner tonight? I don't believe it was to just share information. Was it just so you could test me for weaknesses? Find out how to get rid of me, if you had to?"

"Of course not."

"Did you just need a date for the evening?"

He let out a bitter chuckle that no one would mistake for a laugh. "On the contrary. If that was the case, I would have met you somewhere else. Your appearance here is already unprecedented."

"What do you mean?"

He fixed me with a stare. "Vampires do not date humans. We stalk them, we manipulate them, and we eat them. We do not invite them to our domain to share a meal." His eyes roamed around my body for a long moment, making me squirm. "Vampires only mate with vampires. The whole world is watching me, to see who I will choose as my mate. The fact that I am having dinner with someone who appears to be mortal… Well, that is already making waves within my realm. It is unprecedented."

My mouth was suddenly dry. "I'm not mortal."

"Yes. *That* news is most definitely making its way around the supernatural community by now, since you vanquished the Bloodlord."

I put my hand over my face. Great. So much for keeping my head down. Rafael had me over a barrel now. It had been several millennia since I'd been world-famous in the Supe community. I suddenly had a big target painted on my back. Rafael, being the most powerful creature in the world, was the best person to protect me.

I wondered if this was what the dinner was about. He was shaking me down, like a mafia boss demanding protection money for keeping me shielded from the other thugs. Sooner or later, he was going to want payment for the protection.

I wondered what form that payment would come in.

I shouldn't have been surprised. Rafael was a chessmaster like his father, moving his pieces into place, protecting his most powerful weapons and keeping his pawns close.

I turned back to Rafael, frowning. "Something has been bugging me. Sonja told me that you saved her, when she betrayed your father. You lied for her, brought her home, and let her mate with Brick." I stared at him. "Why did you do that? Was it so you could win her loyalty?"

"No." He shrugged. "That would be a pointless exercise. You know as well as anyone how flimsy loyalty could be. Before Sonja met Brick, she was unquestionably loyal to my father. He was cruel to her, yes, but she was loyal."

"Her love for Brick destroyed that loyalty, though."

"Yes. Love destroys everything."

I raised my eyebrows. "That's a little dark, even for you, Your Fangliness."

"It's true." He leaned towards me. "You know it as well as anyone."

I opened my mouth. Nothing came out. I shut it again.

I *did* know it. It was burned on my psyche. I opened my mouth again to deny it, though, just to be contrary. Before I could get the words out, a distant rumble caught my attention. It came from below, down in the valley.

I cocked my head, listening carefully. Thunder? No, the skies were clear tonight.

I looked down at my wine glass. The dark liquid inside trembled. Glancing back up at Rafael, I frowned. "Earthquake?"

The muscle in his jaw twitched. "No. And yes." He frowned. "I feel... *something*."

I didn't feel anything at all. I glanced around. None of the other guests seemed to notice the distant rumble, or the ripples in their wine glasses. The man next to me had his shirt sleeves rolled up, and I could see the hair on his arm standing on end. While I was watching, the man looked down at his arm. A slight furrow appeared in his brow.

Rafael had gone very still. "The portal." His voice took on a dangerous edge. "We must go." He balled his napkin. "Something is coming."

CHAPTER 5

The streetlights on Main had blown; the little town was in complete darkness. My eyes ached while they adjusted. It was disorientating. I let Rafael take the lead, and we ran towards the town square like ghosts in the wind. Rafael was fast; faster than any vampire I'd come across. Possibly faster than me. I wasn't looking forward to testing that.

Sonja and Brick followed closely behind us, leading a team clad in black combat gear. The rumbling had stopped. It had only been a few minutes since we'd been sitting on the patio at the country club, watching the dark liquid tremble in my wine glass.

We blazed through the streets and stopped abruptly at the edge of the town square, taking cover behind the pillars of the council chambers. I glanced behind me. The vamp combat team swept the area, their assault rifles following the motions of their sweep, carefully checking everything around us.

The town center was deserted. Perhaps subconsciously,

all of Emerald Valley's residents stayed home in their cozy houses with their doors shut tight when night came, not risking creeping out their doors and running into something unknown. None of them had any idea that a portal to all other worlds lay above their heads, swirling ominously, liable to spit out a nasty creature with pointy teeth. Unlike me, though, they could feel it; they could sense the danger that crept within the darkness. No human soul risked venturing out at night time here, and the town was empty.

I snuck around one of the marble columns of the town hall, watching the dark shadows carefully. Slowly, we crept forward, until the full view of the town square was in front of us.

My eyes instinctively went towards the portal, the spot that had sucked the skin off my body only a couple of months before. It was invisible, of course, around twenty feet in the air, at the back end of the town square behind the statue of Sir Humphrey.

A monster lay at the foot of the statue.

Enormous, with a long trunk-like nose and completely covered in white hair, the monster looked like the result of a threesome with an elephant, a whale and a polar bear. While I watched, transfixed, the monster wrestled with its stumpy claw-tipped legs, attempting to climb to its feet. The gangly trunk flopped from side to side, smashing holes in the earth where it hit the grass. The monster let out a deep, ominous rumble.

That thing was *big*. I had no idea what it was, but it had obviously fallen through the portal.

"Do you know what it is?"

I jumped at the low voice beside me; Rafael was too close, his back against the white pillar, looming over me with his enormous presence. He'd snuck up on me in perfect silence.

"I have no idea," I breathed out softly. "You don't know?"

He shook his head. "I've never seen anything like it."

"It's *huge*. And it obviously packs a lot of power. Look at what that trunk is doing to the grass."

The creature must be disorientated from falling through the portal. It looked as though it was attempting to gain control over its own limbs again. The trunk flailed around, a long thick muscle that destroyed everything it came into contact with. The creature's claws dug huge furrows into the earth around it as it tried to scrabble to its feet. As soon as it figured out how its own body parts worked, we might be in for a world of trouble.

I hissed up at Rafael. "It's the size of a damn Mac truck. I don't think my knees are up to the effort of throwing it back into the portal."

He frowned. "We must destroy it, then. We do not know what it is capable of."

"I hope that that thing's flesh is not toxic. We'll have to blow it into chunks to get rid of it. We'll be picking up chunks of polar-whal-phant for days." I shuddered, feeling sick at the thought. "I wonder if there's any chance we can somehow get it to jump up through the portal."

"It does not look like it's built for jumping," Rafael murmured, his eyes darting back towards the monster.

No, indeed. The body was thick and heavy, and his stumpy legs were tipped with sharp claws. Definitely *not* a jumper.

I swallowed roughly. We'd have to kill it, and quickly, before it got scared and tried to run. It would destroy anything in its path. "Okay," I whispered. "Let's go. Slowly, now."

We broke cover and edged towards the monster. I took point, stepping onto the grass of the town square, keeping my feet light in case the thing in front of us could sense my footsteps. Rafael followed, and moved in front of me, a sword in his right hand, and a dagger in the other. With a flick of his wrist, he tossed me the dagger as he crossed in front of me.

Oh right, weapons. Good idea.

In front of us, the creature struggled to its feet, rumbling mournfully. We approached it from the rear, so it wouldn't see us coming. I assessed it carefully, checking for the weak spots, trying to find a place to thrust my dagger. The neck was far too thick to cut through without some pretty determined hacking. Its skull was covered in dense white fur which didn't move at all as the creature swung its head around, which probably meant that its brain was encased in very thick bone. The brow was heavily ridged; I couldn't see a temple to slide a blade into.

While I watched, the creature rumbled again. Its slit of mouth opened up, revealing enormously fat, molar-like teeth. This beast ground up its food whole, instead of tearing flesh off bones.

I sighed inwardly. Even when you couldn't see any soft spots on a strange beast, it always had *one*.

It had been a long time since I'd had to go up a creature's anus to kill it. Sometimes, the best way to kill something was also the worst.

Oh, Lord. Why me?

I grimaced, and crept closer. The beast threw its head around, groaning, facing away from me. The thing was huge, and digging deep pits in the earth around it. Pretty soon, the whole town square would be a mess.

I jerked my head at Rafael. "Take the front. Distract it. Poke an eye out, if you can. If you see an artery, sever it. I'm going to take..." I swallowed. "The rear."

Rafael nodded, and moved to the right in a low crouch, silently stalking the beast, his sword arm out and held in a relaxed grip. His soldiers followed close behind, their assault rifles up and ready to fire. Bullets wouldn't do any damage at all, though; that hide was at least a few yards thick.

I slid forward, keeping on the balls of my feet, moving as quietly as possible. In a few seconds, Rafael and his team would be exactly in the beast's line of sight, and I'd have to act quickly while it was distracted.

I crept closer. The darkness hemmed us in from all sides. I could barely see anything beyond the beast - just the head of Sir Humphrey, the statue, which sat just beyond it.

Rafael and his team were almost in front of the monster now. It had stopped swinging its huge trunk around. It stilled, its thick white hair vibrating as it tested the air around it.

Rafael raised his sword in the air. It glinted in the starlight.

Wait…

I froze. The statue of Sir Humphrey was destroyed.

I'd seen it myself; it had lain in mangled twists of bronze and marble rubble for weeks before they'd cleared it. The plinth was still there, but the statue was gone.

But now, I could see the bronze statue as clear as anything. What the hell was going on?

The beast caught sight of Rafael, and it jolted. An enormous bellow rose up out of its trunk, whipping the trees at the edge of the town square, stripping off leaves with the force of the blast. Its legs whirled; it was fast as well as big, and its claws dug deep into the soft earth at its feet. It looked like it was trying, and failing, to run away.

Rafael raised his sword and moved, spotting an opening at the beast's throat as its huge head swung backwards.

All of a sudden, I caught sight of the beast's eyes – the size of dinner plates, widened in fear, with a distinctly human expression. The intelligence in those deep, brown depths stopped me in my tracks.

I recognized those eyes.

Oh, shit.

I shot forward, meeting Rafael's strike with my dagger. "No!"

The shock on Rafael's face as I blocked his blow was understandable, but he pulled back straight away. In the next heartbeat, he'd wrapped his arm around my waist and whipped me sideways, out of the way of the beast's flailing trunk. It smashed a huge hole in the ground where my feet were moments before.

"Imogen," he snarled. "What are you doing?"

"Don't hurt him!"

He pushed me behind him, and faced the beast, holding his arms out to protect me. "What do you mean, don't hurt him?" The monster, apparently getting control of himself, pushed its front legs out. He managed to snare his flailing trunk between his claws and hold it in place. "What is it doing?"

"It's not a monster from the portal."

Rafael glanced back behind him, meeting my eye. "What is it?"

I pointedly looked up at the statue.

Rafael followed my gaze. Understanding flared in his eyes. He held up his arm and made a fist. The soldiers around the beast stopped their advance immediately.

He bent down and murmured in my ear. "Who is it?"

"I think..." I stared at the monster. He'd brought his trunk in closer and clutched it to his body between his claws. He hunched in on himself, crouched down on his knees. His skin trembled.

The poor thing was terrified, and trying not to move, in case it hurt any of us.

I heard a noise behind us, and risked a glance to confirm what my ears already told me. The shifters had arrived – Backman, in the lead, holding Marigold behind her protectively. Marigold's blonde hair peeked out in a curtain as she tried to peer out from behind her wife's muscular shoulders. Next to her, Debbie, the camp mother, had already shifted into her lion form, and was pacing back and forward at the edge of the town square.

I held my arms out, palms facing outward, in an obvious 'don't move' motion. Backman growled; her teeth showing, but she nodded at me and stopped her advance.

Silence stretched out into nothingness, pulled taunt by the darkness that surrounded us.

I turned back to the monster, looking into his eyes again. The resemblance was unmistakable. "I think," I whispered again. "I think it's Leroy."

Rafael's gaze flicked back to the beast, and ran over the massive body. His face betrayed nothing. After a moment, he raised his hand. His soldiers' eyes shot towards him. He cocked his head towards the statue.

They crept forward.

The tension in the square bloomed, as they stepped forward, their rifles raised, ready to fire.

Boom.

The statue exploded, blowing us all off our feet.

Only Rafael managed to stay upright. I landed on my butt, and quickly cataloged my injuries. Sonic blast only, no debris, no shrapnel wounds anywhere. I scrambled to my feet, looking up.

Instead of a statue of Sir Humphrey, a young man stood on the plinth. His very white skin glimmered softly in the starlight as if it were bioluminescent. He had dark hair, the color of a raven's wing, and big black eyes, very prominent, almost alien in his pale face. High cheekbones, pointed chin, and...

I swallowed. Pointed ears.

Goddamnit.

CHAPTER 6

*T*he young man put his hands on his hips, tipped back his head, and roared with laughter. He sounded *almost* human, there was a tinge to the timbre in his voice, an extra resonance that marked him as not from this dimension. "Oh," he chuckled merrily. "I should not laugh. You ruined my fun!" His eyes twinkled. "Although, watching you animals scramble in the dirt almost makes up for you not killing this beast here."

I quickly cast my eye over his clothes. He wore dark trousers tucked into shining black boots, a black shirt and a gleaming silver belt with a dagger in a sheath. A dark-green cloak covered his shoulders. Everything shone, perfectly made, not a crooked stitch or ragged hole anywhere. His expression was absurdly arrogant, and overwhelmingly, bizarrely attractive.

A fae kid, and a high-born one, too. I didn't recognize anything about him, not the cut of his clothes or the design of his dagger. He seemed like a young man; in human years I would put him at around twenty, but if he was fae, he could be anywhere from a hundred, to thousands of years old. He was bigger than an average human, too, probably matching Rafael in height.

The oddness of his gleaming skin and the power of his magic scared me to the core. He would have to be from somewhere far, far away from our earthly dimension.

This was bad. This was very, very bad. Leroy, the size of a whale, flopped down in front of the fae. He'd curled his long trunk underneath his body, and was attempting to put his claws over his head, trying his best to be invisible.

I had to keep the fae's attention on me. I was the only one that could survive the torture that he might dish out.

I stepped forward. "Who do we have the pleasure of hosting on our earthly plane?"

He laughed arrogantly. "Oh, is this Earth, is it? I've heard of it, I'm sure. Never had the pleasure, of course." He raised his chin. "I am Prince Atonas, heir of Dayanvan." He looked down his nose at me.

I squinted at him. "Do you... Can you be a little more specific? Where, exactly?" I didn't want to antagonize him. I needed to know as much as possible. So I'd know how to kill him.

Atonas narrowed his eyes slightly. "The kingdom of Dayanvan," he repeated, as if I should know exactly what he was talking about, and sigh in wondrous recognition.

I'd never heard of Dayanvan, though. There were as many fae species as there were animals in the animal kingdom. I just had to get this guy classified in terms of where he sat on the food chain.

"Yes, I got that," I said patiently. "Are there... uh, any other kingdoms around you? Or is yours the only one?"

He frowned. "There are two."

"And... ah... what's the other one like?"

His expression fell into a snarl. "The kingdom of Upier is full of flighty fools and morons," he spat out. "They are of no consequence. We are the *mondsuteryn*, the foundations of the world."

Now that word was something I recognized. I almost smacked my face with the palm of my hand. Mondsuteryn was a word that appeared throughout a lot of fae languages.

It meant Underworld. I was looking at a Prince of the Fae Underworld.

Awesome.

"Prince Atonas," Rafael said, stepping forward. "I am Rafael Stefano Di Stasio. I am the Vampire King in this realm." Rafael made a brushing motion with his hands on his forearms, running them upwards from wrist to elbow – first one, then the other. It was a fae handshake; he was showing Atonas that he had nothing up his sleeves to stab him with. It didn't really matter that there was a sword stuck in the ground next to him. For a fae, it was the gesture that mattered.

Atonas raised his chin again. "Ah, someone who understands good manners. Not like this ignorant whelp here," he said, carelessly brushing his hand against Leroy's enormous hide.

"An interesting illusion," Rafael inclined his head towards Leroy. "How did you do it?"

"It is a projection, sweet Vampire King," Atonas said haughtily. "My magic is born from the depths of the victim it is worked on. This silly child thinks of himself as a giant idiot, who, although potentially very dangerous, is essentially worthless, and a danger only to those he loves. *Briolo!*" Atonas clapped his hand. "Thus, he is the very thing he imagines himself to be."

I ground my teeth. What an asshole. "Is it permanent?" I growled.

"Of course not," Atonas said airily. He looked down at me and frowned. Leaning over, he peered at me closer, his brow furrowed. "Who are *you?*" He inhaled through his mouth, as if sampling the air around him. "You are not a vampire, nor a half-breed animal."

I pursed my lips. "My name is Imogen."

"You smell like a human." He narrowed his eyes. "There's something else here, though. Something not from this realm. I know that scent…" He tilted his head on the side. "What is it? I cannot remember." Slowly, he ran his eyes up and down my body, assessing me carefully, suddenly very interested in me.

Okay, now he was focused on me. It was exactly what I wanted, although now that it was actually happening, I was already regretting it.

With a lithe movement, the fae prince leaped from the plinth and landed in front of me. Rafael moved imperceptibly; a little in front of me, shielding me very slightly.

Atonas circled me, running his eyes up and down my body. "You look human. But maybe…"

Rafael cleared his throat. Atonas' eyes snapped towards him. "Prince Atonas," Rafael said. "If I may be so bold, how did you come to Earth? I understand it is almost impossible to navigate the barriers between realms, and our realms are further away from each other than should make any travel possible."

Atonas smiled; his haughty mouth curled up in a devastating smirk. "I am a fae prince, my sweet Vampire King. We have deep magic; more than you can possibly imagine. And, of course," he shrugged his shoulders languidly. "I was invited here."

"You were invited?"

The fae prince's eyes snapped back to me. "I was." He gestured up, towards the portal, and chuckled darkly. "It was not intended, which makes this all the more amusing. Your child there–" he pointed at Leroy's huge, furry white ass. "He sent me an invitation by accident. From what I understand, he meant to install a look-away charm, to stop strange creatures falling through your portal."

I glanced up above Atonas' head, and narrowed my eyes, trying to focus. A tiny bundle floated in the air, around twenty feet up, right where the portal should be. Somehow, Leroy had managed to anchor a charm in mid-air.

I peered closer. Just above the bundle, a tiny drone buzzed.

I let out a groan. He'd solved the puzzle on how to anchor the charm, and, excited to try it, had gone ahead and installed it himself without checking the wording of the spell.

Atonas chuckled lightly, clearly amused. "The spell, when viewed in this dimension, gives a sharp push back, and says: *Go away! Don't come here, you'll have a bad time, I promise you.*"

I groaned again, and my shoulders slumped. Rafael nudged me in the back, maybe trying to remind me that there was a very dangerous creature in front of us that might take offense to me being so dramatically unhappy that he was here.

I couldn't help myself, though. This was bad. Atonas came from the fae underworld; his realm was inverted. Leroy's intentions would be viewed backwards. The spell would have pulled at Atonas, enticing him, calling to him in big loud letters ringed in blazing white lights: *Come here! I'll promise you a* great *time!*"

From behind me, I heard Marigold sigh. "Ugh. I *told* him..."

The great white hairy monster groaned. He knew he'd screwed up, too. Now, what did we do?

I held out my arms in a pleading gesture. "I'm sorry you were deceived, Prince Atonas. As you know, that spell wasn't Leroy's intention. We were trying to keep innocent creatures out of our realm, so they wouldn't be caught in the portal."

He stared at me, amused. "That's what your little baby said, too."

"So..." I swung my arms back and forward awkwardly. "Did you... you know... wanna head home now?"

He threw his head back and laughed. "Oh no. No, my strange girl, who seems human, but is not." He put his hand on his chin and stroked it. "Your scent has a hint of the stars to it, so I will call you Starsmell."

I ground my teeth. It was the stupidest name I'd ever heard. "My name is Imogen."

"Nevertheless, Starsmell," he went on, ignoring me. "I was invited here for a good time. I will not be leaving *until I have a good time.*" His huge black eyes met mine. He stared at me intently, right into my soul.

The prince's words echoed around the town square. Every single one of us froze in place, wondering what he meant. I couldn't sense the danger that must be radiating from the fae, but I knew the atmosphere was thick with fear. Rafael's limbs were tensed; the muscles in his jaw taunt. Backman's skin rippled; she was trying hard not to shift into her bear form. Marigold's skin was deathly pale. Sonja and Brick stood close together, his hand on her wrist as if he were about to pull her away and run at any second.

I looked back at the prince, and frowned. "What kind of good time? What do you mean?" For a fae, it could be anything from mini golf, to a spot of genocide.

He licked his lips. "I think you know what kind of good time."

"Oh." I exhaled. "You mean a *good* time. A time of a sexual nature. Sexy fun times."

I should have guessed. Sex featured very highly on the list of recreational activities for the fae. Boating, camping, hunting, orgies. Sex was a fun game. Murder was a fun game, too.

In fact, anything that involved loud grunts and warm bodies was a fun game for the fae.

He nodded, smiling at me. "I'm glad we understand each other."

"So you'll go home if you get laid."

Atonas inclined his head. "You have my word. It is as you say. I will go home if I have a good time."

"Okay." I pondered for a moment, and shrugged. "Sure," I said. "I don't see why not."

Rafael's head whipped towards me. "Imogen!"

"What? I've had worse." Atonas might be a little alien-looking, but he was still devastatingly attractive. We looked a similar age, even though he was probably a few thousand years younger than me. "I might be the only person on this earth close to his age bracket," I said out loud.

Rafael, next to me, actually growled.

I turned to him. "Oh, come on, Rafael. We've been on *one date.*"

He ground his teeth, his muscles still clenched.

Atonas chuckled. "I don't mean *you*, Starsmell, as lovely as you are. No."

"Oh." I frowned. "Who do you mean, then?"

"Him." He pointed at Rafael. "The Vampire King. The handsome creature with the perfect manners. *Hmmm.*" Atonas let his gaze run all over Rafael, and he slowly pulled his bottom lip through his teeth in a suggestive manner.

"Excuse *me?*" I clapped my hands towards the prince, trying to get his attention back. "No."

Atonas frowned. "No?"

"No. Not happening."

Atonas cocked his head, and pursed his lips. He put his hand on his chest. "You *dare* defy me?"

"Oh yes, I absolutely dare. You're not having him."

Rafael, next to me, snickered. "Imogen, we've been on *one date.*"

I whirled around. "You're meant to be dark and brooding, Your Majesty," I snarled.

A rage had built in my chest that I'd never felt before; a burning fire that electrified me. I couldn't quite understand where it came from. Even as the words were leaving my mouth, I knew it was a bad idea, but I couldn't stop myself.

I turned back to the fae prince. "You're not having him. You can choose another type of 'good time'. Someone else, maybe."

Atonas pursed his lips. "It is the Vampire King, or no one."

"Then it will be no one," I jerked my chin towards the portal. "Game over. Go on, get. You can go home to Dayanvan now."

"He is not yours," the prince hissed. "I can tell. You are not mated, and vampires only mate with vampires. Even I know that. Who are you to say who he cannot sleep with, if he chooses?"

"He does not choose you, sweetheart."

The prince snarled. Suddenly, he leapt backwards, ten feet in the air, and landed in crouch back on the plinth, towering above us.

"Then I will stay," he declared. "And find other ways of having a good time!"

Straightening up, he pulled his arms out wide, gathering sparks from nothingness. He clapped his hands together, and the sonic boom that followed knocked me back on my ass again.

The prince had disappeared.

CHAPTER 7

*R*afael pulled me to my feet. I brushed myself off. "Well, that didn't go as well as it could have," I told him, shocked at the acid burn that had flared up in my chest. "I'm not sure what came over me. Deep fae magic, maybe, or something like that."

"You were jealous, Imogen." Rafael had his back to me. He stared intently at the plinth, where Atonas had disappeared.

"Ha! No, I wasn't." I brushed the dirt off my knees. "I've never been jealous in my whole life. I was just annoyed, that's all. The nerve of that man, thinking he could demand a roll in the hay with us."

"With me, you mean." Rafael glanced back at me.

"Well. To be fair, it was your own fault. You have perfect manners," I said, imitating Atonas' voice childishly.

Rafael turned around to face me. I sighed heavily, and looked him dead in the eyes. "I apologize for answering for you. I was willing to sacrifice my body to get rid of the prince, because I'm the only one that would survive it. But that would have been my decision. You have a right to make your own decisions."

"You were jealous," Rafael murmured, stepping closer to me. He looked down at my face, towering above me, a hint of a smile on his lips. "It was sweet."

"Fuck off," I said. "I'm not the jealous type. I never have been. Anyway, now what are we going to do? We've got a rogue fae loose in our realm, looking to stir up trouble."

My eyes drifted over to where Leroy lay, a mighty behemoth trying to curl himself into a ball and become invisible. "More trouble, I mean," I sighed.

Marigold edged towards us, Backman holding her close. "Is he okay? Leroy, sweetheart, are you alright?"

The monster groaned. He shuddered and pulled his head in tighter.

"Is he stuck like that?"

Rafael shook his head. "The projection should fade, now that Atonas has left the area. It might take a few hours. He will soon be normal."

I patted Leroy's enormous hide. "Do you hear that, buddy? You'll be back to your own weedy little kid body in no time at all."

Marigold looked at him with wide eyes. "How are we going to get him out of here?"

"I'll walk him back to the cabin. He's already smaller. He was the size of a humpback before, now he's more like a big orca." I gave him a nudge. "His claws are shorter, too. I'll be able to get him home."

"I'll walk with you." Rafael said.

"Suit yourself. Leroy! Come on buddy, on your feet." He trembled. "Let's go, Moby Dick," I patted him again. "Walk it off. On your feet. Your claws are shorter, so you should be able to stand up properly."

The giant beast swayed from side to side. He slid his stumpy fin-legs out from under him and flopped them to the ground. The claws made little dents in the ground, not near as much damage as before, though. Slowly he rose in the air on his legs. His trunk flopped to the ground, and trembled. "Just try not to move it," I told him. "I don't need you smacking me in the head with your trunk while we're walking."

The grass around the statue was a mess. Big holes had been gouged in the earth, and little mud pits had sprung up where Leroy's claws had tried to get purchase in the ground. I grimaced; the asshole cop who stopped me earlier was going to have a field day. I glanced at the cameras on the corners of the town square apprehensively.

"They will not capture anything," Rafael murmured, watching me. "Fae magic can knock out electrical equipment. Besides, the security feed comes through my team before it gets downloaded to the police servers."

"Of course it does. So why does the local cop have footage of what happened with the Bloodlord?"

"He does not have anything. The feed has been corrupted."

"He said he was getting it cleaned up," I muttered, frowning.

"Imogen," Rafael said, a twinkle in his eye. "Unless he has an endless supply of Kleenex and a whole ocean of bleach, there's no chance he will be able to clean up that footage enough to see anything of note."

Leroy swayed his huge body towards me. He'd got the hang of walking, so I met his eyes and gave him a nod. "We'll take it slowly, okay?"

A normal walk up the valley to our cabin might take just over an hour. With Leroy in this form, it might take days. Once we started walking, however, he got into his stride with his legs, swinging them around more efficiently.

Rafael walked next to me. His guard arranged themselves around us; a handful up front, scouting ahead, and the rest covering our rear. "You were very quick to say yes to sleeping with the fae," he said, his voice casual.

"I was bluffing, Your Fangliness. I figured that I might be able to get him into a vulnerable position and subdue him, somehow, and try to throw him back through the portal."

"Ah." Was I reading too much into it, or did the tense lines in Rafael's shoulders ease? "We must be wary," he went on. "This fae prince could be very dangerous."

I patted Leroy's furry ass. "You think?

"We do not know what he is capable of."

"Well, we know he's from one of the outer realms, and we know he's from the underworld which essentially makes him a sort of demon. We know he's a trickster, and we can guess what his sense of humor is like. He turned Leroy in to a monster and disguised himself as Sir Humphrey so he could watch us murder our little boy. Ha. Ha, ha, ha." I chuckled lightly, thinking of how I had planned to try and go up the monster's butthole so I could kill him by cutting him up from the inside. Atonas would have loved that. My heart squeezed painfully, but I giggled at the same time.

The hairy beast's head swung towards me; I ducked to miss the flying trunk. His monstrous eyes narrowed. Leroy was glaring at me. "Sorry, buddy," I chuckled. "I wasn't laughing at you. It's nervous tension. You had a very lucky escape. I'll tell you another time."

Hysteria was a funny thing.

Luckily, the spell seemed to be rapidly dissipating. Leroy's trunk had gotten much shorter, and he was the size of a polar bear now. Most of his hair had disappeared, leaving wobbly white skin on his hide.

He looked hilarious. I quickly snapped a couple of pictures while his back was turned.

Next to me, Rafael swung his arms as he walked. His posture was impeccable. It made him seem taller; his shoulders impressively broad. "We have a fair idea of the prince's magic, too," he said. "In true underworld fashion, his magic is dependent on his victim. He will likely torture us with our worst fears."

I shrugged. "All my worst fears have already come true, a million times over, so he might find me a tough nut to crack."

The vampire gazed down at me, his eyes hooded. "I seem to acquire new fears every day. Just as the old ones dissipate, something new takes its place."

"Hmmm. Good point," I muttered. If the prince touched Leroy again, I'd use his entrails to tie up my gutter. It had come down in the last heavy rainstorm, and I'd used a pair of old tights to fix it back up. "How are we going to get rid of him?"

"From what I understand, Leroy's spell was an invitation to the prince, and by answering it, it's also serving as a contract. The prince cannot leave here until he's had a good time."

I nodded. "And only he can decide if he's had a good time or not."

"Exactly."

"Do you think that the contract is bound to you, too? He stipulated quite clearly that only *you* can satisfy him." I winked at Rafael, and made a stupid kissy-face.

Rafael did not rise to the bait. He seemed unbothered by the idea of sex with the fae prince, which made my chest prickle uncomfortably again. I stopped with the stupid kissy face and frowned. "Will there be any kind of contractual rebound if we managed to tie him up and throw him back through the portal?"

Rafael's stride lengthened. We walked quicker now; Leroy's de-spelling had reached a sweet spot where he was still big, with a nice stride, and his claws were completely gone, so we used the advantage to pick up the pace. "I don't think so," Rafael replied. "He did not say out loud that the 'good time' had to be of a sexual nature, and it was not in the wording of the spell, either. I think that if he manages to satisfy himself by playing a few unpleasant tricks on us, he will go home."

"He'll do some damage," I said, watching Leroy's butt slowly shrink in front of me. "And not just physical damage." The poor kid had turned into a useless, dangerous monster because that's what he thought he was. "Emotional damage. Financial damage," I muttered. The amount of money I was going to have to spend on his therapy sessions was going to severely deplete my bank account.

"We'll get through it," Rafael said, looking down at me.

I glared at him. "You're a little too optimistic, your Majesty. Are you... excited by the idea of Atonas propositioning you?"

Rafael smirked for a split-second. "It took me by surprise, I must confess. I was initially concerned that I would find myself in a fight to the death with the prince if he insisted on sleeping with you. I was very cross that you agreed so readily."

"I wasn't actually going to, though, I told you that," I said. "So, you're not *opposed* to sleeping with him?" I demanded. "I mean, I don't judge. I'm not going to yuk someone's yum. You can get your freak on with the weird fae prince if you like." I tossed my hair back. "I don't care. I couldn't care less."

He laughed out loud. "Your tone and expression tell me otherwise."

"I don't," I muttered.

Weirdly, I *did* care. It wasn't like me. I wasn't the jealous type. Rafael wasn't even mine – in fact, he had been quite emphatic about that fact. Vampires would never mate with anyone but a vampire. Oh, sure, they'd sleep with humans for fun, but that was always a precursor to feeding. They only ever kept humans as pets – it was never anything more than a vampire and his faithful service animal. The relationship was never on equal footing.

Vampire relationships were only ever with other vampires. They would never mate with another species, and definitely not inferior humans. They despised shifters even more than humans. And the few vampire-fae couples I'd ever heard of in my whole lifetime had all torn each other to shreds within days of declaring their love for each other.

It just didn't happen.

My chest felt hot. I cleared my throat, waiting for the uncomfortable, tight feeling to go away. I wanted to say more. I wanted to ask Rafael if he actually considered sleeping with Atonas. I wanted to demand that he didn't. It wasn't for me, though. It wasn't my place.

We walked in silence for a long time. Leroy's body shrank slowly. By the time we made it to the cabin, he was back to normal, wrapped in one of the vamp team's flak jackets.

"Thanks," I said to Rafael as we reached the porch. "I'll take it from here."

Rafael touched my shoulder, sending a little zing through my body. "We will meet tomorrow," he said. "To discuss the fae problem."

"Oh. Of course. With Marigold and the shifters."

"Yes."

He looked into my eyes and nodded. "Goodnight, Imogen Gray."

His words sounded like a lullaby.

CHAPTER 8

$\mathcal{I}$t was a dazzling sunny day; far too bright to be on my hands and knees, rummaging underneath the floorboards of a flimsy weatherboard chicken coop. Benson had called me earlier about a strange demonic creature that was killing the hens at Christine Curtis's hobby farm, and because I was a sucker of the highest order, I'd gone out there to check.

It turned out to be a fox, which was unusual. It was the first time I'd been called out to get rid of an animal that turned out to be an animal.

Once I'd cornered it, I wasn't sure what to do with it. The savage little bastard had murdered all the chickens already, and was lying, bloated and bloody, on the floor of the coop.

It was funny, really. There were all these supernatural monsters in the world that, according to Benson, took the highest priority to get rid of, when it was actually the earthly animals who were the worst ones.

Same with humans. We invent demons and blame horrible acts on Satan, when it's always humans to blame. No one does inhumanity like humans.

Eventually, I bundled the fox into one of my catcher bags and handed it to Christine Curtis to deal with. After a quick chat to check to see if there were any male members of her household that had gotten back from holiday recently, I was on my way.

Atonas had thrown a spanner into the works. I'd planned to focus harder on finding my dad. With the danger of the portal in the heart of the town, it was becoming more and more important to find him and find a cure for my immortality. It was only a matter of time before I was crushed to pieces again. It might take me years to get another chance to find him. He'd be somewhere else again, wearing another body, and I'd have to start from scratch.

Sometimes, the panic made my heart race, and I had to stop, and bend over, put my hands on my knees and take a few deep breaths before I could go on. It was an awful, tearing feeling, to feel like my time was running out, but at the same time, it stretched on forever, with no relief in sight.

I was in a terrible mood when I left Christine Curtis's hobby farm, headed for Marigold's. We'd arranged a meeting at her shop - a war council, of sorts, to share what we'd found out about the fae prince, and to decide a plan of attack. Leroy would be there already. He'd left early in the morning to go through all Marigold's books.

The poor kid had cried for a long time once we'd gotten home. It was his fault that Atonas had invaded our town, and, as I expected, to have his deepest fears projected onto himself had been very traumatic for him. He didn't even cheer up when I told him that I'd planned to go up his butt to try and kill him when I thought he was a monster.

Leroy got up early, washed his face, and took off to Marigold's to go through her books, to look for a way to get rid of Atonas. He was determined to make up for his mistake.

He was still suspended from school, so he might as well make himself useful.

The poor kid had barely slept. When he finally dozed off, he woke up screaming a few more times than usual. We didn't talk about it, though. We never talked about our nightmares. I knew I screamed in my sleep, too. It wasn't something that we needed to talk about.

As I drove onto Main Street, I saw that the car parks outside Marigold's were all taken up by a road crew. I grumbled as I crossed the street and parked further down the road. I stopped the van, unbuckled myself, and opened the door.

A police cruiser pulled in beside me, flashing its lights. I turned towards it, narrowing my eyes. I couldn't see inside the car – the glare hit the windshield exactly the wrong way, so I couldn't see who it was. Was it Officer Harman, flexing his muscles again? Looking for another little power-trip?

I waited.

For a long time, nothing happened. What did he expect me to do, wait for him to get out? Was he trying to provoke me to do something crazy so he could arrest me? Rage bubbled up in my chest. I took a breath, slammed my van door, and turned to walk off.

The police cruiser's siren blared, cutting through the silence. I turned back and glared at the cruiser. More anger rushed through me, flooding adrenaline into my limbs, making my fists shake. The loudspeaker clicked.

"Stay where you are," the magnified voice ordered.

It was *so* loud – clearly designed to intimidate and cause the most embarrassment possible. An older lady coming out of the butcher's shop turned to look at me. Two little kids watched me from across the street; their mom caught them gawking and hurried them away.

My stomach churned.

I could flip the cruiser with Harmann in it, and run away. But I'd have to run and leave Emerald Valley for good. Leroy would be taken back to his mom.

I'd take him with me, of course. I'd never be able to come back, though, and I wouldn't get to find my dad. Ugh.

It had been a while since I'd felt this feeling. I was so physically powerful – I could tear this asshole to pieces and play polo using his head as the ball and his legs as a mallet. Yet right now, I was completely helpless.

I clenched my fists, trying to stop the trembling. If Harmann got under my skin too much, I'd do something stupid, and jeopardize everything.

After a long minute, the cruiser door opened and Harmann got out, moving as slowly as humanly possible. I stood still and arched my brow. Play it cool, Imogen, I told myself.

He sauntered over. "You have your ID on you today, Imogen Gray?" He said my name in the stupid baby voice again. I wanted to hack off his head with my bare fingernails.

I shook my head. "No, I don't."

Slowly, he pulled out his notebook and took a full thirty seconds to scribble something down. He looked up at me with a smirk. "Where were you last night?"

"Why?" I crossed my arms over my chest.

"Answer the question."

"Have I committed a crime?"

He chuckled. "Oh, most probably." He wrote something down. "I would say it's very likely."

The rage burnt my throat. "What crime?" I said through clenched teeth.

He shifted his weight, popping out a hip and placing his hand on it, drawing my attention to the SIG in the holster. "We had another incident last night in the town square. The dirt got tore up pretty bad, all the grass has been ruined.

Looks like another deliberate attack on the statue to me." He narrowed his piggy little eyes at me. "You know about that?"

"No." I forced myself to keep cool.

"Where were you, then?"

I arched my brow. "I was not digging up the town square, I can tell you that much."

He smirked again. "So you were there."

I exhaled. "No." Damn cop. I knew I was no good at lying, so I tried to tell the truth so I wouldn't be caught out.

"Where were you?"

"It's none of your business." The rush of fury was making it hard for me to concentrate. I couldn't come up with a lie on the spot, and he was too good at poking holes in my words.

"Oh, it is, girl. It is my business. Where were you?"

"At home," I replied. I had gone home. Eventually.

He wrote in his notebook. "Can anyone verify that?"

"My kid, Leroy."

Another sarcastic chuckle. "He don't count. No one would take the word of a known bully." He looked up. "You don't have an alibi for last night?"

"I don't need one," I spat through my teeth. "I didn't do anything wrong."

"Oh, I doubt that. The lawn on the town square is ruined." He scribbled something else in his notebook. "Someone has no respect for the history and culture of my town," he added idly. "Someone, who hates our founder Sir Humphrey, destroyed the statue. It wouldn't have been a local. Folks around here love Sir Humphrey. Most folks are very unhappy the statue got destroyed. You didn't seem to care much when I asked you about it yesterday, did you?"

I kept my mouth shut.

He waited. When it became clear that I wasn't going to say anything else, he hoiked up a loogie, and spat it on the ground next to me. "After I asked you about it yesterday, someone went and ripped up the grass around the remains of the statue. Looks like they took a hammer to the plinth, as well, that seems a bit more damaged. Strange, that." His close-set eyes roamed around my face for a second, and dipped to take in the rest of my body.

"I had nothing to do with it."

His eyebrows raised. "I think you did. I got good instincts, girl. I think you know exactly what's going on."

As if I needed any more examples of life being horribly unfair, this asshole had good instincts, and he'd learnt to trust them.

He gave me a hard look. He was waiting for me to say something, and he'd wait all day if he had to.

I forced my mouth open. "You have no evidence." I struggled to keep my voice calm.

He watched my face carefully. "I will soon. We're getting that footage from August fifth cleaned up. Last night's footage, too." He glared at me. "Security cameras are on the fritz. Can't blame you for that. I doubt you'd have the know-how to sabotage the electrical equipment."

I felt a crunch, and a jolt of pain in my mouth. I'd broken one of my back teeth, I'd been clenching my jaw so hard. The pain did nothing to help temper my fury.

Think of Leroy, I told myself. Think of your dad.

"You know what, I think I'm going to take you in," he said, closing his notebook and shoving it in his top pocket. "Your tongue might get a little looser once we're in the station."

"I didn't *do* anything!" I yelled, losing my temper. "You can't arrest me. You have no cause and no evidence."

"Oh, I can. Who's gonna stop me?" He laughed, a deep, hearty chuckle. "I know about you, Imogen Gray. I know you live in that messed-up cabin up on the ridge, and you drive this clapped-out thing. The only public defender within a hundred miles is a buddy of mine." He smirked. "You say you're in town to trace your ancestors – that's a lie, I can tell. You're here to make trouble somehow. I know you had something to do with Sir Humphrey's statue. Even if you didn't," his voice dropped to a murmur, and he ran his eyes over me suggestively. "At the very least, I'll have you on your hands and knees, resowing the grass seeds."

Rage overtook me; my vision went blurry at the edges. I could feel the glow within me begin to flare. My fists shook uncontrollably.

Harmann pulled out his silver handcuffs. "Turn around," he snapped.

"Officer Harmann!" The voice was sharp, male, and commanding. It came from right behind me. "What is going on here?"

The cop's piggy eyes flared, just slightly. "Nothing, Mr Jamieson. Just asking this new girl here a couple of questions."

I exhaled, and closed my eyes, desperately trying to push down the glow inside of me. I felt like an overheated nuclear reactor desperately trying to cool down.

"Well." Jamieson lifted his chin and eyed the cop steadily, no hint of a smile on his normally-cheerful face. "It looks to me like you're harassing her."

Harmann took a step back and clicked the clasp of his handcuff pocket closed again. "Not at all, Mr Jamieson. I'm investigating what happened to the statue. I thought this new girl in town might know something about it, that's all."

Jamieson, the current vet and ex-mayor of Emerald Valley. The funny old man who had put me into an induced coma a couple of months ago, when I'd lost the lower half of my body to the vicious tractor-beam of hell. I hadn't seen him since then – he had left shortly after I woke up to go hiking in Peru.

I should have been happy to see him, but it was hard to get a handle on my trembling limbs.

Jamieson stepped up beside me, so I could see his shiny grey beard and full mop of hair in my peripheral vision. Today, he was wearing a bright-red shirt with white script on it. I turned slightly to see what it said. *"I'm going to have to put your dog down. No, he's not sick. He's just really heavy."*

"I thought it was a lightning strike that broke the statue," Jamieson said. "That was the rumor, anyway. There was a lot of electrical activity around that night, that's why the security cameras malfunctioned."

"I'm investigating alternate theories, sir. Besides, the ground around the statue was defaced again last night. I was just asking Miss Gray here a few questions about it."

Jamieson turned to look at me, a look of absolute bewilderment on his face. "Why would she have anything to do with that?"

"Just doing my job, sir." Harmann's face had shut down.

The old man frowned. "It was a pack of racoons that dug that ground up. I went and had a look on my way to the surgery this morning - I saw the claw marks and everything."

"Well, that's your opinion," the cop muttered. "Others have their own opinion on what happened. It didn't feel quite right to me. It would take a pack of racoons to do that."

"A family. Just a small family of racoons could do that much damage."

"I was just asking questions, that's all."

Jamieson moved, so he was standing more in front of me, shielding me. "I think you're done asking questions here, Harmann." He eyed him steadily. "Leave the girl alone."

The cop set his jaw stubbornly, and glared at the older man. After a tense few moments, he backed off the sidewalk. "I'll be seeing you, Imogen Gray," Harmann said to me. He made it sound like a threat. He opened the car door, got in, and slammed it so hard behind him the windows rattled.

Jamieson turned to me, his face somber. "I'm sorry about that, Miss Gray," he said.

I exhaled heavily. "It's okay." The adrenaline was already beginning to drain. I felt shaky.

"Officer Harmann has a reputation for fixating on his 'persons of interest,'" he said, bringing up his hands to do the speech marks in the air. He turned, and stared in disgust at the police cruiser as the engine started with a roar. Harmann backed up the cruiser with a squeal of tires, hit the siren, and sped away.

Jamieson sighed. "Officer Harmann can be single minded in pursuing what he calls justice, and slightly heavy-handed." He turned back to me. "I'll have a word with the captain over at Cedar Hills."

"Oh, don't bother on my account."

"If not for you, my fine lady, then for the next person who captures Harmann's interest," Jamieson muttered. "I worry that the power of being the only policeman in the Valley has gone to his head."

"Well. I can always take his head off later." I froze. Did I say that out loud? Whoops, I did.

Jamieson roared with laughter. "Oh, ho ho ho." He laughed just like Santa Claus. I almost cracked a grin myself. "Young lady," he chuckled. "I shouldn't laugh. Considering your condition only a few months ago, you're probably being serious." He laughed again.

I shrugged. "I *was* being serious."

Jamieson doubled over in laughter again. "Ho ho *hoooo*."

After a few minutes, he seemed to laugh himself out. He straightened up, and wiped his eyes. "Please," he said. "Let's refrain from decapitating our only police officer in the Valley, just for now," he said. "Maybe wait until he's crossed you off his suspect list." He chuckled again. "I wouldn't want you getting into any more trouble."

"I'll keep that in mind," I said dryly. I patted him on the arm. "Thanks for helping out."

"No problem." Jamieson's eyes twinkled brighter than ever.

I walked away, leaving the funny old vet chuckling behind me.

CHAPTER 9

*M*arigold's shop was as pretty as ever. An apothecary-slash-beauty boutique, she made her money by brewing cosmetic potions and crafting herbal teas that were in high demand not just in the exclusive country club, but all around the world. As a result of some rare ingredients, the price tag on her eye creams were eye-watering.

The shop had a light, airy vibe, less witchy and more spiritual love and light. She'd redecorated for Samhain, which was only a month or so away. Crispy amber and mulberry-red leaves hung from the ceiling in banners, and she'd decorated every spare surface with artful arrangements of bleached branches, pinecones, and beeswax candles.

Marigold herself was seated on the floor in the middle of the shop, where she'd cleared a space for the meeting. In true witchy fashion, instead of chairs, she'd arranged a wide circle of cushions, with an altar in the center made up of statues, purple candles, and a handful of big pointy amethyst crystals. Everything looked Instagram-worthy.

Behind the counter, Backman stood, arms crossed and with

an intense scowl on her face. She peered at the little screen on the desk, tapping on the keyboard with two fingers, painstakingly slowly. It looked like she was helping with the stocktake. She looked up when I entered, and her scowl deepened further.

"What's happening, Berenstain Bear?" I tipped an imaginary hat at her. "How's it going?"

She scowled even more.

Marigold got up from her knees. "You're first to arrive."

"We're not sitting on the floor, are we?" I'd gotten used to using chairs in the last few thousand years; I wasn't fond of sitting cross-legged anymore.

"Of course! What else would we be doing?"

"Sitting on chairs, like normal, civilized people?"

Backman growled. "She's given you a cushion."

I made a rude noise. "Can I just stand up, instead? Sitting in a circle and singing kum-by-ya really isn't my thing."

Marigold gazed at me, a puzzled expression on her face. "We're not singing. This is a meeting about the fae prince. Remember?"

I exhaled. "I know that, Marigold. I just don't want to sit on the floor, that's all."

"Cranky old lady can't get up, Mar," Backman rumbled. "Her knees are all old and worn out."

"Oh yeah?" I nodded at the bear shifter and cracked my knuckles. "Want to test out my knees, Backman? You can test out my fists too, if you want."

"Anytime, little drill bug."

"But seriously, as soon as this fae prince has gone home, me and you are due for a rematch."

She looked up lazily from the computer screen. "You're on. Human or bear?"

"Come as you want. I'll destroy you either way. Maybe as the bear. I need a new rug for the cabin floor."

"You'll have a hard time getting back up to the cabin after I rip your kneecaps off."

"Ha. Jokes on you. They grow back."

She chuckled. It would have sounded to anyone like we were joking, but we really weren't. Sparring with Backman was an amazing release of tension for both of us. Neither of us could spar with anyone else without doing severe damage, and she was so used to holding back with her students. It felt good for her to let go.

It was painful, yes, but sometimes you have to beat the shit out of someone to feel better about being alive. She might get a few shots in, but it would be worth it.

Fighting her as a bear would be much harder, but I looked forward to it. A lot of it was because I knew something about her that she didn't know about herself. She thought she was a grizzly bear. She wasn't.

Typically, shifter animals were larger than the normal version of that animal. For example, werewolves were usually twice the size as normal wolves. They just accepted this fact and didn't question it too much.

Because I was a cranky old lady, I knew a little better. Shifter animals were mostly from that animal's prehistoric species, and that DNA didn't ever go extinct. Humans carried it on within themselves.

Although she didn't know it - I would never tell her because I didn't want her getting a big head - Backman wasn't a grizzly. She was *Arctotherium angustidens*, the largest known carnivorous land mammal that had ever walked the earth. That species that, in its purest form, went extinct around 11,000 years ago. It looked like a grizzly, but it was much, much bigger. I hadn't fought one for over fifty thousand years, and it made me a little nostalgic.

I looked around the shop. "Where's Leroy?"

"He's picking up some snacks," Marigold said. "Here he comes now."

The doorbell jingled and Leroy walked in, carrying a box in his hand. "Hey, kid." I waved at him. "I'll take that." I took the box out of his hand. "Gotta keep it away from the hungry bears." I lifted the lid. "Ooh," I sighed. "A bear claw. Look at that, Backman!" I held up the bear claw and turned around, suddenly finding myself staring at a wall that appeared out of nowhere.

The bear claw disappeared from my hands. Backman had snuck up behind me, quiet as anything, and snatched the donut out of my hand. "Mine," she growled.

I chuckled, picked out a jelly glazed one for myself, and settled down on one of the cushions. Leroy plonked himself down next to me. "How did the research go?" I asked him.

"Okay," he said, in between mouthfuls of cinnamon roll. "I found out a few things about Atonas' world." He stopped, and looked up at Marigold, who had settled herself onto a cushion opposite us. "Are we getting started? Should we wait for the Vampire King?"

Marigold carefully placed a laptop onto the cushion next to her, the screen facing us. "He's late," Marigold said, frowning. "I mean, you were very late, too, Imogen. The King is even later."

"I'm surprised he agreed to come," I said. "I thought he'd push Sonja and Brick to come instead."

"They're coming, too," Marigold indicated two cushions, both flatter and less comfortable-looking than the fat red one between them. "Sonja tried to move the meeting somewhere else, so she'd be in charge, but she didn't want any of us in the country club. We argued about locations for a while until she finally agreed to come here. And the King *wanted* to be here. He's supposed to be in Venice, opening some new art gallery, but he blew it off to stay in Emerald Valley. He might be worried about luring Atonas too far away from the Dip. It would make it harder to get him out of our dimension. Anyway, I mean, it's him that the fae prince wants, so he feels like he needs to be involved. He doesn't seem too worried about that part, though."

I felt a hot flare in my throat. I coughed to try and clear it.

Opposite me, Marigold tapped on the laptop. A split screen appeared; two very different, but strangely similar women appeared.

"Everyone, meet my aunts," Marigold said. "Mabel and Mavis. They're my mom's sisters. They grew up here in Emerald Valley, and moved to Europe when they were in their twenties."

The two women on the screen nodded their heads. "Merry meet," they both said in perfect unison.

The witch on the left-hand side had a wild mane of curly white hair that puffed out in a perfect circle around her head, filling the screen. She placed her hand on her heart. "I am Mabel Rose Dupont-Laurent," she said her name formally, with a touch of an accent. "I am high priestess of *Femmes Vertes de la Terre*, here in Lyon. I established the coven here over fifty years ago. We are green witches, hearth witches, we honor the plant and root. I have met a handful of fae over the years, creatures that journeyed through France. I hope that I might be able to help you. Blessed be." She nodded deeply again.

The other witch waved merrily. Her bone-white hair was dead straight. "I am Mavis De Vries." Her voice was slightly accented, too, but sounded completely different to her sister. "I am High Priestess of *Hou Van Magie* coven here in The Hague. I have had sexual relations with two fae, one man, and one woman. I hope that I might be able to help you."

I sniggered. "Blessed be!"

Mabel, with the wild curly hair, turned to glare at her sister. "Always the showboat, aren't you, Mavis?"

"I'm just saying, I think I'm going to know a little more about them, that's all."

"I engaged with the fae with respect and honor. I have a vast knowledge of their magic systems and their flora they use to craft their spells."

"The fae they've got there isn't trying to take over the Emerald Valley Rose Club, Mabel. He's trying to get his dick wet."

"Why must you be so vulgar?"

Mavis put on a sooty voice. "Why must you be such a stick in the mud?"

"Aunties." Marigold tapped the computer screen. "We need both of you. Please behave." She turned and faced the rest of us. "My aunts are joining the circle today to help us with our little problem." Marigold looked at her watch, frowning. "We might have to get started. We'll get the King caught up when he gets here. Okay," she took a breath. "I've filled in my aunts on what we know about Atonas already. We know what realm he's from, and we know it's an underworld realm." She nudged Leroy. "Go ahead."

"We know about his magic," Leroy continued. "His primary power is in his projection magic. He can read his victim's energy and pull out the darkest version of themselves. When he turned me into a monster, I felt it happening." Leroy's jaw tensed. "I felt him inside the part of my brain where my nightmares live." He stopped, and blinked a couple of times. "I think you all know what I'm talking about."

"We do, buddy," I said. "We've all been there."

"He pulled out an abstract version of myself and turned me into that... thing. I kinda felt like I could have stopped him." he frowned. "I have a feeling that this particular power of his is weak, like, he had to have my participation to turn me into a monster. I think… if I had really felt the feelings he was bringing to the surface, then I could have stopped the transformation from happening. You know what I mean?"

I nodded. None of us said anything. It was classic underworld mojo. Even spirits in our underworld get off on tormenting people with their worst fears.

If you can face your worst fears, then they don't hurt you as much.

"The other weapon he has in his arsenal is his manipulation of sound. He can make shock waves using sonic energy. It's a blunt instrument, but it's powerful. That's his primary physical weapon."

"We'd need to assume that he's skilled in hand-to-hand combat, too," I said. "Most high-born fae don't screw around. They're always fighting for their thrones, so they learn how to swing a fist in the cradle. Fae martial arts were similar to a lot of earthly ones, but a lot showier – lots of knife work, sometimes maces and other flashy weapons that they can swing around."

"We can take him," Backman rumbled. "He'll find it hard to whirl that shiny white ass of his through my pack of shifters."

"You were watching his ass, were you?" I gave her a smug look. "My, my. Watch out, Marigold. Your wife might be switching teams."

Backman growled low in her throat. "You're just jealous he wanted Di Stasio, and not you."

"That's where you're wrong, Fozzie Bear."

"Hush," Marigold said softly. "I think the thing we need to worry most about is his illusion magic. He can change himself into other things easily, both looking and feeling like whoever he wants to be."

Leroy stirred. "He turned himself into the statue of Sir

Humphrey; it was a perfect replica. He can also imitate any living thing easily. It's just like the Bloodlord, but worse, because the Bloodlord couldn't really imitate people we already know. Atonas can, up to a point. He could be impersonating anyone.

I turned to glare at Backman. She was already glaring at me.

"Don't even think about it, little drill bug."

"You gotta admit, you're acting a bit weird. Fixating on Atonas' ass like that."

Leroy gave me a nudge. "Concentrate. We also know that Atonas does not have to see or be close to someone to replicate them. He can construct an image from other people's memories."

I nodded. "Even I was fooled by the statue of Sir Humphrey. He never would have seen that statue. He replicated it perfectly."

"He saw it in my thoughts," Leroy explained. "So that's everything we know about Atonas' personal strengths. He can project your worst fears, he has some pretty high-powered illusion magic. He has a sonic bomb in the palms of his hands, and he is, most likely, an expert in martial arts. We know he's got a sick sense of humor, and that he's not going to leave until he's had a good time. We also know that the "good time" is probably going to kill a few of us."

"Great," I said. "Now we just have to dig into his weaknesses, so we know how to kill him instead." I shrugged. "Or get him out of our dimension, at the very least. I haven't heard of Dayanvan, but we can gather from his appearance that it's one of the outer realms of Faerie. Most of the inner realm fae can pass as human in our realm, as long as they cover their ears. Atonas would never be mistaken for a human."

"His skin is luminescent, like a pearl, and his eyes are far too big," one of the witches said.

"That's more of an indication that he's from the underworld, though," I replied. "I meant the shape of his face, the curve of his ears."

Mabel cleared her throat. "I have a coven sister who has heard of Dayanvan. Her grandmother remembered her own grandmother talk of dallying with a trickster fae from that realm, a hundred or so years ago. She re-read her grimoire, looking for notes. There's not much, and the information that was there was... unsettling. Dayanvan is a small realm, and the upper and lower houses are always at war, and constantly slaughtering each other. The upper kingdom, apparently, is arrogant, more traditional and colder. There was a reference in the grimoire to the visitor cutting off the hands of someone who fumbled the fae handshake. The punishment for most offenses is death."

They love their manners, I thought wryly.

"The underworld fae are less rigid, but they are worse troublemakers, apparently," she went on. "Either way, we know they are very dangerous. Even more disturbing, my sources lead me to believe that these fae might be cannibalistic. They mostly eat raw meat from slaughtered game, but they also eat the flesh of their enemies in ceremony."

Mavis, the witch with the ruler-straight hair, nodded. "My experiences with the fae–"

"You mean, your whoring," her sister muttered.

"–Would confirm this information. The male fae I made love to did talk about the other realms. He said that the further out the realm is, the more of an indication it was to stay away. He said that some of the outer realms have almost no regard for the life of their fellow fae. They only care about the lives of their close family members, and they would happily cut off the head of a neighbor if they snuck extra bottles into their recycling." She gave her sister a sly side-eye glare. "They'd run you through with a lance if you turned their algebra homework in as your own."

Mabel bristled. "That was fifty-four years ago, Mavis. When will you let that go?"

"When you apologize!"

The two witches began shrieking at each other.

Marigold sighed deeply, reached out, and turned the screen around. "This is why I didn't give them their own screens," she said apologetically. "They're worse if they can see each other."

The doorbell jingled. As a glorious counterpoint to the tinny, light jangle of the bell, Rafael stalked into the shop – tall and broody-looking, his luscious mouth set in a deep frown.

He was smoldering more than usual. I could almost imagine cartoon-like thunderclouds hovering over his head.

Brick walked in behind him, visibly tensed. He had to turn sideways so he could get his overly-muscular shoulders through the door. Finally, Sonja came in, holding a crossbow in her hand. It was loaded with a dull-gray bolt, cocked, ready to fire.

"Your Majesty," Marigold got to her feet. Backman, too, rose, and nodded. Leroy also scrambled to his feet. "Thank you for coming," Marigold said.

"Thank you for having me. I apologize for my tardiness." He nodded around at each of them, then looked down to me, where I lay propped up on one elbow on my pillow.

I gave him a salute. "You took your time."

An odd expression came over his face. Did he... was he... *blushing*? Vampires don't blush, but I could have sworn I saw a soft bloom of color in his cheeks.

"I was waylaid. I apologize."

I was immediately suspicious. "Waylaid by what?"

Rafael glanced down at the cushions on the floor, and folded himself gracefully, like a panther settling down for a nap. The two vampires behind him threw themselves on the floor, keeping their heads lower than his.

Sonja sat directly in my line of sight. She glared at me and raised her crossbow. The iron tip shone dully in Marigold's downlights.

"Sonja, is it me?" I asked her. "Or do you seem more aggressive than normal? Expecting trouble, bestie?"

Her eyes narrowed. "I'm watching you. You can't fool me."

"I'm not trying to. You do a pretty good job making a fool out of yourself, though."

She snarled and lifted the bow higher.

Rafael, without turning, held up one hand. "We know that it is her, Sonja."

Sonja cocked her head, the crossbow still poised to shoot me. "We cannot be sure, Master."

"Oh, I can be sure," he replied, the hint of a smirk on his face. "She did not rise when I came in."

The vamp blinked like a robot, and she lowered the crossbow. "That is a good point, Master."

I shuffled forward until I was sitting up. "What's going on?"

"Your lack of manners is a defining feature of you," Sonja replied, gently placing the crossbow on the floor.

I swung my gaze to Rafael. "Did something happen? What have I missed?"

"I had a visit from our fae friend."

Marigold gasped. Leroy went noticeably pale.

Two tinny voices screeched from behind Marigold, in unison. "Turn us around! We want to see!" Marigold swung the laptop back around to face the rest of the circle. "Your Majesty, these are my aunts, Mabel and Mavis. May I present Rafael Stefano Di Stasio, Vampire King of the North."

Mabel's eyes fluttered, and she bowed deeply. Mavis smoothed her hair down and waved. "Well, hell*ooo* Your Majesty!"

"Don't be a tart, Mavis."

"Oh, lighten up, Mabel."

"You always have to turn any room into a bordello, don't you?"

"It's called having fun! Something I know you don't know much about–"

Marigold, blushing furiously, leaned over and stabbed a key on the laptop with her index finger. The voices cut off. "I apologize," she said. "We'll leave them on mute, I think."

I sat upright and swept my legs underneath me. "Okay, Your Fangliness," I said. "Go on. What happened? You seem like you're all in one piece.

"I was in a meeting at the club when I was informed that you had arrived, and you wanted to see me."

I frowned. "Me?"

"Yes. One of my security team vetted you and passed on the message to me. I had no reason to believe it wasn't you. I instructed that you be brought to my office, and I wrapped up my meeting. When I arrived, you were in my office, reading the correspondence on my desk. It looked like you, it smelled like you..." For a brief moment, he inhaled through his mouth, and looked at me. My stomach squirmed. "The fact that you were reading my mail made me believe it was you."

The squirmy feeling disappeared, only to be replaced by a dull, yawning ache. "It wasn't me."

He nodded. "I know that now."

I took a deep breath. "At what point did you realize that it wasn't me?"

The silence in the circle was deafening. Rafael gazed at

me, his eyes so hot that I could barely stand looking at him. The ache in my stomach swelled to my chest.

Oh God, what were these damned feelings? I'd gone centuries barely feeling anything except boredom, and the occasional bout of unbearable physical pain. Now I had all these *emotions*, I'd forgotten what it was like to feel anything.

It was *not* nice.

Rafael opened his mouth, and shut it again.

I pursed my lips. "Oh, I get it. Did he get his 'good time'? Has he gone home now?"

"No. As soon as I realized it was Atonas, wearing your visage, I stopped him. I am not going to lie to you, Imogen. I was enchanted by the idea of you propositioning me on the desk in my office."

The hot flare in my chest burned brighter. "Did he kiss you?"

Rafael tilted his head. "As far as I was concerned, it was *you* kissing me. Almost the instant that I realized it wasn't you, I stopped him."

"Almost? *Almost?*"

Marigold cleared her throat. "Ah, Your Majesty... What gave it away? How did you realize it wasn't Imogen?"

"A feeling. When his lips touched mine."

I snarled.

Sonja cut in. "I had stationed myself outside my master's office. I was suspicious of you the second you appeared at the country club. You did not arrive in your stupid van. You did not set any booby traps for me. Our bedroom window had been wide open, and there were gardeners outside, fertilizing the roses. You did not steal one of the bags of cow manure. You did not toss it through my bedroom window. I was suspicious," she repeated.

Even the thought of lobbing a bag of cow shit through Sonja's window didn't cheer me up. I turned back to Rafael.

"He kissed you? What happened after that? Did he take his clothes off so you could touch him?"

Rafael pinched the bridge of his nose. "It wasn't you, Imogen. I stopped him. He realized immediately that I suspected him, so he morphed back into himself and tried to seduce me again."

"Go on," I said peevishly. "Cut to the chase. Did you give him a 'good time'?"

"No," Sonja said. "I kicked in the door and shot at him with my iron arrow. I missed."

"Would you have carried on if Sonja hadn't busted in?"

Backman chuckled. "I don't think that's the point here, drill bug. Atonas is already doing what we were worried about. He's impersonating us."

"He's impersonating *me*," I muttered, looking down. "He's going to do anything he can to get his 'good time'." I looked up and glared at Rafael. "You should just go for it. Give him what he wants, so he can go home."

Rafael looked at me, his face hard. "If that is what you desire."

"No, it isn't!"

"Why did you ask it of me, then?"

I clenched my fists in frustration. "I don't know!"

Backman chuckled. I whirled on her. "You can put a lid on it too, Humphrey B. Bear."

Leroy patted my arm. "Immy. Focus. We need to come up with a plan."

"I've got a plan." I folded my arms over my chest. "I'm going to find him, and I'm going to pull out his lungs, and wear them as a waistcoat."

Everyone was silent for a moment. Maybe they were thinking of a plan. Maybe they were visualizing me wearing Atonas' entrails as formalwear.

Marigold cleared her throat. "Well, we don't know where he is."

"I have an idea," Backman said. "We found a couple of deer carcasses in the woods up above the north ridge. We thought it was hunters, but there was no sign of deer shot anywhere on the bodies. The animals had been butchered strangely – the cheeks and eyeballs had been sliced off precisely, and some of its organs were missing. I thought it might be our fae."

Marigold nodded. "It sounds like him. He's probably hanging around on the ridge, watching over us."

There was a bang on the door. Marigold looked over. "Who is that?"

A person stood outside, someone short. I couldn't see their head; it was blocked by the 'open' sign that Marigold had flipped to 'closed'.

I looked down at the body, and grimaced.

The door banged again. "Open this thing! Put a spring on it. It's too heavy for me to move."

"That's on purpose," Marigold muttered. She got up off the floor and walked over, opening the door. Father Benson stood in the doorway, glaring. "We're closed, sorry, Father."

"I'm coming in," he grumbled.

"We're closed," she repeated, gently, but firmly. "And since when have you ever wanted to visit my store? You keep calling it a den of lies. Satan's domain. The House of Evil."

"Yes, yes," he replied testily. "Ye having a war council here without me, about the ghosts and whatnot. I want to be here."

"I don't think that's a good idea, Father."

"Course it is!" He nudged her aside with his stick. "I've more experience with ghosts and ghouls than any of you." He caught sight of me behind Marigold, and used his stick to stab in my general direction. "She'll tell you. She helped me get rid of a vampire girl that was tearing up Terry Becker."

Everyone turned to look at me. "Well. He helped *me* get rid of her. I literally did all of the work."

"See?" Benson glared at the room. "I have to be involved. I'm the senior exorcist in charge here."

Rafael nodded at him. "Father, don't you have to take vespers?"

"Not anymore. The seminary school sent me a new deacon. He's a suck-up, little goody-two-shoes, which is good for me. He can take them." He turned to Marigold and narrowed his eyes. "Let me in, harlot."

"Well, Father, as much as we'd like to have you, we're almost done."

Benson looked dejected. "Oh, are ye? What was the meeting about?"

Marigold glanced back at me.

I shrugged. He might as well know all about it. He was already knee-deep in it, as far as I was concerned. I was slightly annoyed I'd gone to so much trouble trying to cover up the cryptid infestations, pretending they were normal animals. I even dislocated my knee trying to pitch the cu sith through the portal. Next time, I'd make Benson do it.

"There's a strange man running around Emerald Valley," Marigold explained, leading him inside. "He has some... uh, extra powers. He's not from here."

"A devil swain, is he? A demon?"

"Actually, yeah, kind of. He's from an underworld realm, so I guess he does count as a demon."

Benson brightened. "Well, that's my wheelhouse! I'll help you find him." He shuffled in, and settled down on the cushion next to Rafael, with some suspicious creaks and some very loud groans. He patted Rafael's shoulder. "I'll find this demon of yours, my friend."

Behind Benson, Sonja raised the crossbow, aiming straight for his head.

* * *

THE MEETING DRONED ON. We went around and around in circles, discussing Atonas' strengths and weaknesses, what he might do, and how we might kill him, but we didn't come up with a concrete plan other than "if he pops up, shoot him in the head with an iron arrow."

That was Sonja's plan, anyway. Her plans usually involved blunt force trauma of some sort.

Atonas could turn up anywhere, pretending to be anyone. We would have to watch each other carefully and listen to our instincts. According to the popular science articles Leroy googled, it takes around three minutes to spot a fraud in your midst, which was around the amount of time that it took for Sonja to stop aiming her crossbow at Benson's head.

Nobody could fake his mad crankiness for that long.

Three minutes, though, was a long time to spend with a homicidal fae. If he was among us, we'd have to get rid of him as soon as possible.

Nobody brought up the possibility of giving Atonas what he wanted. I watched Rafael carefully, to see if he would offer.

He didn't say much more. His eyes seemed to be fixed on me, whenever I looked over. Once he caught my gaze, I found it very hard to look away. Eye contact wasn't usually my thing. Too intimate. But somehow, Rafael's eyes were very easy to look into.

When I looked into his eyes, I forgot everything. I forgot my immortality, my desperate search for my father, the one person who could help put an end to it. I forgot about Leroy, and the near-constant gnawing worry I felt for his mental health. I forgot about Atonas, and the damage he could do, not just to our little town, but to the world in general.

All I saw was Rafael. His eyes were fathomless, an endless depth, a warm, comforting stillness. It felt like meditation. I felt like I was staring right into his soul. When I looked into his eyes, everything else disappeared.

Then, Benson elbowed me in the ribs when I failed to answer his question, and I was brought uncomfortably back to the meeting.

Finally, we ran out of things to discuss, and the meeting wrapped up. I felt oddly depressed. More depressed than usual, I mean.

Benson gripped my arm as I stood up, using it as a moving ladder to help him to his feet, even though I hadn't offered. I usually hate other people touching me, but I'd gotten used to Benson using me as a mobility aid. "Imogen, me lass. We've got a job first thing tomorrow."

"We do?"

"We might have another beastie to get rid of."

I frowned. Normally he was in a mad rush to call me out to a job. "It's not urgent?"

"It probably is," he said. "Sanjay Sarko has a strange bull set amongst his herd. He swears it's not one of his, and its behavior is… odd, to say the least."

"A bull, huh?" I scratched my chin. "You don't want me to go have a look now?"

"It can wait," he chuckled, shuffling off to the door. "It can wait. It's dark now; and by all descriptions, you'll need bright lights and your wits about you. And Imogen?"

"Yes?"

"Wear old clothes."

CHAPTER 10

*S*anjay Sarko was an interesting character, to say the least.

A young man, in his early thirties, an entrepreneur and former tech billionaire. After a sex scandal got him voted off his own board, he swore off the rat-race, left the corporate world, and became obsessed with breathwork, ice baths and psychedelics. He bought a big property on the west ridge of Emerald Valley, coincidently just down from the country club where he used to be a member, and got straight on Instagram. The staggering arrogance that worked very well for him in the corporate realm spring-boarded him into the spiritualist world, and he quickly became a hugely popular spiritual guru.

He was now one of the leading spiritualist influencers on the platform. Thousands of followers tuned in to his daily 'cosmic energy updates' and to hear the latest about his dedicated veganism and batshit-crazy ideas about expanding consciousness.

Benson and I drove up in my van the next morning, when the sun had just started to peek over the eastern ridge. It had rained in the night. The ground was soft and spongy, and the lights bounced prettily off the raindrops sprinkled on the leaves. I parked the van outside, and looked up at his house – an enormous three-story structure built entirely around an old oak tree.

Benson seemed animated as I helped him out of the van. "Been dying to have a poke around up here, Immy, me good lass. Such a pretty house."

It looked like a fairytale, like something out of Enid Blyton – the Magic Faraway Tree in real life. A closer inspection quickly told me that the house itself was steel reinforced with foundations that went into the ground. Sanjay Sarko, it seemed, was all smoke-and-mirrors.

"It is nice," I agreed.

"It's a pity that Sarko is a godless heathen," Benson added.

I gave him a nudge. "You're just annoyed he hasn't invited you to one of his parties."

Sanjay Sarko had briefly been a key suspect when I was hunting the Bloodlord, so I knew exactly who he was. He'd only lived in the valley for five years, and he had a revolving door of young 'truthseekers' who made the pilgrimage to stay with him at his farm. I thought he might be building a cult of young hippies to sacrifice, but a quick look at his millions of followers on social media had me crossing him off the list immediately.

Sanjay Sarko hosted wild 'Go Within' spiritual retreats, where gangs of skinny young people would gather at his treehouse to do large amounts of psychedelic drugs, play in the forest, and puke their guts out. They'd head home, posting ecstatic videos about their ego-deaths. They neglected to mention the brain cells they'd lost, and the emotional trauma from having childhood memories dragged up and exploited by a stoned-out-of-his-mind ex-tech billionaire.

"Aye," Benson admitted, as I helped him up the aesthetically haphazard path towards the front entrance. "I wouldn't mind joining in on one of his full moon parties. It sounds like a riot. Been a few good years since I've had the funny mushrooms."

I smirked. "We'll get him to invite us next time, as payment for this job. What are we here for, anyway? A bull?"

"That's right. He says there's something not quite right about it."

"Not quite right, huh?" I mentally flicked through the filing cabinet in my brain. "Does it breathe fire? Have wings? Does it have a bull's head, but a man's body?"

"No, nothing like that. Apparently, it just has... some..." Benson frowned. "Incontinence issues."

I stopped in my tracks. "Incontinence issues? Benson, I'm not a vet. Go and pick up Jamieson, he can help you."

Benson tugged me along. "No, it's you I need. Sanjay Sarko might be divorced from reality, but it sounded like he might have a funny beast on his hands." He gave me another tug. "Besides, I want to check out his house."

I sighed. "Fine."

We reached the front door of the treehouse. I picked up the heavy old-fashioned brass knocker and let it fall a couple of times. A *boom boom boom* sound came from within the house. It sounded suspiciously electrical. Probably a recording wired up to the knocker. Smoke and mirrors.

After a moment, Sanjay Sarko opened the door, shirtless, wearing a pair of tie-dyed yoga pants, and a joint between his lips. Two beautiful blonde girls wearing hot pants and crocheted bra tops curled sleepily around his shoulders.

He was so stoned he could barely open his eyes. "Father," he drawled, smiling happily. "Thank you for coming." He let go of one of the blondes and passed the joint to her. "From one spiritual leader to another, I welcome you." He put his hands together in the prayer position and bowed deeply.

"Greetings," Benson said chirpily, eyeing the blondes. "This is Imogen. She'll be helping me today."

Sanjay turned his head towards me, and his eyes widened slightly. "Imogen..." he breathed out. "Wow. Such energy. Such potency. Wow." He waved his arm around, gesturing to my body.

I stopped myself from rolling my eyes. I was getting good at this socialization stuff. "Hi."

"You haven't come to visit me before." He let go of the other blonde and stepped closer to me. "Why haven't you come to visit me?" The blonde whined a little in protest, sagging slightly. The other girl moved behind Sanjay and hugged her. It looked a little like they were supporting each other because they were too wasted to stand upright.

"I can't think of one reason why I'd want to visit you," I said.

"Imogen!" Benson nudged me in the ribs. "Don't be rude. She's just eager to get down to business," he said to Sanjay.

"Oh yes," Sanjay drawled. "Business. The cows. Yes." He nodded to himself a few times. "The cows. You see, Imogen, I've got these beautiful desi cows, they're a symbol of life, you know. I keep them to remind me of the deep beauty of nature. And they're so pretty. Big, dark eyes," he said suggestively, looking directly into my eyes while he said it. "Huge horns. A big *hump*." He paused, and raised his eyebrows.

Was this guy for real?

I eyed him steadily. "One of them has got diarrhea, I hear."

"Well, yeah." He shifted uncomfortably. "Something like that."

Another tall, beautiful dark-haired girl came from behind him, and wound her arms around Sanjay's waist. "Are you talking about the cows, baby?" She nuzzled her head into his neck for a second, her thick curtain of pitch-dark hair hid her face. "That new one with the crazy horns?"

"Mmmm hmmm." He nuzzled her back. "These two fine people are here to check him out."

She flipped her hair back and looked at me, with big dark eyes. "That thing looks wild, man. I never seen a cow that looks like that before." She clearly wasn't as stoned as everyone else here.

"Okay," I said. "I guess we'll go have a look."

Sanjay plucked the joint out of the blonde girl's mouth and waved it in a circle, pointing it towards the path outside to the left. "Let's go!"

I backed off the step, helping Benson down. The two blondes whined incoherently, but Sanjay patted them back inside.

"I'll come too," the dark-haired girl said. "I want to have another look." She wound her arm through Sanjay's and they walked ahead of us.

We wandered through a pretty apple orchard, taking a gravel path towards the little farm at the edge of the property. An old-fashioned red barn came into view. Beyond that, a herd of cows moved idly in a paddock, within a circle of rustic-looking fencing.

We stopped underneath a huge sycamore, twenty feet away from the barn. Sanjay crouched under the tree and settled himself in yogi-style underneath it. "My cows," he pointed.

I looked. Around six huge beasts loitered in the paddock, their heads down, chewing on the grass. They were definitely impressive; big heads, long horns stretching out for several yards either side. Their bone-white hides shone in the sunshine.

I looked back down at Sanjay. He looked like he'd settled

in. "Are you going to show me which one you're worried about?"

"Ah, no." He shook his head and took a puff on his joint. "You'll see. Go on."

Benson sat down next to him. "Off you go, Imogen. Let me know how you go."

Lazy bastards.

I shrugged. Okay, if this was going to be a one-woman show, that was fine by me.

The beautiful raven-haired girl took my hand, winding her fingers through mine. "Come on, I'll show you."

I tried not to flinch as she pulled me forward. Her hand felt so weird, so casually intertwined in mine. It was such an intimate gesture.

I struggled with being touched at the best of times, and having her fingers wound around my fingers, our palms touching... it felt... explosive. *Dangerous*. A strange rush of fear ran through me, combined with something else. Apprehension? Confusion?

I wasn't sexually confused, I knew that. I had always preferred men, and apart from acknowledging that this girl was physically stunning, I didn't think I was sexually attracted to her.

I was so busy trying to diagnose my feelings, I didn't notice we'd reached the fence posts. The girl pulled me forward, and pushed me in front of her. "There you go," she cooed.

I looked.

One of the cows *did* seem strange.

I peered closer. It was bone-white, like the others, but instead of a mop of hair on the ridge of its head, it had a mane running down its spine, like a horse.

I stiffened. Its horns didn't curve out to the side. Instead, they curved back, and curled in on themselves, obviously useless in a fight.

I groaned. No. Not a bonnacon. *Not* a bonnacon. Anything but that.

I'd rather fight the Jabberwocky than have to try and get rid of a bonnacon.

I opened my eyes, hoping that the curled horns had miraculously uncurled and had fixed themselves to point outwards. No such luck.

"Goddamnit."

The beautiful girl giggled beside me. "It's pretty, though, isn't it?"

I pinched the bridge of my nose. A damned bonnacon, hiding right here in between Sanjay Sarko's cows.

Bonnacon were common in medieval times – whole herds of them would roam the forests of Europe in the Dark Ages. They'd been hunted to extinction here on Earth, for several different reasons. The first was because, at one stage, they'd been exceptionally popular to hunt and mount. The other was because they caused so much damage, it was too dangerous to have them roaming free.

The horns of a bonnacon were useless for defense, so they'd somehow developed another extraordinarily disgusting defense mechanism.

When it was chased, the bonnacon could shoot a stream of lava-hot dung out of it's ass. It would kill everything behind it, torching the hunters into charred skeletons and burning whole forests to ashes.

I put my head down on the fencepost and groaned. How the hell was I going to get a bonnacon back to the portal?

The raven-haired girl leaned in close behind me and put her lips to my ear. I shivered. She whispered to me. "What do you think, Starsmell? How are you going to get rid of that?"

CHAPTER 11

*J*jerked around, turning to face her. "Atonas?"

She laughed out loud. "You didn't recognize me? You're a fool. I'm wearing almost exactly the same face." The face shivered; her eyes grew slightly larger; the skin glistened, then, it returned to the human-girl visage that she'd taken on. "This form is easy," she said. "I like it. I thought it might be better to use this one to seduce the lovely Vampire King." She giggled again, and looked me up and down. "Since he didn't want to have sex with me while I was wearing *your* form. How does that make you feel? Knowing that he does not want to have sex with you?"

I backed up, putting three feet between us, and pulled out my knife from its sheath in my boot. "What are you doing here?"

She waved her hand towards the bonnacon, chewing its cud mindlessly in the paddock. "Trying to have a little fun. Your little doctor friend over there is fairly enjoyable."

I cocked my head. "Doctor friend?"

"The one who distributes drugs."

I pursed my lips. "He's not a doctor. He's just a narcissistic attention-whore."

"Well, he was relatively enjoyable for a bit. The party we had last night was good, clean, wholesome fun."

I had no idea what the fae underworld prince would call 'good, clean wholesome fun'. "Those girls looked stoned out of their minds," I said through clenched teeth. "What did you do to them?"

"Nothing they didn't want me to do." She shrugged. "Well, they didn't say they weren't enjoying it."

"Have you ever heard of consent, Atonas?"

She looked confused. "Excuse me?"

I exhaled, and backed up a few steps, giving myself room in case she wanted to fight. Just then, something occurred to me. "You said you had a good time?"

"No, I didn't. I said that I had good, clean, wholesome fun."

"Wholesome for you, you mean."

She waved her hand dismissively. "Whatever. I'm still owed my time with your Vampire King. And I will have him."

The burning feeling reared up in my chest again; suddenly I was so mad that I could choke. I bared my teeth at her. "You will not. He is not yours to have."

She sniffed dismissively. "He's not yours either. You have not claimed him, and he has not claimed you. Besides, I came to him wearing your body, and he refused me."

"Exactly," I pointed my finger at her. "He refused you. As soon as he realized you weren't me."

"Irrelevant," she shrugged. "I will have him, no matter what. He may find this body more to his liking."

The hot feeling threatened to overwhelm me. She was right – Rafael wasn't mine. I wasn't even sure if he liked me very much. He'd made it clear that he was only interested in other vampires and wouldn't date a human or shifter. I wasn't either of those things, and I didn't know where I stood.

And he hadn't mentioned fae.

Rafael was free to do what he wished, but the idea of him making love to this beautiful body in front of me made me feel homicidal with rage.

I pointed at the herd of cows. "Did you put the bonnacon in there?"

"Of course. He was easy to lure through the portal. I turned myself into a female bonnacon and promised him his own good time, and led him here. I thought you might have some fun getting rid of him, while I go off to pleasure your Vampire King, Starsmell."

I gritted my teeth. "Stop calling me that. It's the stupidest name I've ever heard."

"It's fitting," she laughed. "You smell of the stars. No wonder you are so jealous. The stars are always jealous."

"What the hell does that mean?"

She laughed merrily, like I'd missed a very obvious joke. "You're so funny. Acting all silly and ignorant."

"No more games." I lifted my knife and moved into a strike pose. "Get rid of that bonnacon, right now."

She tilted her head to the side. "Come now, Starsmell. Why would I do that? I put him there on purpose, to distract you, while I seduce your king."

"You'll find it hard to seduce him with a hole in your gut," I snarled.

She giggled again, and bent down and picked up a pebble. She tossed it in the air idly. "Are you sure you want to do that?" The pebble soared into the air again. On the next throw, she tossed it at the herd of cows.

It hit the bonnacon right in the head.

The huge creature jolted, then froze. The herd around it shot their heads up, tensed. I held my breath. After a loaded, tense second, I heard a tiny *pffft* sound, coming from the bonnacon.

An insane stench hit my nostrils; I gagged. It was rotten egg in a used diaper. It was dead whale and seagull poo on a beach. It was cyclops' asscrack after spin class on a hot day.

Atonas picked up another pebble.

"Don't," I hissed, holding out my knife.

She laughed softly. "You're not going to stop me. I'm going to take your man, Starsmell. I'll have him, every single way I can."

She tossed the pebble at the bonnacon, and disappeared.

The bonnacon lifted his head and bellowed.

CHAPTER 12

*T*he Imogen of three months ago would have chased her. No, the Imogen of three months ago would have tossed her knife on the ground, got in her van, and drove far, far away from Emerald Valley.

But this was now. The bonnacon were nervous creatures. The pebble had startled him. He tossed his head, snorting, teetering on the verge of a stampede. If he started a rampage, he would start shooting burning poop everywhere, torching the other cows, destroying the barn, and burning Sanjay's house to the ground. If he took off down towards the town, he could kill hundreds of people.

I shot a glance towards where Benson sat underneath the sycamore, exhaling a puff of smoke. He passed the joint back to Sanjay. My eyes narrowed for a second, but I shelved the thought, promising myself I would yell at him later.

The man had asthma. Smoke was bad for his lungs.

I had more important things to worry about. If this bonnacon got loose, he'd kill everyone.

Within the paddock, the beast stamped his hooves, teetering on the verge of a downward spiral. The other cows moved nervously away. "It's okay, big guy," I said, trying for a soothing, relaxed tone. He tossed his head and glared at me. Another *poot* sound came from his rear.

I gagged. The smell was unbearable. I doubled over, and dry-retched a couple of times before I got control of myself.

I had to get this damned creature contained, and back through the portal. Or I could just kill it. I could kill it, couldn't I?

Leroy would be disappointed. And bonnacon were very rare, even on other planes of existence.

Think, Imogen. *Think.*

While I took too long thinking, the bonnacon backed up. Unfortunately, he backed his ass into another cow's horn.

Oh *no.*

A small squirt of bonnacon shit came out its rear. Intense, scorching heat blazed out like a flamethrower. The stream missed the other cow by inches and hit the grass, instantly burning a deep hole into the ground, the dry grass crackling like tinder and burning at the edges of the scorched furrow in the ground.

I vaulted over the fence. The herd started to stampede, headed in a circle around the paddock, unable to get past the fencing. Another hot squirt streamed out of the bonnacon's butt, this one caught one of the cows across his ribs, burning straight through the poor beast like it was a lazer. It gave a tortured scream and fell to the ground. The herd ran faster, going around and around and around in circles.

I had to stop them. Sooner or later, the bonnacon would shoot enough burning shit to burn down the fence. He'd escape and wreak havoc on the town.

But how do I stop him?

Oh, *damnit.* I launched myself into the middle of the stampede.

I felt a hot rush of pain as sharp horns sliced through my

left arm. Even the damned normal animals were hurting me, now. It was too dangerous to get behind the bonnacon, so I turned, facing the incoming stampede as they ran around the paddock. The bonnacon stomped right in the middle, small squirts of shit shooting out of his ass like a flamethrower. Another squirt hit the cow behind him. Her face instantly disintegrated, and she tumbled to the ground. The herd screamed, and ran faster.

I missed the bonnacon as it came around again, having to dodge the giant horns of another incoming cow. I felt like I was in a video game - duck, jump, step left, duck again.

In the distance, I could hear Sanjay screaming. "My cows! What are you doing to my cows!"

"One of them is not a cow, you idiot," I yelled back. "Go get me a rope. Steel, if you have it."

Steel wouldn't really help – the bonnacon's dung was hotter than lava, and it would burn through it. But if I could subdue the stupid thing and keep it still, hopefully I would not get any shit on the rope. I could hold it still until it calmed down. I couldn't risk taking my eyes off the running herd, but I sincerely hoped that Benson was still waiting under that sycamore tree.

After a few long minutes of ducking and weaving through the stampeding herd, I saw my chance. I threw myself around the sharp horns of one cow, got the bonnacon by the neck and wrestled him to the ground.

The big bastard was stronger than he looked – much stronger than a regular cow, anyway. He jerked and thrashed in my arms; a trail of putrid hot dung squirted out his rear in a gush. I gritted my teeth, dug my heels into the ground, and held him still, so the jet of poo only went in one direction. It gushed out, burning the same deep furrow into the earth. "Sanjay! Where's the rope?"

"Here!" A coil of rope flew towards me and landed next to the struggling bonnacon.

"Get the rest of these cows out of here!" I shouted at him.

"What *rest?* They've all melted," he sobbed. "They're melted. Melted!"

Give me strength. "Pull yourself together, man!" There were still two cows left, running in a terrified circle, trying to jump the huge flaming furrow in the grass. "Get those two out!" I jerked my head towards him. If they stayed in here, they were going to die. Or they would trample me while I was trying to hold the bonnacon down, and I would probably kill them in frustration.

Terrified, crying and shaking uncontrollably, Sanjay crept closer to the fence and opened the gate with a trembling hand. He squealed in fright as the cows came around towards him. I heaved the bonnacon, and aimed the creature's flaming poo to scare the cows in the right direction. They galloped out of the paddock and ran towards the orchard.

I held the bonnacon steady. Great jets of poo still squirted from his rear, showing no signs of slowing down. The long, narrow crater in the earth was getting deeper and deeper. "Any minute now, he'll stop," I muttered to myself. "Any minute."

The beast thrashed. More lava streamed out. I ground my jaw. "Relax, you asshole," I snarled. "Relax."

Okay, that didn't work. We needed a plan B.

I eyed his skull. It was very thick. I couldn't knock him out without killing him.

I groaned in frustration. The crater in the earth was several feet deep now. "Stop shitting yourself, you idiot."

A bonnacon was a magical creature. There was a good chance that he was never going to stop. It was like holding an uncontrollable flamethrower that never ran out of gas. I snarled out loud in frustration. I was going to have to slit his throat.

I took a moment to consider how strange it was that I felt bad before I had to kill something. That hadn't happened in several millennia. I didn't want to kill this beast. I would rather it be Atonas. Atonas, who brought this poor creature in here, and set me up so he could go and seduce Rafael.

Fire burned in my stomach again, almost as hot as the shit coming out of the bonnacon. When I got hold of that fae prince, I was going to string him up by his toes. First, I'd make him explain to me what he meant by 'the stars are jealous,' and then, I'd...

I spotted Sanjay out of the corner of my eye, tears running down his face. Atonas had called him the doctor, because he had a lot of drugs. An idea crept into my mind.

"Sanjay!"

"Wha-wha-what?" he sobbed back.

"Do you have any sleeping pills on you?"

"What?"

"Sleeping pills!"

Bewildered, he rummaged around in his yoga pants. "Uh, no," he shouted back. "I've only got a little bit of molly and... some ketamine."

"Did you say ketamine?!"

"Yeah!" He held up a handful of vials. They clinked together in his shaking hands. "I've got lots. We've got a bus of breathwork students coming in later, I thought we'd head down the K-hole."

I almost rolled my eyes. Ketamine was an anesthetic, quite literally used as a horse tranquilizer. "Bring them all here," I snarled.

"No way! I'm not coming near that thing!"

"Bring it here, or I'll let him go, and your pretty fake tree house will burn to ash."

"Okay, okay!" Slowly, crouching down, he crept towards me, shaking like a leaf. The bonnacon jerked his head, almost getting his feet underneath him, but I wrestled him down again. Sanjay shrieked like an old lady, dropped the vials on the grass, and ran away.

"Okay," I said, gritting my teeth. "Here we go."

It's one thing avoiding the fiery poo of the bonnacon. It's another to wrestle his mouth open and jam a glass vial down its throat. It was the hardest thing I'd done in a long time - getting my weight flat on his body to keep him still, while I forced his jaw open. I emptied one vial and waited a couple of seconds.

Where's Jamieson when you need him? Knowing him, he was probably backpacking in Puerto Rico.

The bonnacon jerked, still shooting poo. I jammed another vial in and emptied it down his throat.

He jerked his head. The poo jet lost a little of its force. Suddenly, his body stopped bucking wildly, and he lay almost still underneath me.

I looked down at his long face. His next bellow morphed into a sad moo, then, a pathetic gurgle. His eyes rolled into the back of his head.

He was out.

I exhaled in relief. Cautiously, I opened his mouth and pulled his tongue out so he wouldn't swallow it. Blessed silence fell around me, broken by a soft crackle of smoldering grass.

I got up and looked around. Long, deep slashes marked the paddock, spreading up into the trees beyond the paddock where the poo had splattered. Four seared cow carcasses smoked around me, sending an unsettling smell of barbecue into the air.

"My cows," Sanjay whispered. "My farm."

"Well, personally, I think we got off lightly." I stood up

and brushed myself off. "It could have been a *lot* worse. Now, you'll have to help me get him back to my van." I had to get this thing back into the portal before he woke up. I could carry him myself, but it would be nice to have someone open the gates for me.

I looked around. "Sanjay... where's Benson?"

I followed Sanjay's pointing finger to where Father Benson lay under the sycamore tree, asleep, with his hat over his eyes. He snored softly, oblivious to the devastation surrounding him.

CHAPTER 13

I loaded the unconscious bonnacon into my van and called Rafael on the drive to the portal. He answered immediately. "Imogen," he said, his voice low. "Is everything alright?'

"Not exactly," I said, swerving the van around a tight bend. "I had a visit from our fae friend. And by friend, I mean 'homicidal maniac who is trying to kill us all'."

Rafael exhaled. "I was worried about something like that. I had a business meeting with one of my shipping partners in the dining room at lunch. He brought his daughter with him, a beautiful young woman with long, dark hair."

"Beautiful, huh? How beautiful was she?"

There was a beat of silence. "Not beautiful enough for me to lose my wits. As soon as I saw her, I returned to my office immediately and left them sitting in the dining room."

"Sonja didn't shoot her in the eye with an iron bolt?" I asked, while sliding the van sideways down towards main street. "That's not like her."

"We couldn't be sure. Atonas has a way of masking his scent. The dark-haired young woman might have been my shipping partner's daughter, for all I know, and I would have a diplomatic nightmare on my hands. Besides, we were in full view of several Fortune 500 company owners and a handful of royalty and heads of state. You can't just shoot a guest in the eye. It's not polite."

"Of course," I said dryly. I swung the van into a park behind the town square in a secluded spot, keeping an eye out. A few townsfolk were lingering on the green, eating sandwiches on the grass. I'd have to wait until they were gone before I tried to pitch the bonnacon through the portal.

My knees creaked in protest at the idea. God, I needed a rest.

"So you hid in your office. What happened then?"

"The daughter made several attempts to follow me. My security team took her into another area, ostensibly to bring her to me. We attempted to seal her in one of the holding rooms."

"At what point did you find out if it was a real mortal girl with a crush, or a fae madman?"

"When he blew up the holding room."

"Ah."

"Several of my security team are wounded. The sonic blast has damaged their eardrums."

"Oh." That wasn't great. "Is Sonja ok?"

"She'll be glad of your concern. No, she was not with us, she was running another errand for me. Brick was in his death-sleep, recovering from the last encounter with Atonas."

"What? Did he get hurt?" Brick was Sonja's mate, a vampire himbo. "What did I miss?"

"Brick was badly concussed in the confrontation with Atonas, when he was pretending to be you. He took the full force of the sonic blast that Atonas aimed at Sonja."

"Aw. That's love for you, isn't it," I said idly. "Always sacrificing yourself and getting hurt."

"Indeed."

I heard an odd noise through the phone. I listened, trying to place the sound. "Are you on a helicopter?"

"*Si*. I am on my way to Washington."

"Of course you are," I said sulkily.

It was almost easy to forget Emerald Valley wasn't the center of Rafael's universe. Whenever I spoke to him, he made me feel like I was the only person in the world, and Emerald Valley was a little bubble, a pocket universe where nothing else mattered.

A bitter taste ran in my mouth whenever I remembered who Rafael Stefano Di Stasio really was: The world's most eligible bachelor. Vampire King, mega-mogul, billionaire. Ruler of thousands of vampires, and direct boss of millions and millions of lowly humans.

The reality check gave me vertigo.

"I have an important meeting this evening," he said. "I will be back by morning."

"Why a helicopter?" I asked. "Don't you have a private jet?" I knew that he did. He had his own airline, for God's sake. I had no idea why I was being so bitchy.

"Helicopters are more maneuverable. I can land wherever I want to. Besides, there is no runway in Emerald Valley."

"Yes. Good point." I glared at the two women on the town square lawn. They were taking their sweet time, finishing their sandwiches.

Rafael was silent for a moment. "Imogen, are you okay? You said you had a visit from Atonas, too?"

I sighed. "You know that job I had at Sanjay Sarko's house? Turns out, Atonas had lured a bonnacon through the portal and set it among his desi cows. Benson and I showed up to check it out, and Atonas was there, in Sanjay's house, looking like a pretty hippy girl. She taunted me, ground my gears real good, threw some rocks at the bonnacon before running off to seduce you."

He exhaled sharply, and swore in Italian. "Did he touch you? Are you hurt?"

"I'm fine," I said, quickly checking to make sure the bonnacon was still out cold. "I handled it. The bonnacon is unconscious, and I'm about to toss him back through the portal now."

There was a pause. "Is Sanjay Sarko's house still standing?"

"Mm-hmm. I managed to limit the damage to his paddock. A few of his cows bit the dust, though."

"I am pleased to hear that. He is still a member at the country club, and we have several long-standing business arrangements."

"Why am I not surprised about that?" I muttered. Sanjay was all smoke and mirrors. On his Instagram, he pretended to be a communist.

The two women were finally leaving the lawn behind the ruined statue. Soon, the coast would be clear, and I could throw this giant cow through the portal and get rid of him. "I've got to go," I said into the phone. "I've got to get rid of this monster before he wakes up."

"You are at the portal now?"

"Yep."

"My team will clear the security cameras."

"Thanks."

"Imogen..."

"Yes, Your Fangliness?" These two ladies were taking too long clearing up their lunch.

"Nothing. It is not important."

"If you say so," I said absently. I wasn't going to beat words out of him. It wasn't my style.

I heard him inhale. "Imogen, please let me know if anything else happens with the fae prince. I was hoping that by removing myself from the Valley for the evening, it might draw him away."

"I hope you packed your chastity belt," I muttered under my breath.

"*Scusi?*"

"Nothing. Bye, Rafael. Bring me back a present. Bring me whatever Washington is famous for."

He chuckled. "I don't think I can fit confused tourists and bad traffic into my carry-on."

I gasped. "Your Majesty. Did you just make a joke?"

"The world is clearly ending," he said smoothly. "I must go. *A presto.*"

"See you soon," I echoed.

The two women finally threw their leftovers into the trashcan and wandered off. The coast was clear. I sighed, and cracked my neck. Cow-tipping, eat your heart out. Time to try a little cow-tossing.

CHAPTER 14

The bonnacon went through the portal on my second throw. It was a good thing, too; he was starting to twitch in my arms as the ketamine wore off. He'd be fine when he got back to his own realm. Maybe. Probably.

I walked back to my van, and stretched my calf muscles as I got in my seat. Even with my strength, it was no easy feat tossing an unconscious twelve-hundred pound cow twenty feet in the air.

I belted up, and started the van, wondering where I should go. Leroy was up at the outdoor education center, doing research with Backman, so I'd head there.

Surreptitiously, I sniffed myself. No, I'd probably have to go home for a shower first. I put the car in reverse and pulled out of my parking spot.

Suddenly, all hell erupted.

A siren screamed, ear-splittingly loud over the squeal of tires. Flashing blue and red lights appeared behind me. The police cruiser blocked me in.

Harmann had come for me again.

This time, he didn't make me wait. He shoved the car

door open and flew out of the cruiser, hand on his holster. "Don't move! Hands where I can see them!" He ran towards my window, pulling his SIG. "Hands where I can see them!"

I put my hands on the steering wheel. What the fuck was he doing now? I glanced back at him where he was cautiously moving up towards my window. "What are you doing?" I shouted at him. "I'm not armed."

"The hell you're not armed," he spat back at me, pointing the gun at my head. "Don't move."

"I'm not moving!"

"I said don't move!" He jerked the gun higher.

I flinched, adrenaline flooding my limbs. "I'm not moving!"

"Get your hands on the wheel!"

"They are on the wheel!"

"I said don't *move!*"

"I'm not moving!" I glared at him.

"Your mouth is moving. Your head is moving." He jerked the gun. "Turn around. Eyes forward."

An acid taste flooded my mouth. I turned my head away slowly, looking out the windscreen. "What the hell is this all about?" I said through clenched teeth.

"I said don't move that mouth, girl. You're done asking questions." He shifted the SIG into one hand, freeing up the other one. "I'm opening your door. Keep your hands on the wheel. Stay still."

I looked out the windscreen, and blackness started to creep in on my vision. Stay here, I told myself. Stay focused. Don't lose it.

I couldn't lose it. If I ripped this cop's head off, I'd have to leave Emerald Valley. I had to stay here. I had to find my dad. My hands gripped the steering wheel tighter.

Harmann opened the door and reached past me. He turned off my engine, took out the keys, and put them in his pocket. "Do you have any weapons on you? Any guns?" I shook my head. "Knives?"

I had a bunch of knives. "I have a hunting knife in my boot." And I'm going to shove it into your kidney as soon as I know I can get away with it. "Are you arresting me?"

"Shut up," he snapped. "Where's the weapon?"

"In my boot." I looked down.

"Don't move!" He jerked the gun up again, this time pressing it against my head. I gripped the steering wheel. The wheel bent under my fist. With superhuman effort, I forced myself to relax.

Harmann bent down and patted my legs. He found my knife in the sheath in my boot and pulled it out. "Why do you have this on you, huh? Why are you carrying a knife?"

I didn't trust myself to speak. I stared stonily ahead as he patted the other leg.

"Okay, girl. Hands behind your head. Get out of the vehicle, slowly."

I placed my hands behind me and slid out of my seat, fixing him with a venomous glare. "You better have thought this through clearly," I snarled. "I hope you know what you're doing. I'm going to rip you to shreds."

"Is that a threat? Are you threatening an officer?"

"Metaphorically speaking." I straightened up and eyeballed him. He glared at me.

"Turn around. Put your hands behind your back."

"You arresting me?"

"Sure am." He grabbed me roughly and pushed me around, pushing me hard against my van. He held my wrists together, snapping on cuffs. They were pulled too tight. They dug into my skin.

"What the hell for? I haven't done anything."

"Oh, girl, you have," he chuckled. He turned me around to face him. "I've got you. I've *got* you." He holstered his SIG and laughed in my face. "That footage cleaned up, just like I thought it would. The camera footage of the night Sir Humphrey's statue was busted." He chuckled. "I *got* you."

"What?"

It was impossible. There was no footage. Rafael said it would be unsalvageable.

"It shows you, clear as anything, smashing up the statue." He moved closer, peered into my face, and laughed again. "Oh, I see you're surprised. You thought you were going to get away with it."

My mouth dropped open. "But that's not…"

"Shut up," he snapped. "You can shut your mouth, little girl. You don't gotta say anything, in fact, I better read you your rights, because you're going away. You're going away for a long time." He pushed me around again, and marched me to the cruiser, reciting the Miranda right as he shoved me in the back seat.

CHAPTER 15

I sat in the back seat, oblivious to the sharp pain in my wrists where the cuffs dug into my skin, the screaming siren, the flashing lights. What the hell was happening? There was no chance in hell he had footage of me breaking the statue of Sir Humphrey. I hadn't even touched that thing. Sir Humphrey had shattered under the weight of the evil knowledge that streamed down out of the portal. He'd been the Tashk's first casualty. The second had been the flesh that was stripped from my legs.

I was so confused, the incoherent rage I'd felt when Harmann had first pulled up took a backseat in my mind. All this for destruction of property? He was going to violently arrest me, handcuff me, throw me in a cruiser and threaten me with jail, just for destruction of property?

He drove to the station like a maniac, unnecessarily sliding around corners. He shot into the station car park and slammed on his breaks. I wasn't belted in - I was knocked around like a piñata.

I barely felt it.

"Out of the car," he snapped, opening the door. He

marched me into the station, taking the front steps. An elderly lady walked past with her dog; a young couple gaped at me as Harmann pushed me up the steps. Maximum humiliation. Ultimate shame. It was all on purpose.

He walked me into the station and held me against a wall while he booked me. The station was tiny – just one big room with a reception stand, a couple of desks, and a cell along the back wall. I was roughly fingerprinted, photographed, searched and shoved into the one tiny cell at the back of the station.

The cell was bare, save for one rusty bed frame, bolted to the wall, and a metal toilet with no seat.

The toilet stank. There was no window. I could punch my way through the brick. It would take some time, but I could do it. The iron bars were thick. I could bend them and squeeze out quite easily.

I wanted to break out so much that my stomach hurt. I wanted to smash the whole building, tear Harmann's heart out of his chest and stomp on it on the way out the door.

Old Imogen would have done it.

Then again, Old Imogen would have got caught again. She'd get overwhelmed, and end up getting torn to shreds, either by a mass of bodies and bullets, or by the Ancient who hunted her.

It was always hard to run from the Ancient. It was getting harder to run from humans. Facial recognition, body cams, helicopters, heat sensors. The technology of the modern age was great in some ways, although it made my life a lot more dangerous. Gone were the days where I could burn down a village, pop on a headscarf, change my name and move on to the next town.

I wanted to kill Harmann so badly it hurt. I had to wait.

Maybe I *was* getting smarter.

I turned, and watched Harmann through the bars. He

sauntered through the office, ignoring me. He made himself a cup of coffee and idly sat down at his desk.

"You've got nothing on me, you know."

He huffed out a laugh and tapped on his keyboard.

"All this for a simple property damage charge? Seems excessive, don't you think?"

He chuckled, and picked up a piece of paper. "Listen to this, sweetheart: *Any person who willfully injures or destroys, or attempts to injure or destroy, any structure, plaque, statue, or other monument on public property commemorating the service of any person or persons in the armed forces of the United States shall be fined under this title, imprisoned not more than 10 years, or both.*" He swiveled around in his chair and met my eye. "You're going away. Sir Humphrey is a national hero. You're going *down*, girl."

"You've got nothing on me. You're not going to have a job when I'm done with you." I gripped the cell bars tighter. "They're going to kick you out of the force so hard that your head will spin, and you'll be on night security at Dominos for the rest of your life." If you're lucky, I added silently. If you're not, I'll rip off your legs and use them as croquet mallets.

"You think I've got nothing? You're delusional, girl."

He seemed so confident. I frowned. Maybe he had fabricated some evidence. Cops did that. Forensics, too. I remembered reading about a case where a lazy scientist from the police forensic labs had rubber-stamped all the drug samples the cops had seized as illicit substances, when they were benign things like tea, or powdered sugar. Hundreds of innocent people had gone to jail before she was busted.

"I want a lawyer."

"You got a lawyer?"

I didn't know any lawyers. None that were alive anymore, in any case. My heart kicked in my chest. I'd have to call Jamieson. He had been the mayor here, he'd get me out of this. My heart sank again when I remembered he'd gone backpacking. Marigold, then. She'd be sure to know someone. I had to get out of here before I lost my temper, as well as my grip on reality, and destroyed the whole building.

Harmann watched the frustration on my face, and he chuckled. "You think about that, girl. You'll have some time to come up with your story before a public defender comes out here, anyway."

I scowled at him. I remember him saying the public defender was his buddy. No way I'd be taking him. "I want a phone call," I said. Marigold would know a lawyer.

He smiled at me. "Fine." He stood up and walked to the wall, where a fixed-line phone sat on a shelf. He picked up the receiver. "Who am I calling?"

"Marigold."

"Marigold who?"

Oh Lord, I didn't even know her last name. Why was I so bad with names? "Marigold, from the store down the road."

He smirked. "I don't know who you're talking about."

I ground my teeth. "Marigold from Marigold's Tea and Beauty Supplies. Harmann, it's literally on the next block. There are only a handful of businesses in this town, you know them all. It's right there, on your list above the phone." I glared at him. "You can't deny me my phone call."

"Fine, fine." He hit the pre-programed number and passed the receiver through the bars.

I put the phone to my ear. It rang and rang. No answer.

Marigold should be there. It was nearing late afternoon, but her store should definitely be open.

After a moment, the phone clicked to the answering machine. I'd have to leave a message. Harmann eyed me, an amused smirk on his face, while I spoke into the phone. "Marigold, come and get me. I'm at the police station. I've been arrested. Come get me out."

Harmann laughed. "That's your call done. I hope she checks her messages soon." He reached through the bars and snatched the phone back.

"You can't keep me here."

"I can keep you as long as I want to."

"You've got nothing on me."

"Oh yeah?" He walked back to his desk, and picked up his cellphone. "You wanna see? Maybe, once you see it, you'll settle down and accept it. You're *done*, girl. I watched everything. I watched you smash that statue with a sledgehammer."

His expression turned thunderous. "I watched while you desecrated the monument to the greatest founder in our nation's history. You broke him to pieces and walked away, whistling."

My mouth dropped open. He was delusional.

In one of his bizarre quick mood changes, he grinned again. "But no matter. I've got it all on video. You're screwed."

He tapped on his phone, and held it up so I could see the screen. "This is the footage from the night of August fifth. It's clear as daylight. Even my blind grandma could ID you from this."

He pushed the screen towards me. A video started playing.

A tiny kitten walked across a carpet. Its little foot stepped on a piece of tape, and it got stuck to its paw. It jumped in the air, a little fluffy ball, doing a somersault.

I glanced up at Harmann, puzzled. "What is this?"

"Just watch."

I looked at the screen. A fat ginger cat walked along the top of a fence. From the corner of the screen, a frog jumped out, landing right in front of the cat. The cat leapt three feet in the air, falling off the fence and out of sight.

"Harmann, this isn't…"

"Shut up and watch."

The next video started. Two cats squared up to each other, preparing to fight. Both stood on their back feet, paws raised, waving in time to techno music. They looked like they were dancing.

I dragged my eyes off the screen to stare at Harmann, who was grinning at me. "See?"

"Harmann, that's not footage from the town square…"

"You can't play games with me, girl." He pointed to the screen. "See you, with the hammer, right there?"

On the screen, a tiny fluffy kitten valiantly attacked the twitching tail of a bored, flat-faced British shorthair. "That's not the town square, you idiot. Those are funny cat videos."

"That's you, right there," he pointed to the screen. "You took to Sir Humphrey like a batter in a cage. You can't argue your way out of this. It's damning evidence."

"Harmann it's *not*." I jabbed a finger at the screen. "That's a cat trying to fit into a box, but the box is way too small."

He swiveled the phone around and looked at it for a second. "Oh," he chuckled. "I see what you're doing. You're going for the insanity defense."

"Insanity? Me? You're the one watching Youtube shorts of cat videos, thinking they're security footage."

He ticked his finger at me. "Now, now. You can't deny it." With one finger, he scrolled through the video, and paused it. "See there? Right there. It's you, full-frontal, with a hammer, smashing the sword right out of Sir Humphrey's hand."

It was a cat, with a slice of bread around its head. An in-bred cat.

I gaped at Harmann. "What the *fuck?*"

He nodded, clearly feeling vindicated. "I told you. Clear as day."

I studied his face. He was so confident, so sure. When he

looked at the screen, he saw me destroying the statue of Sir Humphrey.

A cold chill ran through me, and I backed away from the bars. *Was* it me? Had my reality warped again? Had I lost time? Lost control?

Had I finally gone completely insane?

My legs hit the metal bed behind me, and I slumped down to it. I heard Harmann chuckle again. "Finally sunk in, has it?"

My trembling fingers patted the metal bed. Metal. Cold. I sniffed - the smell of urine and bleach hit my nostrils. I concentrated on my ears, and noted the sound of Harmann's footsteps, as he walked away from my cell and sat down at his desk again.

I looked down at my belly. All the organs were inside, where they were supposed to be. I patted my arms and legs. They were still attached.

I closed my eyes. Breathe. Breathe in, breathe out.

I wasn't crazy. I mean, I wasn't crazier than usual. I'd hallucinated before, but it didn't feel like this. This was different.

I knew what I was looking at on that screen. They were definitely funny cat videos; I'd stake my immortality on it. I'd even seen some of them before. How is it that Harmann thought it was me on that screen?

The door buzzed loudly, and I flinched. Harmann gave an annoyed huff, got out of his chair, and walked towards the door. A strange man stood in the doorway.

The stranger was short and thin, completely bald, and impeccably dressed, in a sharply tailored dark-blue suit. In his mid-forties perhaps, with sharp eyes and a curved nose, and skin the color of strong tea. Deep creases etched on either side of his mouth, as if he spent a lot of time frowning.

He spoke to Harmann in a quiet voice. I couldn't hear what he said.

Harmann replied gruffly. I couldn't make out all the words - something about the stranger not being able to come in, maybe. Harmann straightened up, put his shoulders back, and put his hands on his hips. The stranger cocked his head, and spoke in a lower, sharper tone. Harmann lifted his chin, and glared at the stranger. A moment passed. Finally, Harmann stood aside, waving the man inside the police station.

"Go ahead," he said. "She's over there. Knock yourself out."

The stranger walked towards me, taking quick, efficient steps. "Miss Gray?"

I pursed my lips. "Who are you?"

"Benedict Plum," the man said, sliding a business card between the bars.

I took it and frowned. The card said *Benedict Plum*, and nothing else. "What do you want?"

"I'm here to represent you."

I cocked my head. "I don't know you."

Harmann laughed out loud. He picked up his coffee mug and took a leisurely sip. "Girl, you are dumber than a box of hammers. I'd advise you against being rude to your lawyer, but then again, I want you to go away for a long time, so I'm going to stand here and keep my mouth shut."

My lawyer? I looked at the stranger. I'd never seen him before in my life.

Benedict Plum turned around and gave Harmann an exasperated look. "If you don't mind, officer. Please give us some privacy."

Harmann narrowed his eyes. "We don't have an interview room here."

"I don't need you to let her out. That will happen soon

enough. I just need to be able to talk to my client privately." When Harmann bristled, Benedict Plum snapped his fingers. "The law demands it."

Harmann frowned. "Well, as long as she ain't getting out. I'll sit outside, finish my coffee." He turned around and walked out. The door buzzed and slammed shut behind him.

Benedict Plum turned back towards me and smiled. The movement slid oddly on his face. The furrows on either side of his mouth bent into V-shapes. "Miss Gray. It is lovely to make your acquaintance. You seem to have gotten yourself into a spot of bother."

I eyed him carefully. His suit was perfectly pressed, not a wrinkle or a fluff of lint anywhere. "Who called you?"

"I have been retained by the King," he said formally. "I am here to offer my assistance in getting you freed of the charges that have been laid on you."

"Bullshit."

He cocked his head. "Excuse me?"

"You heard me." My heart started thumping in my chest. I backed away from the bars.

Benedict Plum smiled widely again. His skin was the strangest color, like a white person had put on a too-dark foundation. "You seem quite unsettled, madam," he said. "Is there anything I can do to make you more comfortable?"

"There are lots of things you could do to make me more comfortable. You're not going to do any of them, are you, Atonas?"

"Ah." His smile dimmed, but he still seemed amused. "No, I am not." He laughed softly. "You're not as stupid as I thought you were." Abruptly, he sank to his knees. His fingers brushed the floor.

He was activating a ward. I didn't try to stop him. Wards don't work on me. He didn't know that though, so I didn't mention it. "That trick with the cat videos was a nice touch."

He shook his head, eyes twinkling. "Honestly, that human man is breathtakingly stupid. It was barely an illusion." He looked up at me from his kneeling position, and he brushed his hands along the corners of the cell. "He wanted a reason to arrest you. In his heart, he wanted to see you locked away, and hurt quite badly." He rose to his feet elegantly and leaned closer. "What did you do to him, Starsmell?"

"I existed," I snarled. "And don't call me that."

"He was astonishingly easy to convince that you were guilty. I was under the impression that the justice system in your realm favored the innocent. It seems like I was mistaken, and it is far more like Dayanavan than I thought. In my realm, too, we often detain the most likely suspect of a crime, and leave them to rot."

"It's only because of you that I'm in here."

"Indeed," he grinned at me. "I wish it wasn't the case, but I need you out of the way. Your Vampire King is proving harder to seduce than I thought."

"Has it ever entered your stupid brain that he doesn't want you to seduce him?"

His brow furrowed. "No."

"He doesn't."

"Ah, that's where you're wrong, Starsmell. He is a wild and passionate creature, as am I. He's been around for thousands of years. I can imagine he has tried every sexual pleasure this Earth has to offer, and he's bored." Atonas smirked. He put his hands on the bars and leaned forward, staring at me intently. "I can offer him something new. Unheard of sensations. A brand-new experience. I can make him *scream*."

The tightness in my chest threatened to overwhelm me.

I put my face close to his and growled. "You won't get to touch him."

Atonas grinned back. "I will. I just have to get a couple of you annoying women away from him first, so he can concentrate on me. Your witch friend and her shifter are otherwise engaged."

I narrowed my eyes. "What did you do to them?"

"Nothing." He chuckled. "Well, I didn't do anything to *them*. Their little shifter students, on the other hand, are having a hard time controlling their change, on account of all the pheromones I sprayed around their school. The bear woman and her witch have their hands full, trying to get them to change back."

"They're *kids*, Atonas. They are still learning control." I was horrified. Shifter children need a lot of support when they first start changing. There's always a chance that they'd forget themselves, and not be able to change back. Ever. "Do you have any idea what you've done?"

"All's fair in love and war, Starsmell, and this is both love *and* war."

"We're not at war! This is you, making trouble, because you just want to have a good time."

He shrugged. "I have harmed no one."

"You turned my kid into a monster."

"He's fine," he brushed off my comment.

"You traumatized him!"

"Oh, Starsmell, he was already broken. You know that as well as I do. That child has an interesting mind," he mused. "There is so much darkness there. He reminds me a little of me." He frowned. "There is still too much light in there for my liking, though."

"You will leave him alone," I snarled, grabbing the cell bars.

Atonas cocked his head. "I have no interest in your boy child, Starsmell. I am only interested in the Vampire King. In fact, I pledge to leave the boy alone completely, from now on, as a gift to you."

"I don't need you to do me any favors." I narrowed my eyes at him. You never accepted gifts from the fae.

Atonas tossed his head, the movement at odds with the fact that he wore the visage of a bald man. "I will leave him alone anyway. He is essentially useless. I am not a monster, you see. I do not harm anyone that is not a threat."

"Brick was not a threat to you. He has a concussion, which he got protecting his mate from you. That was your fault."

"He's fine too," Atonas laughed again. "Although he may not be once he comes out of his deathsleep."

Oh God. "What did you do to him?"

"A tiny illusion, Starsmell. You see, the female vampire has been too successful in thwarting me. She is suspicious. I had to get her away from her king, so that I may gain access to him." His brow furrowed. "She is far too obsessed with him, you know."

"Tell me about it," I muttered.

"There is only one thing that she's more obsessed with, and that is her true love. What better way to distract her, than to make him disappear?"

"You made him... disappear?"

Atonas shrugged. "I am not a monster, Starsmell. He is in his bed. She just can't see him anymore, that's all." He giggled. "She is going mad, ripping her abode apart, trying to find her love."

I stared at him stonily. "You still won't get to Rafael."

"Ah, that's where you're wrong. I know he has left this Valley, and that he is attending a summit somewhere. One of his business partners will be attending the same summit." Atonas' lawyer-image shimmered in front of me, morphing into a larger white man with a prominent chin. "He will be leaving the country club in his helicopter shortly." He laughed. "Or, he would be, except he is tied up in the lavatory in the staff quarters."

He'd gotten rid of Marigold, Backman, and Sonja. At least I knew Leroy was safe. "You're not going to stop, are you?"

"I came here for a reason, Starsmell. I'm not leaving until I get what I want. And I will get it." He smiled. "You can't do anything about it. You are stuck here."

"You think I'm stuck here?" I laughed. "You're out of your mind. In fact, I think I've had enough of your games." I flexed my muscles, and stretched my neck from side to side. "You think that this cell will hold me?"

"Oh, I know that the *cell* won't hold you." He grinned. "The ward will."

"Wards don't hold me."

"This one will."

I eyeballed him steadily, and went to push my hand through the bars. To my shock, my hand stopped one inch beyond the bar.

I pushed. My fingers bent inwards.

My mouth dropped open. I'd never felt this before, not even the slightest bit of magical pushback from a ward.

I glanced up and met Atonas' eye. "What is this?"

"'Tis a ward, Starsmell. You've never felt one before, have you?" He giggled. "Oh, this is such fun. No human or preternatural creature would be able to create one for you, and I know why." He held up his finger. "You see, in order to key a ward, one has to specify exactly what one wants to keep out. Or in," he added. "Wards have never worked on you because no one knows what you are." He stepped forward and put his face close to the bars. "But *I* do."

I backed away. "No, you don't."

"Oh, sweet denial." He inhaled through his mouth and smacked his lips. "I *do* know what you are. I recognized your scent. And I named you for your parentage. You smell of the stars, for you are part-star."

"What the hell are you talking about?" I shook my head. I could feel my heart thudding in my chest; it made me dizzy.

He wasn't making any sense. Just more made-up bullshit. He was just messing with me, the same way he messed with everyone. "Stars aren't people. They're flaming balls of gas, you absolute fucking idiot!"

He tutted. "No need to get hysterical, my love. We call them stars in our world – I do not know what they are called in this realm. Another name, perhaps. We call them *Aym* in our language, which is the same word we use for the stars. We call them that, because they watch, and they shine." A tiny furrow appeared on his brow. "It's peculiar, Starsmell. You are unique, I'll give you that. I've never known a Star to appear on a mortal plane and join with a lowly beast such as a human. They are complicated, though. They are wild and jealous."

I snarled in frustration. "What are you talking about! These are all riddles!" I stomped forward and tried to push my hand through the bars so I could rip out his throat. My hand hit the invisible ward hard, as if I was punching a brick wall. Worse, in fact, because I'd punched brick walls before, and my hand always went at least part of the way through.

I'd never felt anything like this before.

"Uh, uh, uh, Starsmell. You won't break through. Not in a hurry, anyway. This ward is an experiment for me. It is part-Star, and part-human, like you, so it should hold you for a good long time. Long enough for me, anyway." His face morphed again, shimmering back into the darker, hawk-like features of Benedict Plum. "I'll be seeing you, my love. I'll make sure the policeman keeps you here. And I'll send your regards to your handsome Vampire King."

He turned around and left the jail.

CHAPTER 16

tried punching the wall. My fists stopped one inch from the cinderblock, and it hurt like hell. I tried again and again, until my fists were bloody, but the ward held tight. I searched every inch of the cell, testing every point, but it was useless. I wanted to get out so bad, I felt like I could tear off my own skin.

After a few minutes, Harmann came back inside. I slumped down on the bed and put my head in my hands. The asshole cop ignored me, which I was grateful for. My head spun uncontrollably. I tried to think.

Nobody was coming to help me.

Leroy would be at the cabin. He didn't know I was here. I hoped that he would stay put, and stay out of this. He'd been hurt enough already.

Marigold wouldn't get the message I'd left on her machine at her store; she was too busy helping Backman with her shifter kids. She wouldn't get my voicemail until morning.

Sonja was in her own world of pain, looking for Brick.

Inexplicably, my chest hurt when I thought of her, desperately searching for her mate.

And Rafael was in Washington.

Atonas was on his way there. My fingers clenched around the bed frame, bending it like putty, and I forced myself to relax. Rafael had a security team with him – he wouldn't let himself be alone.

But Atonas was crafty. Who knew what devilish plans he would unleash to get close to the Vampire King?

Harmann tapped away on his computer, ignoring me. I considered asking for another phone call, but he wouldn't give it to me. No one could come and get me, anyway.

I was stuck here.

A star. My father was a star, whatever that meant. It was a supernatural creature of some sort, obviously, something powerful, and not something unique, either, because Atonas knew what they were. My father hadn't been powerful, though, not in the end. He had lived and died just like a human.

Out of the deepest corner of my mind, I remembered a story my mother had told me – the tale of the day that my parents had met.

It was a simple story. She'd been out in the forest with her sisters, gathering roots, when she stopped to get a drink from the stream. When she looked up, there was a man standing there. He shone like the sun.

The way she told the story, I always thought she meant he shone because she loved him the second she saw him. Obviously, she meant it literally. He was a sun. A star. Or, he had been, but he quickly became just as human as she was. By the time I grew up enough to form memories, he looked like any other man I knew.

I'd always known he was different, though. Now, I knew for sure. My father had been a star.

It made no difference to me. He was my dad, the center of my world for the longest time. I kept finding him, and I kept losing him, over and over.

I missed him so much that it hurt.

Sometimes, I was so human that it surprised even me. I'd been arrested, I was in jail, and I wanted my daddy.

My eyes began to prickle, and I blinked furiously. Before I got to Emerald Valley, I was slightly worried that I'd forgotten how to cry. It was almost as if I'd built up a cage around my heart. Several millennia of losing the things that I loved had hardened me, I thought, so I couldn't feel anything.

Somehow, this place had cracked me again. I was feeling things I hadn't felt in years. Loneliness, isolation. Fear.

I couldn't let it go right now, so I held it inside me. I held it, until I could be alone.

After a couple of hours, Harmann got to his feet and stretched. "Looks like you're in for the night," he said to me, grinning. "I'm heading home." He shuffled some papers on his desk, and tucked them into a backpack. "You'll be okay here by yourself. Now, don't you worry, the door here is locked tight, no one can get in." He tossed a couple of protein bars and slid a water bottle along the floor towards me. I ignored him. "There's cameras here, of course, and an alarm, so there's no point trying to bust out. Not that you could, anyway," he chuckled. "I'll see you in the morning."

He switched off the lights and left the station. The door buzzed as the lock clicked shut.

I was alone.

I put my head in my hands and felt the tears trickle down my cheeks, and I cried as if my heart was breaking.

CHAPTER 17

The tears dried on my cheeks. The cell was cold, and I shivered. An hour had gone by, two, maybe, since Harmann had left me alone in the cell. I'd cried myself out. Now, I was just cold.

Night had fallen outside; the high window in front of Harmann's desk had gone dark maybe an hour ago. Harmann wouldn't be back before nine tomorrow morning. I had no idea how long this ward was going to last, but then again, neither did Atonas. I'd promised myself that the second the ward dissolved, I was going to smash through the bars and leave.

To hell with the consequences. I'd kill Harmann and get rid of the body. I'd burn down the station. I didn't care. I needed to get out of here.

The thought crept into my mind that maybe the ward wouldn't *ever* dissolve. That I'd be stuck here forever, trapped in a tiny cell. The thought made me feel even colder.

It wasn't the first time I'd been trapped, of course. It *was* the first time I'd been stuck anywhere with no idea if I was ever going to escape. All the other times, I knew I just had to wait – wait for the ice to melt, wait for an aftershock to tumble the rocks loose, or wait to regenerate, so I'd get my strength back and bust my way out. This time, I didn't know if I was ever getting out. *That* thought was a whole new form of torture.

Every ten minutes or so, I got up and tested the invisible barrier just beyond the cell bars. The ward held firm. I had a long night ahead of me.

Suddenly, my ears pricked. There was a noise on the roof. A soft thump, as if something heavy had jumped on it. A slight scratching noise. I tilted my head, listening.

The noise disappeared.

A possum, maybe. It had sounded too heavy to be a possum, though. I put it out of my mind. Whatever it was, there was no chance it could get in here to hurt me, so it wasn't worth worrying about.

I lay back down on the bed and tried to sleep. It was too cold, though, and I felt horribly uncomfortable. My shirt still stank of bonnacon, and my jeans were covered with mud.

The front door cracked open. I shot upright at the noise, glaring into the darkness. "Who is there?"

I waited for the loud buzz of the door, but it didn't make a sound. The lock had been disabled. A tingle of fear shot through me. I got up off the bed and braced myself.

The door opened. Like an angel stalking victorious from the blackest caves of Hell, Rafael Stefano Di Stasio emerged from the darkness, and walked across the little police station towards me.

He stopped at the cell door. We stared at each other for a long moment. I couldn't believe he was here; right here, in front of me. It was him, though, I was sure of it.

"I thought you were in Washington," I said, finally.

"Imogen," he said, shaking his head. "We must do the passwords first."

"Fuck the passwords," I muttered. "I know it's you."

A crease appeared on his brow. "How do you know?"

I smiled. "The same way you know it's me."

He stared back at me. A complicated conversation was going on in his eyes; in the muscle that flexed in his jaw, in the taunt lines of his lips. I traced each tiny movement, wondering what each one meant.

He didn't speak, so I did. "If it makes you feel any better, the password is *toasted peanut butter.*"

He cocked his head. "That's not the password."

"I was testing you."

"You forgot the password, didn't you?"

"I might have," I said, shrugging.

He chuckled lightly and shook his head. "Imogen. What happened? How are you stuck here? We tried to access the ceiling panels above this cell, but it is impenetrable."

"I'll give you the CliffsNotes version," I said. "Atonas manipulated some video footage to show a vision of me busting up the statue of Sir Humphrey, so Harmann arrested me. I allowed myself to be taken in because I don't want to go on the run again, and I didn't want to kill him, although I am seriously regretting that decision and will rectify it as soon as I am able to. For now, I want to stay here in Emerald Valley, so I can look for my father. I thought I'd be released quickly, once the video footage was revealed to be bullshit. Once I got locked in this cell, Atonas showed up and activated a ward to keep me in."

Rafael frowned. "I thought wards didn't work on you?"

"You've been paying attention. Usually, they don't. I didn't know why, until now." I took a deep breath. "You have to know what to key a ward for, in order to construct it. No one knows what I am, not even me," I explained. "But apparently, Atonas does."

Rafael looked at me. "The Fae knows what you are?"

"Yeah, kinda. He said that I am part-star."

"Part-star?" Rafael frowned. "He couldn't find a proper translation in an Earth language?" I shook my head. "That's not particularly useful."

"It's something, though. And I appreciate you not making any jokes about me being a giant gas ball."

"Well, the stench of bonnacon isn't exactly Coco Mademoiselle..."

I barreled on. "The words don't matter, but the key does. Atonas knows what he meant when he set the ward, so it works. He designed a ward to cage a half-human-half-star, so for now, it's keeping me in."

Rafael moved. He inspected the cell bars, then the wall around them, and tried to push his hand through. His hand stopped at the invisible barrier. "He's keyed it for vampires as well."

"No doubt it will keep out witches and shifters, too, so Marigold and Backman won't be able to break me out."

"We will find a way." He sounded certain.

He stood so close to me, just on the other side of the bars, with the impenetrable wall between us. Somehow, knowing that we couldn't even touch if we wanted to, made me feel wildly out of control, like I was about to lose all the emotions I spent centuries concreting into the impenetrable silo inside of me.

He wasn't the best person to lose my shit around. This was the Vampire King, billionaire, CEO, playboy. Most eligible bachelor in the entire world.

I glared at him. "What are you doing here, anyway? Shouldn't you be rubbing shoulders with socialites? Breaking bread with your billionaire business buddies?"

His eyes darkened, and he chewed on his lip. The movement set off a strange feeling within me, an unclenching; a dangerous, smoldering warmth, right in my core.

God, he was glorious. Atonas was wrong – I wasn't a star. Rafael was. Blazing, out of control, scorching everything in his path.

I forced myself to focus. I watched the motion of his lips, assessing his movements. "If I'm not mistaken," I said. "You're feeling... guilty about something." A twitch of his eyebrow told me that I was right. "What is it?"

"You will not like it."

"Tell me."

"I had a security team watching you."

"Oh. Is that all? I thought you were going to confess to a murder or something."

"I was slightly concerned that you would think it was overbearing. Overprotective." He shrugged. "Controlling."

"Honey, I would have been offended if you *didn't* put a security team on me."

He smiled. "My team saw you getting arrested and contacted me. I assumed Atonas would follow–"

"Ah, *shit!*"

Rafael froze. "What is it?"

"Sorry," I shook my head. "I don't mean to interrupt, but this is important. Atonas told me that he bespelled Brick while he was asleep, to make him invisible. Sonja will be looking for him. He did it to get Sonja out of the way."

Rafael's face darkened. He pulled his phone out. "I was not aware," he said, pushing a button and putting the phone to his ear. He spoke into the phone, a fast stream of Italian. Even I could hear Sonja's relieved squawk at the other end.

He hung up. "I was not aware," he repeated. "She did not tell me. I hope that my country club is still standing."

"I thought she'd be in Washington with you."

"I left her here with her mate. I do not like to separate them."

"That's very nice of you," I said awkwardly. "Anyway,

171

please go on. You put a security team on me to spy on me without my permission..."

His face smoothed out, and he smirked. "You said that you would be offended if I didn't put a team on you!"

"Still." I waved my hand. "Continue."

He cleared his throat. "They watched Harmann arrest you, and they called me. I came back."

"You came back... for me?"

"*Si.*"

I stared at him dumbly. My hands, moving without my permission, patted my stomach to see if it was on fire. It was not. "Why?"

"I was concerned for you. The team watched for a while, and when it became apparent that you were not going to break yourself out, they let me know. I expected you to kick out the back wall of this jail and walk out as soon as Harmann switched off the lights. I have a team of bricklayers down the street, standing by, ready to patch up the damage."

I laughed. "Really?"

"I like to cover all my bases."

"Obviously."

"When you didn't break out, I thought that something must be seriously wrong. So, I came."

There was a lump in my throat. I swallowed roughly, trying to get rid of it. "You came for me?"

He nodded.

My lip trembled. I bit down on it, hard. The jolt of pain helped clear the fog in my head.

"The meeting with the senator was that boring, was it?"

"Insufferable," he laughed. "But if it makes you feel any better, I am losing several hundred million dollars in contracts by leaving the meeting."

I laughed. I laughed some more. Finally, it became apparent that I was on the verge of hysterics, so I bent over, and slid onto my ass, in a sitting position. I took some deep breaths with my head between my knees. After a few moments, I felt more like myself.

"No sign of Atonas in Washington?"

"None that we can see."

"He told me he was planning on going as the guy you were having lunch with yesterday. Your business friend. The one with the daughter. He walked out wearing his face."

"Ah." Rafael nodded. "Mr Dalton. I have not crossed paths with him. There is a gala dinner this evening; I have sent a body double in my place, surrounded by my security. That should keep Atonas tied up for a while."

"Ha." I wrapped my arms around my legs and put my head on my knees. "That will drive him crazy, not being able to get close to you."

"Indeed." His voice took on a sharp edge. "I suspect we may be approaching the point where Atonas loses his patience and does something terrible. Fae princes are not used to being thwarted."

"We need to get rid of him."

"I do not know how."

"Sleep with him, then," I muttered, putting my head on the side.

"Imogen," Rafael murmured. He bent his knees, curling his legs underneath him until he was sitting cross-legged on the floor, with all the dangerous grace of a great cat. I followed his movement, happy that he'd put himself at eye level with me again. "I have absolutely no intention of sleeping with the fae prince," he said.

A knot in my shoulders dissolved. "Really?"

"None at all."

"Not your type, huh?" He paused just a second too long. "Oh, he *is* your type?"

"Not at all. Physically, maybe." He shrugged. "I have lived

a long time, and I am open-minded. I will admit my sexual tastes are broad." His dark eyes flashed, and the warmth in my stomach turned to a swarm of butterflies. "I have had men before, although I definitely prefer women. Atonas is very pretty, but his physical beauty is ruined by his homicidal tendencies."

"That will do it, I guess," I muttered.

Rafael paused. The lines on his jaw hardened. "My father - the General Lucius - was one such vampire. Attractive, narcissistic, controlling... they are traits that I cannot stand."

That made sense. Rafael didn't want to be his father, so he didn't want to appear controlling or overbearing. "There's a line, though, Rafael, and you appear to be strolling it nicely. There's wanting to keep someone safe and keeping them in a cage."

"My mother was kept in a cage," he replied softly.

The admission came out of nowhere. I frowned. "Your mother?"

He nodded. "Luna De Marcona. Lucius found her, and became obsessed with her. He took her out of her human world, had her turned, mated with her, and kept her locked away, where only he could access her talents. As soon as I was of age, he had me turned, too, so I could be used to keep her compliant for all eternity."

"Hang on." I unwrapped myself from the floor and scooted over to the bars so I could be closer to him. "Do you mean to tell me that Luna De Marcona was your *actual* mother?"

He nodded. "My mother was an Omina of Rome – an oracle. He saw her reading fortunes in the piazza and was startled at her accuracy. I was four years old at the time, and I remember it like it was yesterday." His gaze slid beyond me, into the past. "She saw him coming and knew what he would do before he did it. He came to her, and she struck a bargain with him there and then – swear to never harm me; never lay a hand on me, and she would stay with him, and serve only him, forever. She promised to never lie to him."

I exhaled. "Is that why you are the only survivor? Out of all your Made siblings?"

He nodded. "One of her earliest prophecies was that he would die by the hand of one of his own children, but she swore on my life that it wouldn't be me that did it." He chuckled bitterly. "Oh, I desperately wanted to be the one that killed him. He tore my mother away from me, he ruined my whole human existence. He was a monster who murdered without pause, without hesitation. He cared for nothing of the beauty of this world, and thought of humans as little more than dumb animals. I desperately wanted to be the one who tore his heart out of his chest and ripped his head off his shoulders." The light in his eyes dimmed. "But my mother insisted that it wouldn't be me that killed him; it would be another of his Made children. Despite knowing this, he couldn't stop making them; he was enough of a monster that he made vampires indiscriminately, and discarded them when he was done. All except me."

"But he was the one that turned you?"

Rafael nodded. "He had no choice but to turn me – he waited as long as he could. Every moment that I spent as a weak, pathetic human was another chance that I would die, and he would no longer have any control over his Oracle. He turned me, so he could keep me, like he kept my mother. Forever."

Silence settled around us. Rafael shut his eyes.

"I'm sorry about your mother," I said softly. "It never stops hurting, does it?"

He shook his head. "It does not."

"What happened to her?"

He paused for a long moment, then exhaled slowly. "We

were held in a delicate balance for centuries – me, waiting for my chance to kill the General, all the while knowing that it would not be me who got to do it. My father, making and destroying one child after another, testing my mother, asking her each time if this would be the one that killed him. My mother, waiting. Waiting." He shook his head. "Turns out, she was waiting for the right time. She was waiting for the General to start to edge into madness. She was waiting for me to be ready. She was waiting for her chance."

"For *her* chance?"

Rafael smiled. "She was his child too."

My mouth fell open. "Luna De Marcona killed the General?"

"*Si.*"

"Whoa."

"My father was the oldest vampire I'd ever known, and the most powerful, but he was starting to lose the memory of his humanity. When that memory of our weakness starts to disappear, we think of ourselves as gods, and lose touch with reality."

I looked down at the floor. I knew the feeling well. Rafael carried on. "My mother waited until the perfect time. I had all but taken over the running of our business, as my father grew more paranoid and mad, and withdrew from most of our operations. The human world knew my face, and trusted I held the helm. My mother waited until the perfect time, waited until his guard was down, and threw him the most dazzling ball for the Vulcanalia Fire Festival. She had bonfires constructed, as tall as houses, in a ring around the palace. They lit the night sky so well it felt like it was daytime. She fed him blood laced with drugs, and danced him into a blazing inferno. She died with him."

Gristly. Effective, but gristly. A vampire would burn to

ash in the flames. "I'm sorry," I said again. "I'm sorry she felt like she had to die."

"Truly, it was the only way," Rafael sighed. "No one could have bested him - he was too strong, too paranoid. I was never allowed close enough to him that I might kill him myself. He held onto that prophecy with both hands, assured in the knowledge that he would only die by the hand of one of his children. He never thought of his own wife. Not once."

"I bet he's kicking himself in the afterlife, though," I muttered. "You never told anyone he was dead? It's common knowledge about your mom, but most people think that Lucius has withdrawn from society."

Rafael nodded. "I had it announced in vampire society that the General is sleeping, as he attempts to dull the pain of losing his queen. For now, it is essential that we keep up the deception. The time following a monarch's passing is always volatile. The General was the oldest and most powerful vampire I'd ever known. There are old ones like him, though, in the Kingdoms of the East, and rogues spread throughout the South, creatures who would see a vampire monarch fall, and flock like vultures to the feast. I have no wish of any of my vampires or my human employees to die in a war over territory. So, for now, my father is sleeping, and will return one day soon."

I watched him carefully. "That day will never come."

"It does not have to. I just have to hold the throne as long as I am able to, without turning into the monster that he was."

"Ah, Rafael." I smiled. "You would never turn into him. "The difference between you and him is that you were never a monster. He was *always* a monster."

Rafael looked at me. "I keep forgetting what you are. It is unfathomable to me that you are many times older than my

177

father was. You are nothing like him. Towards the end, he was cracked with the misery of existence."

I chuckled harshly. "I've gone through that a few times. You come out the other side. It's almost as predictable as my period."

"Madness? Homicidal insanity?"

I nodded. "Don't get me wrong. I never killed anyone that didn't deserve it."

"You never killed for pleasure? Never tortured someone for the joy of it?"

I shook my head. Rafael smirked. "Oh, sure," I admitted. "I'd chuckle while beheading a child molester, but who *doesn't* do that?"

"Who indeed?"

"They didn't count. There was a big difference between killing for pleasure, and enjoying some well-deserved bloody justice.

"You were never like him, then."

I thought for a moment. He was probably right. "It's funny," I said. "Being a bloodthirsty monster is kind of a vampire trait. You're meant to love killing and eating people."

"Blood is a pleasure," he murmured. "The taking of blood from the neck is an erotic game, as well as sustenance. Only the monsters among us would cause pain for pain's sake. Without the pleasure to go with it, of course. There are many monsters among every species."

"Oh, honey, I know that as well as anyone. There is no black and white. Everything is just a shade of gray."

"Is that how you got your name?"

"Uh, no." I actually chose it at random after I woke up from a regeneration in the early two-thousands. I needed a new last name, so I chose one from a book cover in a store window. I had no idea the book was an erotic novel.

He waited patiently. "I've gone by many names over the

years," I said. "Usually, I choose a variation of Im, my original name." I paused. A chill ran through me. "It meant 'star' in my first language."

Rafael watched me carefully. He didn't say anything.

After a moment, I shook my head. "Huh. I still don't know what it means. Whatever my father was, he wasn't a flaming ball of gas. He was a normal, very human man."

"Tell me about him."

I smiled. "He's so funny. He is always... interested in everything. In nature, in the world, in people, and how they interacted. Everything surprises him, and he is always enthusiastic. He's like that in every single incarnation I find him in. Exploring the world. Meeting people, loving people."

"He is human in every incarnation?"

I nodded. "Every single one. Whenever I manage to find him, I try to get him to tell me what his secret is. How he managed to become mortal." I frowned. "He tells me. He tells me every time... but I still don't get it. He says he must show me, and he tries.... But he always dies before I understand what he means. There's a trick," I muttered. "Some trick that I don't get."

"What does he tell you?"

"He says I must live." My eyes burned. "Every time, he says I must live. I've lived for so long, Rafael. I've done that. I can't do it anymore. I can't keep going." It was only a matter of time before I was provoked into using my hidden power. If Atonas knew what I was, he'd know how to push my buttons.

My glow would come out, and the Ancient would scream out of the portal and rip me to shreds, destroying everyone here in Emerald Valley at the same time. I had to tell him.

I dropped my head onto my knees. "There's something else you should know."

"What is it?"

"I can do... other things."

Rafael waited patiently.

I took a deep breath. "When I first knew my father, when I was very young... he was more Other. That part, the star part, or whatever it was... it dissolved over time, and he died completely human. *I'm* not human, though, not completely. I never have been. I'm strong and fast... and... more."

"What more?"

The way he was looking at me made me feel like I was on fire. I forced the words out. "I can *do* more. I have a... a glow inside of me... I don't know what else to call it. It feels like pure flame, like a nuclear reactor, deep in my core. Wherever I'm forced to access it – or when I'm tricked, or, if I'm overwhelmed and my survival instincts kick in... well..."

"Go on."

I met his eye. "I'm stronger than the planets; I can fly as fast as light. I can read people like their thoughts are written directly on their faces. But... and it's a big but, mind you – whenever I bring that part of myself out... The same *thing* comes and hunts me."

It felt strange to voice the suspicion that had been bouncing around my head for millennia.

"Another star?"

I nodded. "Another... *thing* exactly like me. The same as me, the same as my father, but not like my father. Not like how my father ever was. This thing is the same, but different. No, *that* thing, the one that hunts me, is jealous, and wild, and incomprehensible with rage. I call him the Ancient, because he feels older than me, somehow. He flies out of the Dip like an avenging angel, he hunts me, he finds me, and he rips me into tiny bloody pieces every single time I dare to embrace my other side."

Rafael was silent. He looked down and frowned. He

appeared to be processing what I was saying. "The star part of you..." he said finally. "You can't fight him?"

I shrugged. "I'm only half-star. And I've never really tried. I've got no defense against him. I run, and most of the time, he catches me."

"You have evaded him before?"

"Only a couple of times. I have to keep moving, or else he'll catch me. That's why I live in my van. So I can be ready to run at a moment's notice."

"You outrun an all-powerful celestial creature... in a Ford Transit custom van?"

I chuckled bitterly. "Like I said, most of the time, he catches me. It depends on how far away I am from the Dip. He can only come through the Dip points, at either end. Our protective field squeezes him out within three days, so I have to keep running for three days. The further away I am from a Dip point, the longer it takes for him to find me, so as long as I keep moving, I have a chance."

His face darkened. "You are right under *la porte*."

"I sure am." I huffed out a sigh.

"We must go."

The certainty in his voice puzzled me. "Uh, we can't? Not right now, anyway. Remember the underworld fae who is trying to get into your pants? The other cryptids that keep falling through the portal? My father, who is here in town somewhere?"

His mouth hardened into a grim line. "It is too dangerous to be near the portal right now."

"Rafael..." I curled my legs under and got to my knees, leaning closer. "I'm not sure if you noticed, but I'm stuck in a cell."

He moved closer, facing me. Our faces were inches apart, so close, separated only by thick iron bars, and an impenetrable magical forcefield. "As soon as you are able to, we must leave."

I stared into his face. How is it that something on this Earth could be so glorious? The beauty of his thick lashes, the symmetry of his cheekbones, the hard squareness of his jaw. "Rafael, I *can't*. I'm stuck here. In more ways than one."

The strong jaw tensed again; he ground his teeth. "I am not used to being thwarted."

"I am," I muttered. "Everything I do has been thwarted." I looked up again and was caught in his gaze. He looked at me like he'd never seen anything like me before. I guessed that was true. I was unusual, a mystery, a riddle to decipher. My voice fell to a whisper. "Why are you here?"

"I am here for you." His lips drifted closer.

The door banged; I jumped at the sound. Backman strode into the jail, holding onto Marigold's hand, keeping her slightly behind.

Marigold peeked out from behind Backman's waist. "Need some help?"

I exhaled. "I never thought I'd say this, but boy, Backman, am I glad to see you!"

Rafael rose to his feet and stepped back, blending back into the shadows. As soon as he moved, I shivered. I felt cold again. How is it possible that a vampire, one of the cold undead, could make me feel warm?

I shook my head to dislodge my fuzzy thoughts, and looked up at Marigold. "Is everything okay at the OE center?"

Backman grumbled. "It is now. The kids are sleeping."

"Atonas sprayed pheromones around the center," I told her. "That's why the kids went crazy."

"I know," she said. "I could smell it. He must have cleaned out a vet clinic somewhere. It was only cat and dog pheromones, but it did a number on our wolf kids, and most of the cats, too."

"You didn't lose any?"

Backman's hard face lost some of its intensity. "No. They all changed back. Marigold worked her magic." She smiled fondly down at her wife.

"You're really quite powerful, for a kitchen witch, aren't you, Marigold?" I eyed her carefully, watching her movements, tracking her facial expressions.

There had always been something about Marigold. I still didn't entirely trust her, even though she'd never given me any reason not to. In fact, she'd saved my ass a few times now. But... There were a few things about her that just didn't add up, and I couldn't ignore them. Twice now, I'd seen an otherworldly ruby gleam in her eye when she'd been stressed. It *could* be explained away by red lights, or reflections. I didn't think so, though. That kind of shine looked different. Hers came from within; it wasn't just colored light bouncing around.

Her age was another red flag, so to speak. When we first met, she'd told me that her mother gave birth to her at sixteen years old – the result of a horrifying rape. I'd met her mother in the mid nineteen-sixties, and she'd been around seven or eight years old. According to my terrible math, Marigold was most likely born in the early seventies.

That would make her over fifty years old, but she looked half that. Face potions were her trade, though, so I hadn't asked her about it. Not yet, anyway. For the first time in a long time, I felt strangely reluctant to interrogate her.

I was mostly suspicious about her powers. She insisted she'd never dabbled in blood magic, but her power level was insane for a mere lightworker.

Looking at her now, her face was clear, her big blue eyes wide and innocent. No hint of ruby gleam anywhere.

I peered at her closely, watching. "How'd you manage to gather enough magic to get the shifter kids turned back?"

"Oh, I didn't use magic." She beamed at me.

"What?"

"I peed everywhere."

"You... peed everywhere?"

"Only where Atonas had sprayed the pheromones," she explained patiently. "My human pee diluted the pheromones and confused the scent, and reminded the wolves that they were human, too."

"It worked like a charm," Backman smiled proudly at her. "The kids settled down straight away."

I shot a look at Rafael, standing in the corner of the jail-house. He had his head down, one hand over his face. I couldn't be sure, but it looked like he was silently laughing.

"Okay," I said. "I guess that's one way to do it."

Marigold inspected the ward, testing it with her fingers. "Wow. This is interesting."

"It's not interesting." I climbed to my feet and stretched. "It's annoying."

Backman chuckled. "Never felt a ward before, have you, little drill bug? They're not fun when they're keeping you from being somewhere you want to be."

"It's a crazy combination," Marigold murmured, shuffling along the floor. "I can feel the shifter and human components, but there's something else there that I've never felt before..."

"That's me. My other side." I could feel Backman's curious stare, so I looked up and met her eye. "My mom was totally human, but my dad was something else. I've never known what he was."

Marigold cocked her head. "Atonas knows what you are?"

"Apparently so."

"You still don't?"

I shrugged. "He called me a star, which means nothing to me, but he's obviously met one before. It will be an otherworldly creature of some sort."

"Well," Marigold said. "He's created a Frankenstein ward here. There's shifter and vampire and human, and then the Star part, which I can't budge. It's okay," she reassured me. "The good news is that I can chip away at parts of it, and the other parts should dissolve in time. The shifter and vampire part is easy." She pulled out a few things from her pockets; a handful of herbs, a salt shaker, a packet of band-aids. Tiny rocks and glittering crystals fell out of her pockets as she rummaged around. Eventually, she pulled out a lighter.

I watched her carefully. "The human part is not easy?"

She frowned. "For some reason, I always find human wards the hardest to break. It's usually the opposite in most witches. I don't know why. I'll do the human ward first."

She lit a black candle and settled down, crossed-legged. We watched in silence as she muttered the Words, tiny beads of sweat appearing on her brow. After a few moments, the air just past the iron bars shimmered lightly. Marigold poked a finger through, and exhaled. "That's one part down."

She took a deep breath and started again. I watched her carefully, but I couldn't see or feel anything, no flow of energy, no rush of electricity. She kept her eyes closed, so I couldn't see if her eyes had their eerie ruby tint.

"Barbara," she whispered. Backman marched over to my cell and thrust her hand through the bars. "Good. That's another one down."

A few moments later, she invited Rafael to put his hands through the bars. His fingers passed through easily. I don't know if I imagined the tension in his shoulders easing slightly, but he seemed more relaxed when the vampire ward broke. He stayed where he was, standing beside me, separated from me only by the thick bars that I normally would have no trouble bending.

When Marigold was done, I tried to poke my finger through. I hit resistance. The ward was still holding me.

She looked up. "Can you feel any change?"

I tensed, and pressed again. It wasn't as brick-hard as it had been before. "It feels... softer, I guess."

"That's good. It should continue to soften and fall apart now that the other components have been removed. You'll be able to punch through in an hour or so." She got to her feet, wincing as she stretched her legs. "It's lucky he did a Frankenstein ward. If it had just been human and star, you would be in trouble."

I felt a chill in my bones. "I'd be stuck here?"

"Not forever, but you'd probably be here for a few days, at least. Like I said, I have trouble disabling human wards that aren't mine. Since he did a patchwork ward, it should fall apart soon."

I nodded, and swallowed. "Thanks."

In the back of my head, the old Imogen was shouting at her, demanding answers to the questions I had in my head, laying all my suspicions out bare. Old Imogen was a bitch, though, and now that I had friends, I decided I would like to keep them.

It was nice to have people rescue me. It hadn't happened in centuries. Millenia, even. Usually, it was me doing the saving.

It never made any difference, though. No matter how many times I rescued my friends, no matter how often I saved my lovers from the jaws of death... Everyone I loved always died, eventually.

Marigold gave me a sunny smile; it almost chased away all the ice in the pit of my stomach. "No problem. Now, we'd stay and wait with you–"

"There is no need," Rafael murmured. "Go. Attend to the children in your care."

Backman nodded to him uneasily and pulled Marigold in beside her. "We will."

"Call me when you get out," Marigold said from behind her wife's back. "We need to talk about Leroy. I think he's up to something."

Backman pulled her out of the jail, and they disappeared.

I groaned. "Seriously, that kid is going to be the death of me."

Rafael turned back to face me. He tilted his head back and smirked at me. "You wish."

I cocked an eyebrow. "A joke, Your Fangliness?"

"Ah, Imogen. What better time to make the joke at your expense, when you cannot punch me in the face in retaliation?"

I laughed. He seemed so sure of himself. "I wonder if I could, though," I mused. "Punch you, I mean. I can usually match vampire strength, but I'm always slightly faster, and that's what counts in a fight. No point being strong if you're not fast." I looked at him. "Sonja tells me that you are the fastest vampire she's ever known. Is that her normal insane fangirling, or is she telling the truth?"

His face darkened. "I have worked hard over the centuries to become a formidable enough opponent, so that I may best my father if I was ever given the opportunity. Besides, as Vampire King, I must be able to dispatch anyone who would challenge my authority. So unfortunately, yes, Imogen, she is telling the truth."

"You make it sound like a bad thing. You're the strongest and fastest vampire on the planet, and you're not happy about that?"

"In another life, perhaps I would have been more content to be a lover, not a fighter."

"In another life, I would be *content*," I said bitterly. "But I've never had another life."

He chuckled. "The grass is always greener, as they say. In the meantime, we should enjoy this time. Focus on the micro, rather than the macro."

That kind of bullshit hippy advice really ground my gears. It was easy for everyone else to enjoy the moment, when your days were numbered. My days went on into infinity. "Well, I guess I'll be testing Sonja's theory. I'm looking forward to punching you in the face."

"I would let you," he murmured, a gleam in his eye. "Just for the pleasure of it."

"You would let me punch you?" I laughed. It was hard to hold on to obstinance in the face of his staggering arrogance.

"I'm sure it would tickle. Like feathers."

"Feathers, huh? His face was inscrutable. "We will have to find out, then, won't we?

I pushed at the ward. It was softer; it had gone from solid steel, to brick, and now it felt like wood. "I still can't get out, though," I muttered.

Rafael slipped his hand through the bars. His fingers brushed mine; a shock ran through me. "What are you–"

He hushed me, and tangled his fingers in mine. "I will keep you company until the ward dissolves."

* * *

DAWN WAS BREAKING when we finally walked out of the police station. The ward softened slowly, over the space of a few hours. Rafael held my hand the whole time.

I felt… strange. There was no other word for it. A weird feeling in my stomach blossomed and bloomed, until I felt so restless that I punched at the ward, and it finally shattered.

Luckily, Rafael found the spare cell key and opened the gate, before I bent the bars back and really gave myself away.

"Don't worry about Harmann," Rafael reassured me as we walked from the station. "I will have him taken care of."

I cracked my knuckles. "No need."

"You cannot kill him, Imogen."

"The hell I can't," I muttered.

"Imogen…"

"Relax. I'm not going to. It's illegal to leave a prisoner unattended in a cell. He can't do anything about the fact that I've walked out. Not unless he wants to rat himself out and get fired for his trouble."

"He'll come for you again."

I shrugged. "Let him try."

I just had to make sure I was alone when he did come for me, so I could bury the body without any witnesses.

We walked down the street, headed towards my van. My worries that it was stolen disappeared when Rafael passed me my car keys as we headed to the town square. He'd lifted my keys from evidence in the jail, and I hadn't even noticed.

Rafael's phone rang. He punched the answer button, and put it to his ear, soon engrossed in a furious flood of Italian that I couldn't follow.

My phone rang.

"Hello?"

"Imogen?" She sounded frightened. "Imogen, you have to come!"

"What's happened?"

"The fae prince," she sobbed. "He's got Barbara."

CHAPTER 18

I froze on the spot. "What?"

"He's taken her, Imogen! She was walking me out of the OE center. As soon as we passed the wards, he ambushed us; he knocked us both out with a sonic punch and he took Barbara! She's gone," Marigold sobbed. "I don't know where he's taken her. I woke up, and she was gone."

I bit my lip. "You can't track her?"

"I can't! I can't get a fix on her. I've done all the spellwork I can think of... the closest I can get is that she's somewhere near the country club, but I've looked and she's... she's not there, Imogen! She's there, but she's not. I don't understand!" Her voice rose to a wail.

"Okay, relax." I rubbed at my chest. My heart ached for her. "We'll figure it out. Just... just don't spill any blood, okay?"

"I would never," she replied with a sloppy, wet sniff. "She'd never forgive me. But if it was her life on the line... I would! I would. It's better that she was alive and living on Earth without me than her being dead, I can't, I just can't, Imogen!"

"Stop it," I snapped. "Pull your head out of your ass. She'd rather be dead, than have you risk your soul, and you know it."

"I just don't know where she is!"

I took a breath. "You said she's somewhere near the country club?"

"My tracking spell says she is near the golf course, but it's not showing me exactly where; it's opaque."

"Opaque?"

"I can't describe it properly. Like she's there, but not there. Like she's a ghost. She can't be dead, Imogen..." she wailed.

"Okay, stop it. I need you operating on all cylinders here, Marigold."

She sniffed. "Okay."

"Where are you?"

"I'm on the west ridge above the country club. I thought I needed to get higher, because my tracking spell says that Barbara is above the solid earth..." her voice cracked.

"Okay, wait there. I'm on my way." I hung up the phone and turned to Rafael.

"He has Brick, too," he said.

"Oh, you're fucking kidding me."

"One of our members – an Omani prince – asked him to act as his caddy on a midnight golf round. Brick agreed, and Sonja followed, because she was not prepared to let him out of her sight. She watched as the prince morphed into Atonas on the fourth hole and pulled Brick into nothingness."

I frowned. "On the golf course?"

"*Si*. She cannot locate him anywhere."

"When did this happen?"

"No more than ten minutes ago."

I looked down at the pavement, thinking furiously. Atonas had abducted Backman, and Brick, and disappeared into a spot where we couldn't track him. "Did he know that Sonja was watching?" I wondered out loud.

"I would assume so."

"Marigold said that Backman was somewhere over the country club, but she couldn't get a fix on her. She was there, but she wasn't," I muttered. "Like she was a ghost. She's not dead."

"It will be another of his games," Rafael said, scowling. "If we've learnt nothing else, we know that he loves his games."

I nodded. "He's setting something up; I can feel it. He's abducted both Backman and Brick, knowing that all of us will do anything to come and find them." I rubbed my chin, thinking. "Fourth hole, he said?"

"*Sí.*"

"It's a holy number in fae mythology. It means the four corners: The directions, the elements. I wonder if he used it as an anchor..."

Rafael's brow furrowed. "For spellwork?"

"A pocket dimension," I explained. "Some powerful fae can create them. A small space that exists outside our reality, but anchored to it. The fourth hole on your golf course may be the entranceway."

He nodded. "I have heard of such things. Will we be able to enter?"

"We can try."

I'd gotten into one before. It was thousands of years ago, in Rinn an Scidígh, Ireland . I'd been chasing a sprite who taunted me with information on how to end my immortality, and I'd accidentally blundered into a pocket realm after it. The anchor was a puddle of water in the shade of an old oak tree, and I fell into it while I was trying to catch the sprite. I don't know who was more surprised – me, or the sprite.

I didn't know if it was because I could walk through wards, or if I'd triggered the key accidentally, but I got in.

The pocket dimension opened up into a twilight realm, with a small castle and fields that drifted out into smoke. A rogue Winter Court fae had set up the dimension as a hideaway. Turned out, the sprite was one of his favored pets, and he'd been using it as a scout to lure young mortal women into his dimension to use as sex slaves.

He was *very* surprised to see me. I might have accidentally killed the sprite, but I killed the fae on purpose.

I felt a warm hand on my shoulder. "Are you okay, Imogen?"

I'd been lost in the past, and hadn't moved for several minutes. "Yep, sorry. Just thinking. Yes, I think that's exactly what he's done. Atonas has created a pocket dimension and set up the anchor on the fourth hole. Backman and Brick will be in there, and he'll be waiting for us. We have to go now."

Rafael stilled. "Will you tell me where you went, just then? Somewhere in the past?"

An old memory swam back into my head; my hands around the fae's throat, his skin turning purple, then gray. The blood vessels in his eyes popped slowly, until they dripped red.

"Maybe one day," I told him.

* * *

DAWN HAD BROKEN, but the sun would not poke its cheery head over the ridge for a few more hours. The forest shivered; dew shimmered on fat leaves, promising sparkles once the sun hit. In counterpoint to the serene stillness of the morning, I drove my van like a rally driver around the roads, scattering the wildlife who wandered unwittingly onto the road. The van seemed to roar in protest when I slammed the accelerator, squealed in fright when I jammed on the breaks, and screamed in torture when I flipped the handbrake and drifted around the corners.

"Imogen," Rafael murmured, his soft tone betrayed by his fingers that clutched at the Jesus handle above his window. "You may be immune to the finality death, but I am not."

I side-eye glared at him. "Are you saying something about my driving?" A squirrel chose that exact moment to fling itself into my path; I missed it by inches.

"I would not call what you are currently doing 'driving,'" he said.

I frowned at him and hit the brakes. The van slid to a halt, inches from the heavy wrought-iron bars of the country club. "Well, we're here now."

"I will drive next time."

"The hell you will."

We got out. The gates swung open the second Rafael exited the van; we ran through and up to the reception building.

Sonja met us halfway. Her icy white face was harder than ever. "Your Majesty."

"We'll find him, Sonja."

She nodded, just once. The planes of her face were hard, but upon closer inspection, her chin was trembling. Together we ran to the golf course, set up further on the ridge behind the sprawling palace-like building.

It was quiet, and very dark. Soft, golden lamps dispersed the total darkness, casting a gentle glow on the vivid green grass. The course was manicured to within an inch of its life, not a blade of grass out of place. I ran over the first hole, hit a dewy patch, and skidded for a few yards. It was so satisfying I did it again on the second hole, too.

"*Mia cara*," Rafael tugged my hand. "Must you destroy everything around you?"

"You were the one who said I should try and enjoy every

moment, baby." I ran a little faster, just to show him I could. I'd always been just a little faster than a vampire.

I ground my teeth when he caught me easily. He *was* fast. Sonja wasn't lying. My breath hitched in my throat when the thought occurred to me he just might be faster than me. I had a rule; I didn't date anyone who could knock me out.

We ran to the fourth hole, blazing around the water hazard on the third, and ripping straight through a thick tangle of trees. The fourth hole came into view; a lonely path of green tucked away out of sight of the rest of the club. The burgeoning sunlight didn't penetrate here; a single lamp cast an eerie cold glow over the tiny patch of manicured lawn.

I froze; holding my hand out to stop Rafael and Sonja. "There's no flag in the hole."

Rafael looked. "There's always a flag. How else would they know where to aim?"

"It's the hole." We carefully walked closer. I bent down and studied it. It was four inches across; no wider, and as black as night. I couldn't see anything beyond the lip of the hole.

"What are you waiting for?" Sonja demanded.

"Uh, Sonja, babe," I turned up to face her. "It's literally the tiniest hole I've ever seen. None of us will fit through that. It's smaller than my vagina."

Rafael snorted.

Sonja's head whipped towards him, her eyes bugged out; she quickly dropped her head and composed herself. "I apologize, Master."

"No need," he replied. "You will get used to me laughing one day, Sonja."

I squinted at him. "What do you mean? You laugh all the time."

"Only at you," Sonja's icy glare turned on me.

"What do you mean 'at me'?"

Her eyes narrowed. "My liege finds you amusing."

"Amusing?"

"He has not laughed out loud in centuries," she growled.

I furrowed my brow, confused. "Is that not a… good thing?"

Her teeth flashed. "My master cannot mix with the likes of you," she snarled. "A vampire must never mate with a human. It is beneath us."

Her jibe didn't really sting. I wasn't fully human, for one. I knew she was unsettled by the fact that her king had been acting differently since I came along. I made him laugh, great. I was a new, amusing novelty. There was no chance he'd want to bond with me. She didn't have much to worry about.

I smirked. "You mean to tell me you never hooked up with Brick when he was a human?"

Her lips puckered up in disapproval: I'd hit a nerve. Jerkily, she stalked towards me. "You. Do. Not. Talk. About. My. Mate."

Her arms lashed out; I ducked sideways and threw out my hip, using her momentum to throw her to the ground.

She disappeared.

I looked up and caught Rafael's eye. "Huh."

"*Not* smaller than your vagina, it would seem."

I inclined my head and matched his formal tone. "So it would seem."

"That is lucky."

"Indeed."

His eyes sparkled. He held out his hand. "Shall we?"

I took his hand in mine, marveling again at the strength and electricity in his cool fingers. "We shall."

We turned, and looked down the hole, and jumped.

CHAPTER 19

*I*t felt like we fell forever.

The walls of the entryway to the pocket dimension were thick; made up of fog and magic. My free hand reached out as we fell, stroking the dense smoke of the hole, feeling an alien chill. Rafael watched me as we fell, his dark eyes never leaving mine.

I looked down toward my feet. A light appeared underneath us, thousands of miles away, but coming closer. I put my arm out, feeling my skin touch the uncanny thick vapor and catch.

"Hold on," I told Rafael. I think we're about to hit the bottom of this hole."

He thrust out an arm and dragged it through the thick smoke. It slowed our fall. The light at our feet grew bigger and bigger.

"Brace yourself!" I let go of Rafael's hand as the bottom of the hole came into view; what looked like bright-yellow sand. I bent my knees, anticipating the impact. He followed my lead, dragging his arms through the smoky walls, slowing his fall so much that when we hit the ground, the landing was as soft as if we'd jumped only a couple of feet in the air.

I wasn't near as graceful. I'd over-anticipated the bounce in my landing, so I jumped up and fell back down, landing on my ass.

The sand underneath me felt real, gritty and warm. The light was too bright; I blinked, trying to clear my vision. Noise slammed into my ears, juxtaposed roughly by the eerie silence of our descent. After a second, I identified the ear-splitting racket; it was the sound of a huge crowd cheering.

I looked up, and around.

We'd landed in the middle of an enormous amphitheater; an old, crumbling place. It was made of a vast ring of sand on the bottom, thick walls, and stone tiered seating, the many levels leading up towards huge, vaulted arches that touched the sky.

Each seat was taken. The faceless crowd screamed at us, shouting cheers, jeers and insults.

It was too much. I took a breath. Looking down, I could see the sand beneath my feet, coarse and yellow; I could feel it, rough and grating on my skin. I smelt the blood that permeated it, salty and copper. I heard the screams of the crowd. My breath felt loud in my ears.

My breath was shallow. It didn't satisfy the ache in my lungs, so I took another one. Then another. It wasn't enough, so I took three more in quick succession.

A strong hand gripped mine, I felt him squeeze it softly. I looked up and saw Rafael standing next to me.

"It's not real," he said softly.

I forced my breath to slow. "It's not?"

"No," he said. "Atonas has done this. He has made a replica of the Colosseum for his pocket dimension. It's not real. Look." He bent down, and swept away some of the sand, then a little more, until he'd gouged out a small hole. "There was only a thin layer of sand spread over the floor of the real Colosseum, otherwise the weight would be too much to bear. If this was the real thing, I'd have reached the floorboards of the hypogeum by now."

He moved his face closer to mine. His eyes were so warm, so full of emotion. "It's okay, Imogen. It's not real."

It's not real. The next breath I took filled my lungs a little better.

"You were here, weren't you?"

I managed a smirk. "It was before your time, honey. I was fighting there when it was just a dirty ring with wooden seats."

I'd needed the cash, and being a gladiator paid very well. I was good at it; the fighting, the killing, and I was very good at coming back for more. The crowds loved me, and I loved hearing their cheers. Before I realized it, I'd turned into an absolute monster. I didn't know how bad it had gotten until one day, I stood in the middle of the dusty ring, with my fans cheering around me, and one of my dearest friends was forced out onto the sand to fight me.

I remember looking up in the stands and seeing the Emperor Commodus smirking down at me, guarded by a strong pack of shifter warriors, waiting to see what I'd do.

The memory stabbed me in the belly now. The anger, the guilt, the frustration. I'd wrapped up my feelings in barbed wire, shoved them in an iron box, and bottled it up deep within me. I did what I had to do.

"He's trying to provoke us," Rafael murmured. "He's trying to unsettle us."

"Well, it's working." My voice cracked. I rubbed at my chest, trying to massage the feelings away.

"Imogen." Both of his hands covered mine. He pulled me to my feet and wrapped his arms around me.

He was so warm, it shocked me out of the past, where my

brain desperately tried to yank me back to deal with my unresolved emotions. I closed my eyes, and breathed in his scent; fresh sea air and honey. "It's not real. You can tell me about the Colosseum later, tell me all about it. For now, we need to concentrate."

"Okay, I'm good." I stayed where I was, cocooned in Rafael's arms, with my eyes closed.

"I'll give you another minute."

A roar filled my ears; I opened my eyes and looked. Marigold was over by the stone wall with Backman, who had shifted into her bear form. Her bear was bigger than I could ever dream; she was the same size as my van. She swayed from side to side menacingly, bellowing up at the cheering crowd.

Marigold stood beside her, arms out, concentrating. I was glad she'd found Backman. I'd forgotten we were supposed to meet her at the country club. She must have figured it out before we got there.

Over on the other side, Brick and Sonja stood, embracing, eyes fixed on each other, ignoring everything else.

I glanced up at the sky. It was hot, clear and went on forever.

Atonas wouldn't have had enough time to create anything bigger than this, so I doubted there was anything beyond the edges of the sand floor. He'd built this arena to trap us, so the stone walls would be heavily warded.

Pocket dimensions were usually built as hideaways – they were normally very tough to find, and hard to get into. Once you'd fallen into a pocket dimension, you needed the creator to help you get back out.

Or, you just needed to kill them, and wait until the magic faded enough to break out. If the pocket dimension was hastily made, like this one, it wasn't impossible to break it apart while the creator was still alive. Most of the components would disintegrate if you were strong enough to trash it. But if the creator made thick wards that prevented anyone coming in or out, then there was no escaping.

Speaking of the creator...

I looked around the blank faces of the cheering crowd, searching for Atonas. I found him in the cubiculum - the Imperial Box, surrounded by faceless servant girls.

He saw me, and smiled.

"Welcome!" His voice echoed magically around the amphitheater. "I am glad you finally made it."

Backman growled. Marigold edged forward and entwined her fingers into her wife's fur. Brick and Sonja ignored him completely and continued to embrace, eyes locked on each other.

"What is this, Atonas?" Rafael's voice rang clearly around the amphitheater. The crowd hushed. "Why have you done this?"

The fae prince curled his lip. "I have done this, my sweet Vampire King, because I grow impatient. At first, the hunt for you was amusing enough, but you continue to refuse me. Your evasions, which were coquettish and charming, have become insulting."

Rafael shrugged languidly, looking as relaxed as if he were lounging by the bar at his country club. "I thought I made myself clear. I'm not interested. Your games are that of a foolish child."

Atonas reared back; his eyes bulged. "How dare you," he hissed. "I am a Prince of the Night House of Dayanavan. Millions of souls are ground beneath my feet every day. Who are you to deny me? Who are you to insult me?"

Rafael chuckled darkly. "I don't think you need to be anyone of importance to point out that you are behaving like a petulant brat. And I notice you said you are *a* prince, not *the* prince. You're not even the heir, are you?"

He spluttered. "I am in line–"

"How many before you?"

"That is none of your concern!"

"It sounds to me like there are a lot of princes before you. I'm guessing you have never set eyes on the throne, have you?"

Atonas jumped to his feet. "How dare you! This was a game, a fun game, and you've ruined it all." He tossed his head. "I no longer want you. No man who insults me like this can give me the good time I seek, but then again, I am wise enough to anticipate that. I've seen it coming over these few days, Vampire King. So, I've set up this game to amuse me."

"And what is this game?"

"*The* Games!" Atonas voice boomed around the arena. "A great battle; a battle between all of you. I have some beasts for you to warm up with, but the rules have been sewn into the fabric of this pocket dimension."

"What rules?"

"You must fight each other, and you must amuse me." Atonas grinned. "Since you deny me my pleasure, I will have it here. You will fight each other; you will hurt each other. None of you will leave until I am satisfied."

"You want us to fight each other?" My voice cracked pitifully. He couldn't know my history. He wouldn't know I'd been here before. It must be a coincidence.

He nodded. "There is no escape. In fact, I made sure of it this time, Starsmell. The wards on this dimension are thick, and made up in rings, including a lovely one of star and human. You will not be able to break through unless you use your full star strength to smash the human ward." He lowered his head and smiled at me, his eyes sparkling. "And we both know you will not do that. It would mean risking yourself, and you don't do brave self-sacrifice, do you?"

My face felt frozen. Atonas laughed and laughed. All at

once, I remembered that Atonas was an underworld fae; his talent was bringing out our fears.

He'd set up a perfect way to taunt me. We weren't getting out of this place unless I accessed my deepest powers, and if I did that, the Ancient would come and find me.

And he'd find me immediately. We were only a couple of miles away from the Dip. I wouldn't be able to run fast enough.

He was right; I didn't do self-sacrifice. I'd killed my friend in this very same arena because there was no other option, apart from my pain and suffering. There had been hundreds of times in my existence where I'd walked away from someone I could have saved, because I was scared of the pain.

My worst fear was fear. And that fear, for me, would always trump any love I felt.

"Don't let him get to you," Rafael whispered, tugging my hand. "You saved Marigold from the Tashk, remember?"

My face relaxed. That's right, I *did* do that. I sacrificed myself to save Marigold. It didn't undo my centuries of cowardice, and it was possibly the only good thing I'd ever done in all my lifetime...

But it was a start. I might not ever change physically, but maybe I *was* capable of growth.

Atonas' eyes narrowed as he watched the fear dissolve on my face.

He sat up straighter. "So you *could* smash the ward, but the consequences for you would be catastrophic. And it would take your witch centuries to chip through this human ward," he said, turning his focus on Marigold. "She would find it difficult, especially since she's not human herself."

I glanced over at her. Her face was deadly pale. Next to her, Backman's huge furry body shivered, and she melted back into her human form.

I averted my eyes. Backman naked was not something you could just ignore; she was magnificent on every level.

"So, on with the Games! I was going to call them the Immortal Games, named after your curse, Starsmell. But I will call them the Daddy Issue Games, because all of you have daddy issues."

I almost laughed. "Daddy issues?"

"You cannot deny it, Starsmell. I have been on your plane for a matter of moments, and even I can tell you are all insanely messed up because of your fathers. Look at your witch," he said, thrusting his chin towards Marigold. "She's the product of the most vile and degrading act you can possibly inflict, and her father, like yours, was more than human. I recognize a touch of the underworld within her."

His eyes sparked with interest. "She is unusual, and I would like to inspect her more thoroughly. Maybe I will examine her after she has been gutted by one of the beasts I have assembled for you to fight with. I'm interested to see how much she can do."

I glanced at Marigold. I thought it was impossible to look whiter than she did already, but she was practically translucent.

"Normally, the transference of power wouldn't occur in a human fetus," Atonas went on. "Although, her mother had been a strong witch. Perhaps her magic absorbed a part of him."

Her father had been a visiting tradesman who raped her mother. Now, Atonas was suggesting he hadn't been human. It would explain a lot of my suspicions about her.

I looked at her fingers. They trembled.

He waved a careless arm at Sonja and Brick. "Your two vampire servants there – the female, with her odd passionate obsession with the men in her life. The male, fatherless, letting her take control. And you, my sweet Vampire King," he glanced down at us. "You are the living definition of daddy issues. Desperate not to be like your father but forced to act like him for now. I wonder what the other Vampire Kingdoms would say if they found out that he was dead?"

Rafael's face gave nothing away. He stood, relaxed and uncaring.

Atonas chuckled. "So, you will fight each other. It will be good for you! You need to get some of your aggression out. I will stay here and watch, and when I am amused enough, I might let you go. As a gesture of goodwill, I promise to let the last one standing leave." He stood, and called out. "Bring on the beasts!"

I sighed and ran my hands through my hair. "Oh, this is fantastic."

Rafael took my hand, and beckoned Sonja and Brick closer. They broke apart and walked over immediately. Backman and Marigold followed.

"Are you okay?" I asked Backman as she strode over.

"Fine." She grunted, and stretched her neck from side to side, flexing her arms. I worked hard to keep my eyes fixed on her face. "I'm furious that skinny little bastard got the drop on me. I've been trying to climb up the wall for the last hour or so, in human form, and in Bear, but he has it bespelled. I'm not even sure the wall exists."

"It probably doesn't. The floor is the main component of the pocket dimension, he wouldn't have had much time to construct much else. The rest is just an illusion, and a thick ward." I turned to Marigold. "Have you tested it?"

Her pale face trembled. Her eyes looked out at nothing.

"Marigold!" I snapped my fingers. She flinched; her gaze shot back to me. "Have you tested the ward?"

She took a shaky breath. "No."

"You need to focus. We will deal with all the daddy issue stuff later, okay?"

What Atonas had said today was obviously devastating news to her. She must have suspected something was wrong, but to have someone confirm it like that would be earth-shattering. "Don't think of it for now, okay? You are who you are *now*," I said. "What you are *now* is nothing to do with your father. You need to focus," I repeated. "We need to get out of here, so we need you. You need to test the ward. We need to figure out a way of getting out of here."

"I... I can't..."

"Marigold!" I resisted the impulse to slap her. "Come on, you must have done some therapy at some point. Think! You're literally the sweetest and nicest person I've met in hundreds of years; it's obviously a bit of a coping mechanism. You've had to balance the concept of being half your dad, considering what he did to your mom. Is it so far-fetched that your father had a demon inside of him when he raped your mother? I bet it happens all the time!" I grabbed her shoulders and shook her. "You might be the first person who has ever absorbed some extra magical power from the conception, and yeah, that probably never happens. But we know this for sure; magic itself is not good or evil: People are good or evil. What are you?" I shook her again, and she finally looked up and met my eyes. "Are you good, or are you evil?"

Her chin trembled, but she met my gaze, her eyes full of unshed tears. While I watched her battle with her emotions, a single tear escaped and ran down her cheek. She sniffed. "I'm not evil."

"I don't want to hear that shit, Marigold. Say it."

"I'm not evil. I'm good."

"Yes, you are. You're possibly the goodest person I've met lately. Now, we need you. You're the only unknown quantity here; Atonas said so himself, he's not sure what you're capable of." I narrowed my eyes at her. "You need to concentrate on getting us out of here, okay?"

She nodded. "I think I might have something…"

A ear-splitting rumble came from the side of the wall, I looked behind us to see a gate opening slowly. The beasts were here. My shoulders tensed. What madness had he brought to us now?

The thick wooden gate cracked open further. Suddenly, there was a hard thump as whatever was behind it grew impatient and shoved the door roughly.

It flew open. A strange-looking beast barreled out on short, strong legs: A strange hybrid thing, moving like a rhino, with black scaled skin and horns that curled up and forward, looking like two ready-made spears popping out of its head.

I'd never seen a beast like it before; it was like an odd mashup of rhino and bull, with a black cobra hide and a Siamese cat face. Did he bring fighting animals here from his realm… or did he transform one of the Emerald Valley locals, in the same way he'd turned Leroy into a monster? What were the chances I was about to slaughter the local carpenter or one of the girls from the post office?

Its eyes were black and empty. I couldn't see even the slightest hint of intelligence in there, no fear or confusion.

I shot a glance at Marigold. She turned to me. "It's a real beast," she said quickly. "A Cazor; it's from the fae lands."

Thank God someone had done some research.

The monster opened its mouth and gave an ear-splitting scream; the noise made my ears hurt. It tossed its head, the deadly horns flashing in the sunlight, and it locked its gaze onto us.

It put it's head down, and charged.

Backman shoved Marigold behind her; I quickly stepped

forward. Rafael mirrored me. Brick and Sonja separated and turned to face the oncoming animal.

Behind it, the gate thudded again, and another shaggy horned beast ran out into the ring, circling the perimeter. Another one, until there were three, screaming wildly and tossing their heads.

My eyes shot back to the first beast; he was almost on top of us. The sharp horns glinted evilly in the sun. The obvious choice was to dodge; the thing moved like a great bull, and we had no weapons with which to pierce its hide.

Rafael stepped forward into the path of its charge. The beast, perhaps noticing the movement, focused on him, and lined up its horns to stab him. Before I could wonder what he was doing, Rafael ducked down onto one knee. I watched in horror as the beast bore down on him.

The next movements were almost too fast for my eyes to follow. The beast's horns lowered, and lined up with the kneeling Rafael. Raphael darted forward, reached out and smacked them down at the last millisecond; they dug deep into the sand. The impetus of its charge flipped the huge monster right over his body as if he was a pole-vaulter, and it flew through the air, screaming.

Rafael, still kneeling on the ground, looked up at me and grinned.

I frowned at him. "Flashy, Your Majesty."

The beast smacked into the stone wall behind us and lay in a crumpled heap. Sonja and Brick were on it in a flash; Brick held its horns and pulled its neck back, while Sonja used her claw-like nails to slash at its throat until it was a wet, dripping, mushy mess. The monster gave one last furious scream that dissolved into a pathetic gargle, and the light went out of its eyes.

Backman ran towards the other beasts, shifting as she went; her magnificently muscled human body exploded into a huge mass of shaggy fur and claws. Not breaking stride, she dodged around the thrusting horns of one monster, letting it charge past her in a screaming rage. She bore down on the other, and in half a second, she'd tackled it from behind. Staying well clear of its horns, she sandwiched one of its stubby legs in her paws, picked it up and whirled it around, and smashed it against the stone wall. It fell in a heap onto the sand and struggled to its feet immediately. She picked it up again and repeated the process, whipping it against the stone wall, bashing its head against the wall until its movements grew weaker and weaker. Finally, she lumbered forward, stood on the creature's back, opened her muzzle, gripped hold of the beast's throat, and tore it out.

The last beast ran around the perimeter of the amphitheater, its high-pitch scream echoing through the whole arena. Its horns slashed wildly from side to side, picking a target, perhaps? Brick and Sonja were busy decapitating the other beast; Backman was chewing happily on the throat of the other. In the center of the arena, Marigold stood still; arms slightly outstretched, muttering Words. At first, I thought she was conducting a freeze spell, but as I watched, she knelt quickly and picked up a handful of the coarse yellow sand and ran it through her fingers. The concentration on her face was all-consuming.

She wasn't focused on the monster. She was analyzing the construction of the pocket dimension, cataloging its structure, trying to see if there was a way she could break the wards. In a flash of panic, I saw the beast feint left. It whipped its charge around and went for her. The rough bone horns shone like swords, bearing down, aimed directly at Marigold's stomach.

I ran, ducked my head and charged at the beast from the side. I hit cold, rubbery flesh with my shoulder, and we both shuddered violently from the collision. The thing was heavy, with far more of a solid mass than I'd anticipated. It was like trying to shoulder-charge a Sherman tank. I threw it off balance, though, and its charge was interrupted. It veered around Marigold, who stood frozen in the middle of the arena, her eyes closed.

I glowered over at Backman, still standing over the dead monster, chewing happily at a bloody piece of trachea. "Hey, Yogi!" I shouted out to her. "Come and get your girl. She's going to get skewered over here."

Backman lifted her head and growled at me. I couldn't be sure, but her growl sounded less threatening, and more offended, if that was even possible. She bent down and tore off another piece of the monster's bloody carcass.

I frowned, confused. Backman was usually overprotective in the extreme.

I glanced back at Marigold, and finally caught a hint of a shimmer surrounding her. She'd warded herself. The beast would have bounced off if I had left it to charge. "Oh, right," I called over to Backman. "She's fine. Carry on."

Backman grumbled and licked her muzzle.

It gave me an idea. I turned to see where the monster had gone. It was running the perimeter again, possibly trying to figure out the most vulnerable member of our gang to stab. I eyed it carefully, hunched my shoulders over, feigned a limp, and backed slowly away until I was near the wall.

It stopped, and changed tack, running back the other way, watching me carefully with its beady eyes. I turned my back on it, listening carefully, and pretended to try and climb the sheer stone walls.

I heard the great hooves stomp, it reared, and started a charge towards me. I kept my back to it and scrabbled at the wall, feigning panic. I could almost feel it's hot breath on my neck; I could visualize that horn, lowered, aiming to pierce me right through my spine.

At the last minute I shot to the side. It couldn't stop; its horn stuck fast into the stone wall. It shrieked, and I covered my ears.

No wonder the vampires and Backman had opted to tear out the throats as soon as possible; the thing's voice was a sonic weapon in itself. It made sense, since it was from Atonas' realm, and he had sonic force powers as well. The monster struggled, digging its legs into the sand, scrabbling wildly, trying to pull its horn out of the wall. It was stuck fast. Its hooves couldn't get a proper grip on the sand to get enough purchase to help step backwards. It screamed and screamed; I felt something in my left ear pop. My ears were bleeding again.

Goddamnit. I snarled, and stuck my fingers in my ears, took a few steps back, and wound up a huge kick, directing it straight into the beast's neck. The noise cut off; it let out a revolting gargle and sagged, its horn still stuck fast into the wall.

The noise it made went from being infuriating, to absolutely pathetic. I felt a little sorry for it. It was unfair that Atonas had brought it here to try and hurt us. I hated the fact that I kept having to kill these things that were ripped out of their own world and set amongst us, to cause as much damage as possible. I hated not having a choice. It was either kill or be killed.

I looked at the beast's strange snake-like black scaly skin, and noticed it was striped with scars. He'd probably tortured these things, too, to get them to be more aggressive. The bastard. An icy fury took hold of me, and suddenly the beast's body became very clear. I watched it writhe, and counted the vertebrae on its back. I chose the perfect spot and leapt high in the air. My downward punch popped out the craniovertebral joint, severing the spine from its head.

The scrabbling feet went limp. It died immediately.

I turned towards the Imperial box. "Your beasts are dead. Are you happy?"

Atonas shrugged. "Not in the slightest, Starsmell. You do not have a scratch on you. I was hoping that my Cazor would at least release the sweet perfume of your blood. No matter," he clapped his hands. "I have something else that will do the trick."

The heavy wooden gate swung open. Immediately, we regrouped; I joined Raphael in the center of the arena, Brick and Sonja flew to his sides, arms outstretched, ready for anything. Backman lumbered back towards her wife but kept a careful distance – Marigold was still in her ward, eyes closed, running the coarse grains of sand between her finger-tips and muttering furiously.

We watched the gate. Out of the nothingness beyond the doorway, a large birdcage rolled into the arena on its side, ticking strangely, sounding exactly like a bomb about to go off.

The gate slammed shut. I watched the cage carefully, noticing that the ticking noise was getting slower and slower. We all backed away as it rolled towards us.

It shook slightly; vibrating, in an eerie way that made my skin crawl. While I watched, the cage's roll slowed, and I saw a tiny hatch on the side, complete with a wind-up lock that was quickly ticking down, ready to release. The cage stopped. The ticking sound slowed, then the cage let out a loud clang.

The little door popped open. Two tiny little creatures scurried out; little red humanoid bodies covered in red-ringed fur, with knobbly heads and arms that looked far too long for their little bodies.

I groaned.

Brick let out a chuckle beside me. "What are they? Cute

little things," he said. "They looked like tiny little redhead humans."

Two more crawled out of the cage, and quickly looked around, chittering to each other, then another four appeared. They swarmed on top of the cage, looking around the arena, tasting the air with flickering snake-like tongues.

"Red-spotted borowy," I muttered. "They're the meanest of the whole species. We're so fucked."

"Waddaya mean?" Brick nudged me. "They're tiny."

One of them climbed to the top of the cage, pointed at us and hissed, showing his needle-like teeth in a mouth that was far too big for its head.

Brick leant back, alarmed. "Whoa. Look at those teeth!"

"Beware, my love," Sonja warned him. "I believe they are poisonous."

"Only if they bite you," I told her.

"Still," Brick said, shrugging. "They're only little things. We'll just have to stomp on 'em."

I backed away slowly, leaving the vampires huddled in front of me. I backed away past Backman, who was standing near Marigold's ward, watching her intently, guarding her.

The borowy kept swarming out of the cage.

"How many do you think are in there?" Brick asked me.

"A lot," I murmured.

Borowy had squishy bodies that could squeeze into the tiniest spaces, a bit like octopus. It looked like Atonas had packed thousands of borowy into that cage. They surrounded the cage, covering it completely with their little hairy red-spotted bodies.

"Let's get this over with," Brick said. He punched out his arms, flexing his neck from side to side, and he stomped forward.

Every single little head in the swarm snapped towards

him; they all hissed, baring their teeth. It was the creepiest sight I'd seen in a long time. I took a few more steps back.

One tiny borowy scampered over to meet Brick's advance. He raised his boot, ready to stomp down on the borowy, but quick as a whip, the borowy jumped, landing on his leg, and scampered up his body.

Brick squealed, and swatted out with his hand as the borowy jumped towards him. Almost in slow-motion, I watched the borowy sail through the air, mouth open, needle-like teeth bared.

It landed on his finger and chomped down. Brick squealed again and flung the borowy off him. It flew through the air and hit the stone wall, twenty yards away.

"Goddamn it," Brick gasped. "That little bastard! Those teeth are…" his face went blank; his eyes drooped. "Sharp…" His face went slack.

"My love!" Sonja raced towards him, and he sagged in her arms.

"I told you," I muttered. "And that was just *one*."

The swarm chittered loudly, gathering themselves up, getting ready to attack. Above us, in the Imperial box, Atonas started to laugh.

CHAPTER 20

Two hours later, we were still fighting for our lives. Brick lost a finger to the borowy swarm. I'd ended up having to fight the creatures almost alone, as the poison seemed to knock the vampires out very quickly. The borowy liked vampire flesh, it seemed. They left Backman alone, and they couldn't get to Marigold inside the ward, so I spent most of my time guarding Rafael and the vamps, playing racquetball with their furry little bodies.

I didn't want to hurt them; in the same way I didn't want the Cazor to die. But they made it very clear that they *definitely* wanted to hurt me.

Nevertheless, I tried. After two failed attempts to shove the swarm back into the cage, and one failed attempt to reason with the little bastards, Marigold came out of her stupor and helped me out with a stun charm which confused them long enough so I could squash them all flat. As soon as I'd crushed the last borowy underneath my boot, I succumbed to the overabundance of poison rushing through my veins. I laid down right on the grisly borowy remains and had a nap.

I'd woken to Rafael gently picking me up in his arms, and a scorching heat flashing around the arena. Atonas had brought in a wyrm next, a long wingless beast that slithered all around the arena, trying to barbecue us with its breath.

Eventually, Backman brought it down by riding it like a bronco, while the rest of us ducked in, trying to slice into its soft belly.

Sonja copped a blast of wyrm breath and lost most of her hair. The whole left side of her body bubbled up like pork crackling. Brick caught the full force of its flailing tail, and he was bruised black from head to toe. Backman's fur was stained with blood in a few different places, and she was limping badly.

Rafael had broken a few ribs; he was holding himself more upright, but other than that, you wouldn't know he was injured.

I'd broken my arm and dislocated my shoulder again, but as usual, I was trying to ignore it. I patted my cheek. A group of borowy had decided to gang up and go for my left cheek. There was still a pitted hole gouged out of my face. All of us – bar Marigold – were covered with blood, broken, scarred, and still a little confused from the borowy venom.

Atonas laughed with glee the whole time. When the wyrm's intestines finally slithered out of its body and its eyes rolled back in his head, the fae prince stood up and cheered.

"Bravo! Well done, my fine friends. I must admit I am gladdened by the entertainment you have provided me. Now, to the finale!" He held up his hand. "Wait – I must move closer. We have no more beasts, and it seems you are all well warmed up, and I want a close-up of this bout." He pulled his hands apart; sparks appeared between them. The Imperial box slid down slowly, closer to the arena floor.

"Warmed up? I'm almost fucking dead," Brick put his hands on his knees, leaning over.

I hung my head. Next to me, Rafael swore, holding his ribs. "We must get out of here," he said.

Backman and Marigold huddled up with us. "I think I've got something," Marigold said. "It's good that he's getting closer. It's not something I've tried before, but if he's close enough and distracted, I think I can do it."

"Do what?"

She looked at me, paused, and swallowed.

"You can tell me. Whatever it is." I glared at her. "It's life or death here, Marigold. Well, for you guys, anyway," I added. "I'm going to be doing the moonwalk outta here no matter what happens. But you need to understand that this is self-defense. There's no losing your soul over this. We need to smack Atonas down and get out of here."

She bit her lip. "It's a little on the offensive side, so I'm not... I'm not sure. I've only ever done defensive things before. Just... just let me try, okay?"

"Okay. What about the ward?"

"I can't break it," she said, shaking her head. "Not at all. If I get a clear shot at Atonas, I might be able to... to ...hurt him." She looked up at me with a pleading expression in her eyes.

"I got you, babe," I patted her arm. "You stun him, I'll kill him, and the wards will start to break down. Don't worry about my soul, it's all good."

My soul was ruined anyway. The dusty sand beneath my feet reminded me of that. The last time I was in an arena like this, I'd slaughtered hundreds of people. I only ended my brutal reign as champion when I was forced to kill my friend.

I'd justified it at the time. I'd told myself that he was lucky. At least he got to die. But I'd taken his choice away with a quick slice to his throat.

Brick straightened up and groaned. "Won't we be starting a war with the fae if we kill him?"

"I doubt anyone even knows he's here," I replied, grateful for the distraction from the slow spiral my thoughts had taken me on. "And besides, judging from his laughter while the borowy were gouging chunks out of my cheek, he's already had his good time, so the terms of the magical contract have already been fulfilled. He's just being petty by staying. We've asked him to leave, and he hasn't gone, so he's breaking fae protocols. We're within our rights to try and kill him."

Marigold's eyes bulged slightly.

"What?" I said. "Fae have simple rules. Don't be rude, or you'll get slaughtered."

"Okay," she said slowly. "Just try and keep him occupied for a few minutes. It will take me a bit of time to gather the energy."

Suddenly, a sonic boom ripped through our huddle and blew us all backwards. I landed roughly on my side, and screamed in pain as my broken arm bore the brunt of my fall.

"Now, now," Atonas called out from his new position, just above the sheer stone wall surrounding the arena. "I hate to break up this little huddle, but it's time to fight again. This time, I'll be pitting a battle between you all. I wanted to try a battle between lovers, but I could not imagine how that would work. So instead, we'll go vampires versus the half-humans. Brick, Sonja and my Vampire King," he blew him a kiss. "I haven't given up on you, sweet Rafael. You will fight the shifter, the witch, and you, Imogen. I do not care how you do it, but at least one of you must be out for the count for the next round to begin."

I gritted my teeth and got slowly to my feet. "Or what?"

Atonas cocked his head. "Excuse me?"

"I said, or what? What are you going to do? You've run out of beasts; we've slaughtered them all. You're obviously too much of a chicken shit to come down here and fight us in person."

He tutted. "Uh, uh uh, Starsmell. You cannot provoke me. To be perfectly honest, you are unworthy of me." He shrugged carelessly. "I am a master of the martial arts; I've been training for eons. Even watching you now, fighting my beasts, I'm dumbfounded by how slow and dim-witted you all are. I might as well have released a flock of chickens into the arena and asked you to catch them for me. No," he laughed. "If I step down there, my fun will be over. I couldn't even bring myself to toy with you; my skills are too finely honed, my fighting instincts too sharp. I'd rip out all your spines immediately."

I had no idea if that were true, but I didn't really care. It wouldn't be the first time I'd had to grow my spine back. "I don't believe you," I pursed my lips. "I think you're full of it. You thought you were good enough to seduce the Vampire King, but you failed in that task, too; he saw right through you. We even saw through your first game, where you turned Leroy into a monster and disguised yourself as a statue. That was foolish, the work of a child. You think you're a big warrior boy now? Show me!" I slapped my chest. "Come on down here and show me."

He narrowed his eyes. "Careful, Starsmell. My magic could destroy you in an instant. My fighting skills are unparalleled."

"Come on down, then, you little bitch!" I walked forward. "You're an embarrassment, that's what you are. Your magic sucks, your games are petty and silly, Rafael doesn't want you. I bet no one likes you in your home realm. Am I right? Come on, loser," I shouted. "Show me some action!"

Atonas got to his feet and snarled. "Enough!"

The arena shook; I wobbled on my feet.

He leaned forward, putting his hands on the stone wall.

219

"You will fight each other," he spat out. "And I will watch. You will give me a good show." He lowered his head. "I wish to see you beaten black and blue before I leave this realm.

"You want to see a good show?" I stalked forward and jabbed Rafael in the chest. "Let's go. You and me first."

Thankfully, Rafael seemed to get it immediately. We had one mission; distract the fae prince. I'd already spotted the ruby gleam in Marigold's eyes; she was gathering her strength. Backman, still in bear form, blocked Atonas' vision, so I had to keep them both out of this fight for a few minutes.

If Rafael and I could go a few rounds, and make it flashy and believable enough, we might be able to distract the prince.

Thankfully, he seemed like he understood straight away. He stretched his arms, testing his ribs, and marked out a circle in the sand.

"Master…" Sonja said. "Master, what are you doing?"

"It's okay, Sonja." His warm brown eyes ran over me, sparking something a little more X-rated than battle lust. "Imogen has been getting too… what would you say… impudent lately, anyway." His lingering eyes dropped lower. "She will benefit from a beating."

"Oooh, stop," Atona's eyes sparked. "You make it sound like you're going to spank her. Go on, my sweet prince."

I threw Rafael a glare, trying to keep it menacing, even though I felt a hot flush in my core. "You asshole." I shot forward and threw a jab at his jaw. Rafael swung to the side dodging. He matched my stance and threw a straight right. I raised my fists, blocking. I danced on my toes, and we traded blows in the traditional boxing style, ducking, weaving.

He was *fast*. I struck out again, a straight right, then mixed things up a little. I took a step back and kicked. He moved immediately into a Muay Thai stance and blocked the kick with his shin. The crack echoed around the arena. He moved between the martial arts with his usual confident grace.

Fighting Rafael was like trying to wrangle an oversized, sexy cobra. He was everywhere at once, his muscled arms wrapping around my waist, pinning me down, or sliding over my skin as he tried to get me into a lock. Pretty soon, we'd transitioned into full Brazilian jiu jitsu, and were rolling on the ground, hands sliding everywhere.

Fighting Rafael felt like foreplay, although I was slightly annoyed he was pulling his punches. I wasn't, though. I avoided his broken ribs, just like he didn't touch my rapidly-healing broken arm. But I took the shots where I found them, and felt a strange frisson from him whenever I landed a good hit.

"Do you like that, Your Majesty?" I asked him, as one of my jabs opened up a little cut on the corner of his lip.

He opened his mouth and slid out his tongue, and slowly licked the drop of blood. "*Mmmm. Do you?*"

At one point he got me in a headlock; I flipped out and around, climbing his back like a monkey, I scissored my legs around his neck, dropped, and swung him to the ground. I heard the distant sounds of clapping; I'd almost forgotten Atonas was watching us.

Rafael didn't even flinch when I smacked him in the kidney. "Did that hurt, baby?"

"You wish," he murmured back, tucking his hands underneath me, he had me pulled into a lock. I tried to break it using a release I'd learned when the martial art was still in its infancy, but my jerky movement dislocated my shoulder again. The heat of the fight and Rafael's obvious pleasure at being hit had distracted me; the jolt of pain took me by surprise, and I let out a short, agonized scream.

"Yes! Finish her!" Atonas was on his feet.

Rafael jolted and loosened his arms immediately.

"No!" Atonas screamed, slamming his arms down on the stone wall. "Break it! Break *her!*"

Rafael's arms closed around me again loosely. The agony scorched through me. My head fell sideways, and I saw Marigold, her eyes glowing ruby red, bring her hand up, palms out.

The noise in the arena condensed into nothingness; for a moment, none of us could move. Then suddenly, a blast of red-hot magic poured out of Marigold's hands and hit Atonas in the chest. He flew back, hitting his head on the marble of the imperial box.

"Quick," I struggled to my feet. "We have to finish him."

Rafael helped me up, and I staggered forward. We ran towards the imperial box.

A huge explosion threw us both back, and I blacked out.

CHAPTER 21

*T*he pain hit me before I even opened my eyes. My whole body felt mangled; steamrolled, shoved backwards through a wringer, and tenderized. My eyes cracked open; I took in the dusty sand, the roaring bear in my line of sight, the unconscious body of Marigold lying on the arena floor. Adrenaline rushed through me.

I needed to get up, get moving. We were in trouble.

I'd landed in a heap, my right knee had taken the brunt of the impact, and cracked, bending my whole leg the wrong way. I groaned, and rolled myself flat, feeling my bones crack back into place. God, it hurt. It hurt *so* much. I squeezed my eyes closed, hoping to drift back into oblivion, knowing that I had to get up and help my friends as soon as I could.

"Imogen."

I breathed out what was supposed to be a sigh of relief that Rafael was okay, but it came out more like a tortured gurgle. I felt out with my hand, and my fingertips touched smooth skin.

"You're okay," he murmured.

My normal snarky retorts died on my lips. In the

distance, I could hear Atonas in a screaming tirade. "Rafael," I whispered "We have to help them. We have…"

He nodded. We struggled to our feet. Rafael's head was bleeding; his shirt was stained red. My leg was shattered. I couldn't walk. I blinked sand and blood out of my eyes, and saw Brick, standing near the wall, holding Sonja in his arms. She was unconscious.

Atonas' rage was terrible. "How *could* you? How could you do this? All I wanted was to have some fun, to laugh. And you attack me? In my own dimension? How could you be so stupid? Did it not even occur to you that I would have simple defense spells built-in? Now you are all too beaten and confused, there is no point in this game anymore." He crossed his arms over his chest. "No point at all. You have insulted me," he pouted. "I am offended. No, my friends, you will remain here, now. You will stay here in this dimension until my offense wears off. It might be years before I get over this insult," he snapped, pouting. "Centuries, even. You will stay here and rot, until I am satisfied. In the meantime, I will take the Vampire King's place, so that no one will miss him." He let out a harsh chuckle. "No one will miss the rest of you."

The imperial box began to move backwards, merging with the back of the marble wall behind him. Slowly, with a supercilious curl of his lip, Atonas melted out of the amphitheater, and was gone.

"No!" I hobbled forward and stumbled. Rafael knelt down, gave me his arm, and we limped over to the others.

Brick had sunk to his knees, holding Sonja in his arms. Tears flooded down his cheeks. "She won't wake up," he mumbled, over and over again. "She won't wake up."

"She is in her deathsleep," Rafael said softly. "Remember, in our world, it is day. She is injured, Brick. Just like you were. She will be okay."

He nodded, but kept crying. I stumbled over to Marigold,

who lay on the ground. Backman, in full bear form, paced back and forth and bellowed at me.

"Let me check," I said, my mouth dusty and tasting of blood.

Backman stopped her pacing and pawed lightly at Marigold.

I checked her pulse. "She's alive," I told Backman. The bear let out a huge, painful groan, and dissolved, her boiling flesh and fur compacting in on itself until she was in her human form again.

"Thank the Goddess," Backman knelt next to her, head bowed. "I thought she was gone." Her voice cracked. "I thought she was gone." She stroked her cheek. Marigold's eyelids fluttered.

My heart ached. I looked around the walls of the arena. The crowd had disappeared along with Atonas. All there was left was the sheer stone walls around us, and the empty stand that stretched up into the sky.

We were trapped.

I looked up at Rafael. "What did we do?"

"We should have known." His eyebrows furrowed. He shook his head. "It was a hastily made dimension, but of course it would have protections in place. We underestimated him."

"I should have known," I echoed. "I should have." My voice cracked. "I've been trapped in a pocket dimension before. I know how they work."

Brick pulled Sonja tighter. "Are we stuck here?"

"He will return," Rafael said.

I swallowed, tasting blood and dust. I looked around at my friends; Sonja, unconscious, bald, and with half her face melted away, cradled in Brick's arms. Marigold, lying deathly still, her face so very pale. Backman, with huge scratch marks gouged into every bit of her nude flesh. And Rafael, his shirt drenched in blood, his shallow breath betraying his shattered ribs.

"He won't return," I muttered.

Brick made a tiny squeak. "You don't think so?"

"Not in a long time. If I know anything about fae, I know that they hold grudges. He won't come back, not for years."

"We'll be stuck here for years?"

"Marigold will find a way to break the ward," Backman said.

"She can't do it. She has no ingredients." My voice sounded very harsh in my ears. "She's got no salt, no herbs, no crystals. She's got nothing to channel her powers with."

"She's strong."

"She's *unconscious*, Backman," I snarled. "She won't be doing anything in a hurry."

A thick feeling had settled inside me; it made my voice wobble dangerously. A certain weight, like a yoke around my neck, something that I had to wear. It was for me, and for me only. "And when she wakes up, then what? We've got no salves, no bandages, nothing to help any of us heal. We've got no food. We'll all wither away into dry husks. At least you and Marigold will be fine, Backman." I laughed bitterly. "You get to die."

"Stop it," she growled back.

"It's the truth. And it makes this decision easier for me, anyway. It's selfish, you see, Backman? I've always been selfish, that's the truth. If I can't kill my problems, I usually run away from them. I can't run now, can I? I could just wait this one out, of course, I could hunker down and let myself drift away for a few centuries, but your rotting husks will be decomposing all around me..." The thought was indescribably horrific.

"Imogen, stop." Rafael put his hand on my broken arm. It

felt cool, a light caress. It anchored me. It bore a little of the weight of the yoke around my neck.

I looked up at him. "I know what I have to do."

"No."

"I have to, Rafael. I can break this ward, he said so himself. I have to do it, otherwise you will all die." The tears ran in a river down my face.

"He will find you. The Ancient."

I shrugged; the movement pinched my dislocated shoulder. I barely felt the pain. It was nothing compared to what I was going to be feeling soon.

"I can't let you do this."

"There's no other choice."

He swore, and ran his hands through his hair. "At least wait until the others are awake."

"They might not wake. They might wake, and it will be worse. They might wake, and need water. We have no water, Rafael. We've got nothing. No. It has to be now."

I pulled myself upright, and took a few steps away from the group. "Do me one favor. As soon as the ward is broken, you have to run. Run as fast as you can. It doesn't matter where, as long as it's far away from me."

"No," he pulled me back by the hand.

"Please, Rafael. You'll only make this harder." I shook off his hand.

He let me go. A strange hardness came over his face, the skin around his eyes tightened, distancing himself, perhaps, from what was to come.

I stumbled backwards. "Backman, carry Marigold away. As fast as you can. You take Sonja, Brick." He cradled Sonja closer and nodded to me.

I shuffled away, turning my back on them. It was easier this way. I wasn't sure if I could do what I had to do, while watching Rafael's perfect face.

I put one foot in front of the next, feeling the agony in my destroyed knee, each little pinch of pain in my broken arm and dislocated shoulder; feeling all the stings of the tiny cuts all over my body. I appreciated the pain, because soon, it was going to be a lot worse.

I brushed my fingers up against the stone wall, feeling the odd vibrations of the ward. I could feel the two parts; the human one, which had never really bothered me. I'd always been able to walk through human wards without feeling a thing. No, it was the other part that shocked me. The tiny explosion in the pads of my fingertips, as my skin tasted, for only the second time in my life, the flavor of the creature that had made me.

It was stronger than it had been in the jail cell. That was only a tiny fraction of the power in this ward. He'd made it well, not a Frankenstein ward, but a ward that was fully half-human and half star. Not mixed together, to make something that was the perfect flavor of me, though. It was two separate things. It was exactly as Atonas had said.

I could break it. I just needed to become more star, to break apart the human part.

I closed my eyes, and mentally reached inside myself, to where the simmering lava of my father's heritage stewed. I poked at the scorching heat, letting it bubble, feeling it surge. It rose up with a victorious roar, like a furious geyser blasting into the air, and covered me completely.

The energy surged through me, power infused my limbs, and uncontrollable rawness overwhelmed me. I opened my mouth and I screamed.

I threw back both my arms and thrust them into the walls of the pocket dimension.

All at once, everything shattered, and I fell.

CHAPTER 22

The sweet relief of weightlessness lasted only a brief few seconds, and suddenly, I was lying on dew-wet grass, under the dark night sky. I could feel each blade touching me, licking me with their tiny wet tongues. I could hear every little microscopic animal that scuttled around the dirt beneath the grass. Trillions of limbs. Tiny pincers. Each little impulse pinging around inside their heads.

Power surged through me. I looked down at my hands, feeling the resonance of the earth itself, vibrating beneath my fingertips. I felt all of it, the whole sphere of the globe, and every creature that burrowed and scuttled and limped and swung around on it.

The vastness and beauty overwhelmed me, threatening to tear me in two.

Then suddenly, an enraged roar filled not my ears, but my heart.

He was coming.

CHAPTER 23

I leapt to my feet, desperate. There was no escape. He'd come for me. Even now, I could feel him pushing his way through the Dip, bringing with him the burning rage, the scorching jealousy, the overwhelming shame that he seemed to be made up of. He was bringing it with him, pushing it towards me, letting it seek me out. I felt the ping back as his energy touched mine; he'd found me.

I wished I could die.

So many times in my long life I wished I was dead, and none more than now. It wasn't the anticipation of pain this time, no, because the last few times I thought about what he'd do to me, it wasn't about how he tore me to shreds. I always regenerated from that. My body always bounced back, but he scarred my soul with the emotions he brought me.

He was coming.

There was no point running. My leg was still broken, anyway. My van was at the gate of the country club. I wouldn't make it that far. The Ancient was through now, he'd shot through, and up, as usual, he'd find me from a height and smash down on me like a rolled-up newspaper on a fly. He'd tear me to pieces, and try to use my blood to wash away his sins.

I slumped to my knees and shut my eyes. Waiting.

Suddenly, I was flying. Strong arms held me. Rafael had picked me up and he was running fast.

"It's no... no use..." I stammered. The coolness of his body overwhelmed me; how was it that he was always the perfect temperature for me? He was hot when I needed warmth, and now, with the burning rage of the Ancient bearing down on me, he felt like a cool stream on a hot summer's day.

"I have to try." His voice shocked right through me, thrilling me with its passion, the extra bite in his words was a spit in the face of death himself. It soothed me, calmed the lava pit inside me, the furious geyser gushed, then spluttered, and settled back into a fiery simmer. Rafael ran, holding me tight, straight down the hill of the golf course, headed to the building just beyond the main resort.

I saw where he was headed, and a flare of hope sprung up within me, unbidden. He was taking me to the helipad.

It wouldn't work, though. I could feel the Ancient, high above me. He was locked on, he could feel me, just like I could feel him. Although this time, he hesitated, just for a split second.

What was it that gave him pause? Was it the fact that I was held in the arms of a vampire; an ancient creature himself, who was so desperate to save me? Or was it the fact that my star nature had settled down immediately?

It didn't matter in the end, because he screamed, long and loud, a tortured cry that woke the sleeping beasts that slumbered in the deepest caverns of the oceans.

We weren't going to make it.

Rafael ran to the hanger. A helicopter sat on the helipad;

its propeller still spinning; it had either just landed or it was about to take off.

Rafael flung me inside. It was lucky for us, but not so much the two passengers, who were rudely pushed out onto the tarmac.

I shook my head, feeling the anger, the rage bear down on me. He was high above us, and he was coming.

Rafael didn't bother putting his headset on or waste time strapping himself in, and I loved him for it. We were out of time, anyway, oh God, I loved this man for trying. No one had ever tried so hard to save me before. The Ancient was in the town now, I could feel him plunged to Earth, whirling in furious anger around the town square, I could almost see through his eyes as he blazed up towards my cabin on the east ridge, he smashed through it, blessedly empty, then roared back down the ridge to the main street in town. I felt him as he blazed through the jail, then suddenly, my thoughts were not my own.

Suffering. The tearing, burning pain of jealousy. *Why do they get all this? Why did* he *have this, and why can I not? It is profane, blasphemy.*

He caught me; his mind seized me. *Aberration. Monster.*

I let go and fell back in the chopper seat, holding my head, screaming in agony. He'd locked onto me, he was coming. He shot up the ridge, tearing up towards the country club, with pure destruction in his mind.

Rafael stabbed at the console and grabbed the levers, pulling back, flicking switches above his head.

I was almost shocked when we lifted off straight away.

What the... what the fuck? I watched Rafael as he edged the lever down, and we shot forward.

He was almost on us.

We gathered speed, flying over the town, and I felt him behind us. I turned, and looked out the open doorway.

A great creature chased us, not a man, not a monster, but an ancient beast, made up of wheels that turned into nothingness and covered with thousands of blinking eyes. Black wings made up of midnight sky propelled him forward. While I watched, he dissolved into the shape of a man, a great winged giant, genderless, bald, and made up entirely of pain and suffering.

He reached out his fingertips, his fingers brushed the side of the helicopter, then we pulled away. He screamed.

We were faster.

CHAPTER 24

I didn't sleep.

I wasn't sure what it was I did, but it wasn't sleeping. It felt like my brain had reached full overload, and not even sleep would come to rescue me. I felt like a computer that was supposed to reboot, but had too many applications running. I had to shut everything down before I could restart, but there was too much happening; too many things, too much to process.

My applications were not responding. I could not force quit.

Luckily, I had someone else dealing with my operating system. Rafael effortlessly, intuitively and expertly took charge.

We flew to New York. Rafael already called ahead, and had a jet fueled, started, and taxiing down the runway when we arrived. He simply landed the chopper beside it, grabbed me, jumped out of the chopper, ran and leapt into the jet's open hatch with me in his arms, and placed me gently into the plush tan-leather seats. We flew away, into the bright night skies.

"Where are we going?"

He smiled at me. "It doesn't matter. What matters is that we don't stop."

I nodded, and closed my eyes, desperately trying to make sense of what had happened. I had *so* much to process. Why had the Ancient hesitated when he screamed out of ? Couldn't he find me? Was my energy muddled, or something? It felt like he couldn't quite get a fix on me.

Would he catch us? It didn't seem likely. Most of the time, I couldn't feel him close behind us, but I knew he was still chasing us. I could feel his anger, his resentment; it was so violent and tangible, it almost burned a hole into the fabric of our dimension. It was like a mushroom cloud hanging over a nuclear explosion, I thought it should be obvious to everyone. I was surprised at the easy camaraderie of the pilot when he stopped to chat to Rafael. I was shocked at the gentle politeness of the hostess who served us tiny snacks at all hours of the day and night.

Could they not feel his wrath? How could they not notice that there was a great beast tearing through the sky?

Not for the first time, I wondered if the creature that chased me was *the* Great Beast; the Adversary. The thought had occurred to me before. Although, I knew that he didn't really exist. The tiers of celestial creatures weren't rigid class structures, it was more of a haphazard menagerie. But one thing I knew for sure was that any creature with that much hatred and loathing must be a product of the lowest dimension of reality.

I worried about Leroy. The fae prince was still running around Emerald Valley. He'd promised to leave Leroy alone; he'd sworn it, believing him to be a useless and boring target anyway, but I still worried. I worried about Marigold, even though Backman had called and said she was awake, and recovering from a concussion and some internal bleeding.

At least I didn't have to worry about Sonja. She called often, and took the time to beg Rafael to throw me out of the jet and come home. Her and Brick had gone into hiding, staying away from the country club, so that Atonas might believe that they were still stuck in the pocket dimension.

He was amusing himself, at the very least. He'd discovered human alcoholic beverages, and he'd thrown a Bacchus-type festival up at the country club.

For two days so far, the party raged. Apart from drinking himself into a stupor, he hadn't done anything too crazy. Rafael's security had reported several close calls, and one dead body that was easily covered up. We had to get back to Emerald Valley as soon as possible and find a way to get rid of him for good.

I worried about that the most. Atonas was more powerful and more petulant than I'd ever believed. If we let him stay in our dimension, the bodies would pile up. Over and over, Rafael and I discussed plans; ways to get him back into his own world. We talked about drugging him or tricking him, we discussed faking a message from back at his home, but everything we thought of had the potential to backfire badly, just like it had done in the pocket dimension.

In the end, the best idea we could come up with was to make the whole place as dull as possible, so he'd get bored and go home. Rafael gave the order to send all the country club members away and stop any alcohol deliveries, and try to bore Atonas as much as possible with talk of business.

I worried for the security team. I worried about the innocent mortals of the valley.

There was just so much to worry about.

I worried the whole time that the Ancient would catch us, but I didn't see him again. I knew he was behind us, though, and twice I had the pilot change direction when it looked like he was veering off course, maybe trying to head us off somehow.

I worried that we'd have to stop to refuel, but we never did. When I finally asked Rafael about it, he told me that we'd already refueled in mid-air, several times.

Oh, to be a billionaire, and not have to worry about such things

I stayed on that buttersoft leather seat for three days, cocooned in Rafael's arms. My knee started healing. The deep bloody pit in my cheek started to fill in, and a large scab formed. Rafael's ribs healed.

We flew and flew, circling the earth, while the terrifying creature screamed and screamed behind us, never catching up.

CHAPTER 25

The three days were almost up. Rafael, in his blessed wisdom, had set a timer, and we were on our way back to Emerald Valley under cover of the blackest night sky, flying fast in the helicopter. Suddenly, I felt the Ancient give one last tortured scream as he was pushed back out of our reality, back to wherever he came from.

I looked up at Rafael and sighed. "He's gone."

He smiled at me. "We did it."

"I can't believe it." My voice shook. "I honestly…" I swallowed. "Thank you. From the bottom of my heart."

"Imogen," he said, chuckling. "You sacrificed yourself, again, to save me. You broke us out of the fae prince's dimension. We would have rotted in there without you."

"I would have just stayed there and waited it out, but I was put off by the idea of your rotting corpse stuck in the arena with me." I shrugged. "Best to break out, get it all over with."

We couldn't land at the country club; we didn't know where Atonas was, so Rafael touched the chopper down on the grassy lawn by the lake, just out of the town center. As soon as he'd switched off the rotor, I slipped out of my chair, letting my feet touch the ground.

Ah. Solid ground. Bliss. The three days in the air hadn't been so bad, especially with the Vampire King watching me while I defragged, but it was good to touch the earth again. My leg felt almost healed; my arm was good as new. Apart from some deep bruising around my eyes and an almost flaked-off scar on my cheek, I was back to normal.

Ready to face the fae prince again.

My relief was short-lived. A tremor rumbled underneath the dirt of our feet. I felt a charge in the air.

I glanced at Rafael. Oh God, what now?

"Something is coming through the portal," he whispered.

Whatever it was, it was much smaller than when Atonas came through. His coming was heralded by a great rumble, an earthquake that shook us even high up on the ridge of the country club. This one was tiny; subtle, and the vibration stopped instantly. I doubted anyone else would have noticed, but I still felt some magic in my fingertips from the star surge, and Rafael was tenser than a meerkat watching a hawk circle.

"We need to go," I whispered to him.

CHAPTER 26

The town was dark and deserted. The streetlights struggled to produce even an eerie glow, and the sky was cloudy and devoid of stars. The clouds hung low, brushing the tips of the ridge, enclosing the valley completely.

We raced towards the town square, wondering what nightmare Atonas had brought through this time. He wasn't at the square; we knew that much. Rafael's security team had been on him the whole time, and he hadn't even left the country club.

The streets were empty. We crept closer, using the columns of the town hall as cover. It looked like a maintenance team had started re-grassing the lawn; a big hill of turf was piled in the corner. I slunk over to it, ducking down, feeling the tiny trembles beneath my feet.

I took a quick peek, and gasped.

Leroy stood in the middle of the square, right underneath the portal. He knelt; his head bowed. Above him, a figure loomed – huge, terrifying, wearing a black cloak made of the night sky.

A fae queen.

CHAPTER 27

*N*ow we were *fucked.*

If a minor fae prince could cause as much havoc as Atonas had, a queen could destroy everything. Fae queens possessed unparalleled power.

What was she doing here? Were we about to go to war for the entire earth?

Rafael tried to hold me, but I broke out of his grasp immediately. I ran over to Leroy and threw myself in front of him. I kept my body low, and my eyes averted.

"Imogen!' Leroy said, his voice muffled since I was holding him to the ground. "What are you doing?"

I bowed my head low. "Forgive me, uh... Queen, Your Majesty. Whatever quarrel you have with the child here, please direct it at me."

It was hard keeping my head low while trying to take a peek at the Queen, but I managed it.

She was huge; almost giant-like, around nine feet tall, with perfect proportions, proud shoulders held back and head high. The long midnight-black cloak she wore covered her whole body except for her shoes, which appeared to be made up completely of tiny, glittery diamonds.

Magic shoes, perhaps. Was she going to tap them together three times and wish for home? I was never that lucky.

She gazed down at me at her feet, her expression unreadable. I noted her coloring – her snow-white skin and enormous black eyes. Her raven hair, parted in the middle, fell in a thick sheet down her back.

The power that radiated from her shocked me. She opened her mouth to speak. It took me a moment to decipher her words, the tone and cadence belonged to a far-off world.

"I have no quarrel with this child," she said, her voice low and impossibly regal. Her words carried a resonance, as if her voice were made to carry around the deepest depths of the underworld. "Not yet, anyway. Although I am very curious to know why he called me here to this dimension. I have not received an invitation such as this for many lifetimes." She tilted her head. "No one would ever *dare*. I am very curious, indeed."

I closed my eyes. "You called her here?" I hissed at Leroy.

"Imogen," Leroy hissed back, trying to shove me off him. "Trust me. I know what I'm doing."

"Jesus, kid! You don't know what you're playing with here!"

"You have to trust me!"

"No offense, but you haven't done very well in the earning-trust department," I said, pushing him back down.

"I know, that's why I'm doing this! I have to fix the mess I made," he pleaded, grappling with me.

"Ah *hem*." The fae queen cleared her throat. I stopped trying to shove the kid back, and froze. "You will tell me why you called me now. And your reasoning must be good." Her eyes glinted. "I do not like leaving my realm without good reason."

Although the threat was implied, the weight of it smashed onto me with the force of a Mac truck. A contract was being established. Atonas wasn't going to leave without a simple shag - this queen might demand a tribute of a flowing river of blood.

I felt Rafael beside me. Of course, he'd crept up on us; he wasn't going to leave Leroy and I at the mercy of a vengeful fae queen, no matter how stupid we'd been in throwing ourselves in front of her.

I glanced sideways at Leroy.

"Trust me," he pleaded.

I nodded once. "Okay."

Leroy got to his feet. "Your Majesty, a week ago, here, I made a terrible mistake. As you can see, we have a portal in our town, an access point for the flow of energy."

The Queen's face was unreadable. Her beauty was shocking, almost terrible.

Leroy stuttered, but went on, his voice louder. "We have had a planetary alignment recently, and the portal is wider than it usually is. Strange beasts have been accidentally falling through the portal into our realm. It's been dangerous, Your Majesty, for both the beasts, and for us mortals. I tried to help."

He paused. I made the mistake of looking at the Queen. Her face had an otherworldly stillness; she might as well have been carved from marble.

Leroy swallowed roughly. "I made a mistake. I tried to do a *don't look here* spell, and I messed it up. Instead of telling creatures to watch out, and not to come near, I accidently called another fae here."

Her vast, sparking black eyes rolled slightly, just for a second.

"And, well, that fae is refusing to go home," Leroy went on, his tone growing bolder. "He's been playing terrible tricks on us and making our lives miserable."

The Queen's face hardened. "I do not see how that is any of my concern. Just kill him, and be done with it."

"Kill him, Your Majesty?"

She waved her arm airily. "You revoked his invitation, yes? You asked him to depart?"

I cleared my throat. "We did, your majesty. We were under the impression that a contract of sorts had to be completed. The fae said he was promised a good time, and wouldn't leave until he had one."

She waved her hand again, a graceful, dismissive movement. "Has he laughed in your presence?"

"Many times."

"Then he had a good time. If he refuses to leave, he is impertinent, and you are within your rights to kill him." The elegant shoulders shrugged.

Fabulous. I was hoping that would be the case. We'd been given permission to kill him. It wasn't like I hadn't already been trying, although I may have been holding myself back, considering the consequences might be an interdimensional war. Still, it was going to be tricky. Atonas was already exceptionally difficult to kill.

Leroy bowed his head, his expression uncertain. "Well. Thank you, I guess?"

Her huge eyes narrowed. "Is that all? You called me here to ask my advice?"

"No," said Leroy. "Not exactly. It's not that your advice hasn't been helpful. I just... I don't think you will want us to kill this fae."

She lifted her head and eyed him beadily. I cringed.

"Of course I do. And why not?" Her voice was dangerously silky. "If one of our kind is stupid enough to blunder into a mortal realm, annoy the animals and play silly tricks, then *that* fae deserves to face whatever consequences that come his way, even if that means death." She tilted her head to the side. "To dally with creatures such as you is like burning a scatter of the mite-brownies with a looking glass – it is amusing for a moment, but unnecessarily cruel, and silly to persist with. I care not for some fool who dallies with mortals," she said, insulting all of us breathlessly easily.

"Oh. Okay then." Leroy nodded his head. "Thank you, Your Majesty. Words cannot express how grateful I am to you, your divine highness. We will ask Prince Atonas to leave our realm again, and if he does not, we will attempt to kill him." Leroy's face dropped into a frown. "We'll do our best, anyway."

The Queen nodded her head. "I doubt you will succeed, but you can try. Our kind holds power that you mortals can only dream–"

She cut herself off abruptly. Her beautiful lips turned down at the corners. "Did you say… Prince Atonas?"

Leroy nodded. "Yes, Your Majesty."

"Prince Atonas of Dayanavan?"

"Yes, Highness."

"My *son*, Atonas?"

Leroy nodded. "Yes. He has been in our realm for a little over six of our Earth days."

Silence descended around us like a thick blanket. Leroy wisely kept his mouth shut and waited for the news to sink in.

Finally, the Queen exhaled heavily, and pinched the bridge of her nose. "I did wonder where he was hiding. Oh, why? Why me? Why? The rest of my sons are conquering the upper kingdoms and taking the daughters of emperors as their wives. They are slaying dragons and building their own dynasties. But no, my youngest has to go off and fuck animals in the mortal realm," she said bitchily.

"I'm sorry, Your Majesty."

She gave a bitter laugh. "Do not apologize, child. It is my fault. I dropped him on his head too many times when he was a babe." She dusted her hands. "So. I will pull him out of here by his ears. Where is he?"

"He's up at the palace on the ridge," I pointed up west. "He has taken over and is currently pretending to be the Vampire King. He's thrown a festival. He may still be drunk."

She signed again. "He's *pretending* to be a King? He has not conquered?" I shook my head. "And he's done it just to throw a party?"

I nodded.

She rubbed eyes in that world-weary way that mothers do. "Very well. Take me to him."

"Uh." I glanced at Raphael. "Okay."

"Where is your carriage?" The Queen demanded.

"Your Majesty," Rafael said smoothly. "I can have a fleet of limousines down here to take us to your child in a few moments."

But the Queen was staring at me. "Who are you, child?" She narrowed her eyes. "You are a strange half-breed."

"Yes, I am." My heart leapt. Maybe the Queen knew more than her son did. "I am told I am half-star, but I don't know what that means. My father died when I was very young."

"That's it," she said, pointing at me. "I wasn't sure of the scent at first. You are one of the watchers."

"Watchers?"

"They do not usually interfere," she said. "They are not allowed. That's why we call them stars. They hang from a distance, they watch, and they bitch to each other about our existence."

I nodded. "Okay. How is it that my father came to Earth?"

She shrugged. "He must have been curious," she said. "They don't interfere, because the consequences are usually disastrous."

"I know that's a fact," I muttered under my breath. "Can you tell me anything else about them? Your son made a ward–"

"Oh yes, my son," she cut me off. "Take me to him."

Rafael leaned towards me, his phone in his hand. "The team can't get the limos out of the club," he whispered. "He's not allowing anyone to move."

"Where's my van?"

"I had it brought to the dock where we landed," he whispered back.

"I'll grab it."

"You can't put a fae queen in the front seat of your van!"

We had no choice. Leroy, with his giant balls of steel, had provided us with this amazing opportunity to not only get us out of this mess, but to get some answers for me, so I was going to take it.

"One moment, Your Majesty. I'll bring my ride over." I ran towards the dock at the lake before Rafael could stop me, jumped in, and roared over to the town square in under a minute. I drove straight over the footpath, onto the mangled grass of the town square and slammed on the breaks, skidding impressively over towards where the Queen stood.

I jumped out and held open the passenger door. "Your chariot, my lady."

"What is this?" She didn't sound angry, merely curious.

"It's my carriage," I explained.

She ran her eyes over it. "Fascinating. It is very large." She walked towards me. "Well, if it is a carriage, shouldn't I be sitting in the back of it?"

Rafael was shaking his arms wildly, mouthing at me to stop.

I ignored him. "If you like, Your Highness." I opened the rear doors and gestured with a flourish.

"Is that a bed?" she pointed, frowning. "And that is one of those no-magic ice rooms, is that correct?" She pointed to my refrigerator.

All it had in there was a half-finished bottle of Dr Pepper, and a couple of cans. "That's right. We use solar power for magic."

"Well," she raised her chin regally. "I will make myself comfortable." She climbed into the back of my van and sat down on my bed with a flourish of her cape. "It might be hard keeping balance when we are traveling at speed," she commented. "Perhaps that will be amusing."

She bounced up and down on the bed, her icy-cool face set in a deep frown, but her eyes were twinkling.

"Yes, make yourself comfortable, ma'am," I said. I shut the back and climbed into the driver's seat. Leroy was already there, grinning at me. Rafael got in the other side, looking uncertain.

"The odds of us surviving this journey are very low," he said in a low tone. "Of course, you will survive, but I may not. So, if we make it, Imogen, we must talk."

I put the van in drive. "About what?"

"Our relationship, of course."

"Our what?"

He gave me a look. "You must consent to allow me to formally court you."

"What?"

"Uh, guys?" Leroy, sandwiched between us. "Can you maybe have this talk some other time?"

"What do you mean, formerly court me?" I demanded, ignoring Leroy.

"I wish to have you," he growled. "I *must* have you. I have been patient."

"I don't understand. Why do you need to formally court me?"

"You will be my Queen. You must consent to begin the process."

"WHAT?"

"It is inevitable."

I swung the van wildly around the edge of the town square, and bumped over the sidewalk, headed down to Main Street. A faint *whoop* sound came from behind me.

"What do you mean, inevitable?"

"I decided the second I set eyes on you. You must be mine."

"Rafael, slow down." I took the corner too fast. "You're making me panic. This is *not* the time," I snapped. I pulled back the curtain behind me and took a peek. The Queen was on her feet, bouncing up and down on my bed. "Are you okay back there, Your Majesty?"

She paused for a second and looked at me, her face impassive. "Quite," she replied regally. She bounced again, barreling off the sides of the van.

I flicked the curtain back. "Rafael, this will have to wait."

"I am merely making my intentions clear. Once you have consented to me courting you," he said, his tone lowering dangerously. "I intend to have every part of you, Imogen Gray."

I swallowed heavily, the panic in my stomach suddenly erupting in a slow, fiery burn.

Leroy held out his hands in a pleading gesture. "Imogen, can this please wait? At least, until I'm not stuck in between the both of you and there's not a dangerous all-powerful creature bouncing around in the back?"

I took another peek behind me. The Queen had gotten the half-finished bottle of Dr Pepper out of the fridge and was sipping on it delicately. She screwed up her face, horrified, but she took another sip.

I floored it, before she took offense to the Dr Pepper and blew up our planet.

We rounded the corner up the west ridge and headed towards the gates of the country club. "Security will open the gates," Rafael murmured. "The prince is distracted. We might have to wait a minute." We paused outside the iron gates.

Suddenly, to my absolute horror, red and blue lights flashed in my rear mirror, and a siren started screaming.

CHAPTER 28

Sergeant Harmann got out of the cruiser and ran towards the van, gun drawn. "Out of the vehicle! Out of the vehicle, now!"

Leroy was sitting right next to me. Leroy's body wouldn't handle a bullet. No matter where Harmann shot him, he might still die.

I fixed Rafael with a hard stare and nodded towards Leroy. "Keep him here," I hissed. My hands shook with rage, but I got out of the van and held my hands up.

Harmann stopped a few feet away from me, pointing the gun at my head. "Just you try to move an inch, bitch, and I'll shoot you dead, you hear me?" Little specks of spit flung from his mouth; his expression contorted with rage. "How dare you leave my jail cell? How dare you?"

I edged sideways; Harmann flinched and jerked the gun. "I said don't move! You're coming back to jail, and you're gonna rot there, you hear me? Now turn around." He shifted his grip on the gun and pulled out his cuffs.

I turned. The gun was still pointed towards the van. If Harmann discharged, either accidentally or on purpose, there was still a chance that Leroy would be shot. If that happened, I'd tear Harmann apart, bone by bone, starting from his fingers and toes and working my way in.

"What happened to your face, huh, bitch?" he said as he cuffed me. "Got some bruises, did you? Who did you piss off?"

The Fae Queen's regal voice drifted out from the van. "You there. Why have we stopped?"

I cringed. As if things couldn't get any worse. I had been worried about Harmann accidently shooting Leroy. I probably should have been worried about this dumb cop doing something to piss off insanely powerful creature in the back of my van.

Harmann roughly shoved me around to face him. "Who've you got back there?" He banged on the back of the van. "Come out with your hands up."

The doors clicked, and the Fae Queen stepped out of the van and pointed at me. "You. Star girl. I wish to continue this journey. Make haste."

"I'm sorry, Your Majesty," I murmured. "This idiot has detained me."

She turned her terrifying gaze onto the cop. Harmann's face slackened, his head forced back as he took in her full height. "Who are you?"

The Queen raised her eyebrows, and stiffened. "Who am *I*?"

There was a long, terrifying pause. Harmann's face paled, his eyes flared wider, as his human brain finally took in how *wrong* she looked; her eyes were too big, her skin too white, she was as tall as a giant. He opened his mouth, but nothing came out.

The Queen fixed him with a stare. Her voice deepened, echoing through the forest around us. "Who am *I*?"

There was another long pause; I forced myself to breathe.

A stray wind gusted, shaking the trees. The Queen tilted her head.

"I will tell you who I am," she said softly. "You know of the beasts that give chase in your nightmares, the ones you can never get away from? You recall the shadows that flicker in the edges of your vision, setting your teeth on edge? The stray thoughts that sink into your head as you tremble on the edge of restless sleep? Do you remember the faceless monsters that crowd you at night, while your spirit thrashes and writhes in your paralyzed body, unable to wake?" She leaned down, her face inches from his.

Harmann froze. His skin was bone white.

"*I* am the one who commands them."

His jowly cheeks started to tremble.

The Queen leaned back. "And who are you?"

"He's a pig," I murmured.

"A pig you say?" she glanced over at me. "Swine? He appears to be a mortal man... but, if you say he is a swine, I will take you at your word. Why is this swine holding us up? He has a quarrel with you?"

"He does, Your Majesty."

"Well then." She flicked her hand. "If swine he is, then swine he will be."

The gun shook in Harmann's hand. He mouthed again; no words came out. Suddenly, his flesh began to tremble, and he shrunk an inch, emitting an awful squelching sound.

His eyes bulged. Was his nose... widening? It was. His nose was wider and flatter, turning upwards now, his cap fell off, revealing a balding pink head, and ears that were stretching up and back.

Another huge squelch, and he dropped the gun onto the blacktop where it hit with a clatter. He held up his hands, now black and hardened at the ends.

Harmann fell forwards, landing on his hooves; his face

disappeared as he shrunk again. He screamed and screamed, trapped in his uniform, thrashing and wiggling until his fat pink snout poked out of his shirt. He let out a terrified snort, and ripped his way out of the shirt, and took off into the forest.

I watched him run. "Well. That's something you don't see every day."

"Come now," the Queen turned her back on me and got into the van. "Get in and drive. This carriage is most acceptable. How do you open those metal contraptions in the ice-room? They share the same picture as that bottle I sipped from. I wish to have another."

Wordlessly, I popped the tab on a can of Dr Pepper and handed it to her.

I got back in the van and started the engine. Rafael, speaking on the phone in a low tone, nodded at me, gave one more instruction and hung up. "The team has assembled. Atonas is in the ballroom, on his throne, recovering from the night's excesses. I doubt he'll be on his best form."

"Throne?"

Rafael's face darkened. "Apparently he has redecorated."

I sped through the country club and jammed on the brakes in front of the main building, leaving an impressive twenty-foot skid in the white marble gravel. Rafael opened the back of the van and offered the Queen his arm.

"This realm is most amusing," the Queen said idly as we walked towards the ballroom.

"It is, Your Majesty."

"No wonder my son chose to visit. It is a shame about the daylight," she mused. "You are a creature of the night, are you not? A vampire? And this is your mate?"

Rafael looked at me. "I hope she will be."

She laughed. "I wish you good fortune, Vampire. If I know anything about the stars, I know that they are jealous."

I'd heard that before. I stumbled a little. "One of them hunts me, Your Majesty. Whenever I choose to embrace my star side and access my deeper powers, he comes, and he hurts me."

"I am not surprised. You are unique, child. You may be older than me, but our written history spans millions of years before the mortal realm, and I have not heard of a half-star in all my time. It may be that a creation such as you is forbidden to the stars. I do not know. What I do know is that the stars are jealous. Whoever hunts you does not want you to be powerful, and he does not want you to be happy."

"Can you elaborate, Your Highness? Why would they not want that?"

"They are jealous of humans, of course, and you are mostly human. Humans have the full spectrum of experience available to them. They will not touch them, but they will touch you, as you are half of one of them, so you have the best of both worlds."

I felt like I had the worst of both. Power that I couldn't use, and a body that wouldn't let me leave it, no matter how hard I tried.

I shook my head. "That makes no sense."

"They aren't much for logic, child," she replied. "They are only supposed to watch." She peered down at me. "What happened to the star that created you?"

"He became human," I replied.

"Interesting," she said. "I supposed that would be possible. Why he would want to do that, I don't understand, but nevertheless, it is interesting."

We approached the ballroom. Rafael's security, silent, staring vampires, opened the doors wordlessly. I fell back and let the Queen stride ahead.

Atonas' voice boomed out of the ballroom. "Who *dares* to disturb me? What idiot would–"

He cut off. A chilly wind blew through the ballroom.

I stepped forward. Rafael grabbed my wrist and shook his head.

A short, strangled gasp floated out of the ballroom. "Mother?"

$\mathcal{T}$he fae queen dragged Atonas out of the ballroom by the ear and forced him to walk barefoot down to the portal.

I drove her back down in the back of the van. She told me, her voice full of disdain, that she did not wish him to experience the pleasure of riding in my carriage.

"I think I shall design one for our realm," she announced as we gathered in the town square underneath the portal. "They are most amusing. You cannot see what direction you are going, and you cannot anticipate which way you will sway. I never would have guessed that becoming unbalanced would be so enjoyable. My consorts will love riding through the caverns of the underworld in the rear of one of those carriages."

Rafael bowed. "Your presence here has been most advantageous to us," he said, skirting around the forbidden thank you.

She inclined her head, gesturing at Atonas, who cowered at her feet behind her. "My son will not return. None of my kind will, I will make sure of it."

I bit my lip. "Is there anything else you can tell me about the stars, Your Highness? No one had ever known anything about them until your son showed up."

"They are mysterious, child. I've told you what I know. They are immortal and powerful, and they usually watch from afar."

"How can I stop the one who hunts me?"

She tossed her head. "I would imagine he would be very hard to stop. You cannot fight him, you are only half, and half as powerful."

"I figured that." I sighed. "So I have to keep running."

She shrugged. "You may trap him. If he is enraged enough not to see the trap in advance, as you say, he could be bound for a period of time."

I stopped. "Trap him?"

"My son trapped you."

"Twice. The first one was easier to break."

"I believe the last time you were in a pocket? That may work."

I nodded, understanding. If we managed to create a pocket dimension, I could try and lure the Ancient in and trap him with a ward."

"I will take my leave."

We bowed deeply.

"And I will take your child with me, as a snack for the journey." She grabbed Leroy by the hand.

"*What?!?*"

The Queen tittered. "Oh, this upper realm is making me giddy. I jest, of course. Go, little one." She patted Leroy on the head.

Leaning down, she pinched Atonas by the ear, and with a graceful leap, she shot upwards, disappearing into the portal.

CHAPTER 30

They say it is always darkest before the dawn. The town square was almost pitch black now that the Queen – with her luminous skin and glittery shoes – had disappeared into the portal above us. Leroy, Rafael and I stood alone next to the empty plinth where the statue of Sir Humphrey had stood, in absolute silence.

Leroy broke it first. "Welp." He swung his hands from side to side, acting casual. "I guess I'll be headed back to Marigold's now. Just to check in, y'know."

I looked down at him and pursed my lips.

"You snuck out to summon the fae queen, didn't you?"

He nodded.

"She has no idea you're out here, does she?"

He shook his head.

"We're going to have to have a firm talk, kid."

"Yeah, but not now." His gaze swung behind me, and he nodded meaningfully at Rafael. "I think someone else wants to have a firm talk with you first."

"Leroy, Rafael is a vampire. As long as no one cuts his head off or shoves a pointy stick through his heart, he's going to live indefinitely. He's got nothing but time on his hands. Same as me. You, on the other hand, are not only soft, squishy and easily killable, you also seem to have an insane compulsion to invite the worst kind of danger into our world!"

"Okay, okay, I get it. I'm sorry, okay?"

He didn't sound sorry. I gave him the stink-eye.

"I know I screwed up, but I fixed it! You have to admit that calling his mom was the best idea."

"She could have burned this whole planet to the ground, Leroy. It was lucky that she was as insane as Atonas was." I jabbed a finger at him. "No more spells. None."

"Imogen, no," he whined. "I have to! I'm so good at it!"

I frowned. He really *was* good at it. His talent was insane. Again, I worried what would happen if I stopped him.

I sighed. Parenting was hard. You had to make all these boundaries, and try to stick to them.

"Fine. No unsupervised spellwork, then. Marigold has to check everything you do, okay."

He scowled. "Fine."

"Promise me!"

"I said fine!"

"No, you have to promise. We don't break promises to each other, Leroy."

He scrunched up his face for a moment, and for the first time, I got a good look at the sullen teenager he was about to grow into. With his long, wavy hair and weary, resentful expression, he reminded me of Kurt Cobain.

"Now go. Head back to Marigold's and fill her in, get her to call me when you're done, okay?"

He ran off, melting into the darkness almost instantly. I watched him go, and sighed.

All at once, the relief hit me; we were all okay. We'd lived, no one was badly hurt.

I took a big, deep breath, feeling my lungs expand gratefully. The air around me was thick and wet with dewdrops, the moistness felt so satisfying; it filled my whole body. I could almost imagine every single oxygen atom I took in whirling into my blood gleefully, pushing out the cortisol that seemed to set up shop in my bloodstream permanently.

Is this what people feel when they say the relief was palpable? It felt like a plush heated blanket wrapped right around me. I could imagine each vertebrae of my spine loosening, I could sense the thin web-like fascia around each of my muscles and organs inside my body relaxing, letting the muscle soften.

Ah, sweet relief.

Then, Rafael stepped forward and took my hand, and the satisfied feeling blossomed into something else. A deep, smoldering warmth.

"We are alone," he murmured.

"Ha. No, we're not." I nodded towards the corner of the town square. "Most of your *quattuor* security team are hiding behind that pillar. *Tres* and *quinque* are both up on the roof. I don't know where *duo* are, but I *do know* that we're not alone," I said, chuckling at my pun. No one ever laughed at my puns, so like most things, I had to do it myself. "You're never alone, Your Fangliness."

He rolled his eyes. "You know what I mean. But, if it makes you feel better..." He looked up, and wordlessly nodded his head towards the country club, dismissing his security.

"You would leave yourself unguarded?"

"For you? Yes."

"What if a rogue ancient powerful vampire decided to swoop in and take your crown and enslave all your people?"

He shrugged elegantly. My eyes involuntarily followed the line of his muscles running the length of his shoulders.

The way his chest expanded when he breathed was so sexy, so strong and powerful. I worked hard to keep my eyes on his face.

"Sooner or later, the world will find out my father is dead. Certain things have already been set in motion." For a moment, he frowned deeply; his thick eyebrows drawn together in a furious expression. My hand reached out involuntarily to smooth away the hard lines of his face; I snatched it back before it betrayed me. "My father had made some... arrangements. On my behalf," he added. "I have some things I will need to take care of."

I cocked my head. "What kind of things?"

"Ah, Imogen," he murmured. His eyes glittered. "It is an unpleasant business. Let's leave that for another day. Let's celebrate at least one day with no problems in front of us."

"Oh, baby, I am the *queen* of ignoring bad things," I said, grinning. "You don't need to tell me twice. Speaking of queens, she really did us a favor, didn't she? Dragging Atonas back to his underworld, getting rid of that corrupt asshole Harmann..."

"Hmmm." Rafael stroked his chin. "I wonder where he is now, and if the effect is permanent."

"I couldn't care less," I replied cheerfully. "Even if he does return to normal, he's going to be twelve million shades of traumatized. It will serve him right. Besides, last I saw he was running off in the direction of Jimmy Neil's boutique organic pig farm. He'll be very well looked after."

"I hope so," Rafael chuckled.

"And the queen gave me some great information. There's a chance that I could trap the Ancient. I might be able to figure out how to do it, and ask him why the hell he keeps trying to destroy me."

His expression cooled. "I must admit that the thought of

attempting to trap the one who hunts you makes me…" His voice deepened. "Unsettled," he growled.

I shivered. The temperature seemed to have dropped around me, chilling me to the core. Or… was it the unbridled rage that emanated from the vampire?

No, it couldn't be. I didn't have empathy. It must be just the dawn approaching.

He stepped forward, looking down at me, into my face. The eye contact was so intimate, almost too intense, but at the same time, I couldn't look away.

"I meant what I said." He touched my cheek with his finger; a little electric shock shot through me. "About becoming mine."

"You haven't told me what it means." My voice sounded far away to my ears.

"Bonding yourself to me," he growled. "A Vampire mating. The process takes years, but it is public. You are not Vampire, I know, but the world must see you at my side, and know you are *mine*."

His words echoed around the square, melting into the last dark tendrils of the night.

I bit my lip. "You're right. I am not Vampire. The things you are talking about don't mean the same things to me, and it's not because I'm not a vampire. It's because I'm something else completely."

"That does not matter."

"It does, though. In the big scheme of things, it does. Mating is just sex, Rafael. Bonding means commitment, but commitment means almost nothing to me. These rituals you have – anyone's rituals, really. They're meaningless to me, in every sense of the word. The greatest lovers can come together in the most explosive collision the world has ever seen, but in a few short years, they'll be dead, everyone they've ever known will be dead, and the whole world will have forgotten they existed. The love is lost, gone for good."

I took a deep breath. It felt cold. "There's no point," I added uselessly. "No point to any of it."

There was a long, long silence. His eyes searched my face. "Why do you need a point to it?"

"What?"

"Why do you need a reason? Won't you just... enjoy it?"

"Because it will soon be gone!"

He reared back. I hadn't meant to shout.

It was just so.... Frustrating. Every sweet moment, every delicious budding feeling, even every single filthy dirty horny little impulse that I occasionally gave into... it was always the same. It was always a set-up for a big fall. Whoever the asshole was that said it was better to have loved and lost, than to never have loved at all... well, that person was plain wrong. Losing someone you loved hurt. *So* bad.

Maddeningly Rafael seemed to understand completely. "I know you have loved before," he said softly.

Goddamn him. "I have."

"I know you have lost."

"Too many times," I muttered. "It's easier to be cold."

His hands gripped tighter around my shoulders. "In that case, I will make you a different type of commitment," he said. "A promise. My gift to you, my reluctant gift. Your immortality is your curse, I understand that..."

"You'd be the only man who has ever believed it," I interrupted, my voice bitter. "The only one who has never been jealous. The only one who has never coveted my immortality."

His gaze sharpened. "You believe me? You believe I do not covet your curse?"

I watched his face carefully. Did I believe him? There was no tell, no flickering of the eyes. His pupils were dilated, dark, deep warm brown irises… I would have checked to see if his pulse remained steady, but he had no pulse.

"I do believe you," I finally whispered back.

And I did. Even if I was imagining the sincerity I felt emanating from him.

I obviously *was* imagining it. He'd bespelled me. I felt like I didn't care.

"And so I make you this promise: Despite every instinct and feeling within me, I will commit myself to finding a cure for your immortality. We know that it is possible. Your father completed the transition to human, and so will you. You are already halfway there. We will find out how. I will stay with you." He moved closer. "I will warm you."

He leaned forward, finally closing the last, tiny gap, and he kissed me.

His lips were gentle but firm, pressing into mine, and suddenly my whole world was ripped away, exploded, destroyed completely. His cool sweet breath washed into me, melding with the air in my own lungs and suddenly I felt like I was drowning, not in the usual *I'm underwater and I'm panicking* kind of way, but in the way that people talk about death by drowning, peaceful, serene, being gently tugged away, surrendering, pulled under and far, far away by something I had never felt before and could never explain.

It felt like I was dying. I wanted to stay here forever.

THE END

ACKNOWLEDGMENTS

THANK YOU

From the bottom of my heart, thank you so much. To everyone that emailed me or messaged me to tell me that they loved the series, everyone that left a lovely review, and everyone that preordered each book... please know that my heart exploded with joy every time.

If there was something you hated, or you spotted a typo, please send me an email here info@laurettahignett.com and let me know. I'm human, unfortunately, (and so is my editor!)

If you *did* enjoy it, I'd love it if you could leave me a review on Amazon here. As an indie author, every little bit helps.

Book three in the Imogen Gray series – Immortal World – is due out May 30th 2022. It will be available on Kindle Unlimited, in paperback and ebook on Amazon. Get it HERE!

But wait, there's more! Sandy Becker is getting her own series. **Oops, I Ate A Vengeance Demon** - Book one in my new series **Foils and Fury** – will be out October 14th. Get it here!

Check out the blurb here:

Getting possessed by a demon wasn't on my to-do list. I was just too busy.

I had a 60 hour work week, a hellraiser of a toddler, debilitating morning sickness and a husband who thought his only job was taking out the trash. I was at breaking point.

I don't remember being possessed, or attacking Terry, or my local priest pulling the demon out of me and trapping her in a banana (with the help of a stranger, a badass girl who apparently wrangled supernatural creatures for a living.)

But the aftermath was wild. Terry promised he'd try harder, and give me more support.

He lied. And I broke.

So... I ate the banana. I absorbed the vengeance demon.

She's a part of me now, sharing my body; we're like two people in a car. Most of the time, I'm driving. Sometimes, I let her take the wheel.

She's the rage of wronged women; the vengeance of the vulnerable, wild justice for the oppressed. She can hear bad thoughts, she can sense evil intentions. She can tell when someone wants to abuse their power, and she whispers their secrets to me.

She also eats the internal organs of evil people... which is a little awkward, since I'm a vegetarian.

Her methods might be a little blunt. And bloodthirsty. But she's definitely got my back, and I need her help right now.

My best friend is being blackmailed. Someone's gotten hold of Chloe's nudes, and is threatening to send them to her whole contact list. Together, me and my vengeance demon need to find who did this, and help bring him to justice.

Hopefully, my kind of justice. The kind involving the police and a courtroom. Not the kind where I'm picking gristle and sinew out of my teeth for a week.

But you never know...

In the meantime, take a stroll through my backlist, see if there's anything you like.

Revelations Series

A cursed woman, destined to bring about the apocalypse.
The religious sect, determined to kill her.
The demon who wants to save her.
"It's Good Omens with a Twilight feel"

I don't really need to do this page - intellectual property is already protected so we're good. But, for emphasis:

Don't copy my shit. It's mean, and I can't imagine it's very good karma. I care about your soul, okay? I'm talking outright plagiarism here, not general stuff. If this book has given you some good ideas for your own book, go ahead and get writing. Nothing is original anymore, so don't worry about comparisons.

Also, a PSA: Don't download anything from pirate websites. If you want free books, just ask me. Pirate sites will give you viruses. You wonder why all your old Facebook buddies keep getting hacked? Yeah, that's why.

This is a work of fiction. Characters, places, names and events are all the products of the authors imagination. Any resemblance to people (living or dead), places, events, or organisations is completely coincidental. They are not to be misconstrued as real in any way shape or form.

Cover by MiblArt.

❦ Created with Vellum

Printed in Great Britain
by Amazon

17521844R00157